THE BIRTHDAY PROBLEM

CAREN GUSSOFF

PINK
NARCISSUS
PRESS

This book is a work of fiction. All the characters and events portrayed in this book are fictitious, and any resemblance to real people or events is purely coincidental.

THE BIRTHDAY PROBLEM
© 2014 Caren Gussoff

Cover illustration by Newtasty.

Published by Pink Narcissus Press
P.O. Box 303
Auburn, MA 01501
pinknarc.com

Library of Congress Control Number: 2014902250
ISBN: 978-1-939056-06-1
First trade paperback edition: July 2014

Someplace Safe

Chaaya wasn't surprised when she woke up and saw lips aimed directly over her face. It was beginning. It'd been just a matter of time.

It begins with one, good, solid hallucination.

That was how it had happened to her Nani. This is how it would happen to her.

Chaaya flinched. She'd never been this close to a stranger's lips before. They were pink, heart-shaped: a woman's.

Moist, alive. Like a poster of Nani's that humiliated Chaaya as a child: bone-white teeth biting the bottom of a glossed red lip. It was an ad for a movie Nani remembered, a B-horror flick. From the days before. Nani hung the poster for the shock value, to see how visitors to her home would react to an enormous, naked mouth hanging right over her shoulder: that's how Nani was. When Chaaya moved in with her grandmother, moving that poster was the only thing she asked of her Nani. Nani hung the dirty picture inside the master bedroom closet.

Chaaya was embarrassed by these pink lips hovering above her, but she wasn't surprised. She was finally infected, finally sick.

She was only surprised that it had taken as long as it had. She'd slowly been starving to death. She'd been shitting out bots but she didn't know how many. Days without food, bots were all she passed, her waste odorless and the color of a rain cloud. She pressed her finger into a good sized pile once, and they crunched like bugs.

She'd wondered that day if she was already sick,

playing around with her own shit like that. But now, she knew. Now, she was sick.

It begins with one solid hallucination. One good one you cannot shake away, you don't wake from, that you can reach out and touch and move around inside.

And here it was. Intimately pink, pillows of fat around a dark maw. Close and naked, like a lover.

It only took a few bad bots to fasten somewhere onto the cortex, just a few teaspoons' worth across the sheet of neural tissue, and then, one hallucination. Maybe she'd been able to fight off the intruders before, but she'd shit out bots and there must be too few left in her system to fight. She imagined them like little soldiers laying down their arms. Too few, and the enemy was already at the top of the hill.

So, she was sick, she figured, and this is what sick was like: pink, curved, living, lips.

Chaaya forced herself to look at the lips, to abandon every taboo so deeply ingrained in her. As she focused on them, the lips themselves quivered. Then they transformed into a small little turned up nose, and then a pointed chin. A single mole like a piece of candy stuck to a smooth brown cheek. One elfin eye, then the other, one, the other. Pretty eyes, each one, the whites as white as whites could be, the pupils brown with violet mixed in. All fragments of a beautiful face.

Once the horror passed, after she realized this was her one, solid, good hallucination, Chaaya enjoyed the show. She let the features each come to light, then become another pretty feature.

But the second time the pretty lips hung over her face, Chaaya didn't just see them—she felt hot breath directly on her face, then smelled it too, although it didn't feel or smell like anything other than a pretty girl's breath.

A real girl's breath.

After that, Chaaya stopped enjoying herself. After that, she got surprised and afraid.

She wasn't prepared for a hallucination this solid.

She tried to stop it. She blinked hard and made a

sound. The mouth didn't disappear, but it did pull back a good few inches.

The mouth moved. It said something Chaaya couldn't understand. "Go away," Chaaya said. "Go away." Her body felt heavy, bound down with invisible weights, but her voice was weak as condensation on a cold glass. "Go away."

The mouth didn't go away. If anything, it got bigger. "Go away," Chaaya tried again. "You aren't real."

But spit flung from the mouth felt wet and real. Sweat running down Chaaya's back, pooling between her breasts felt wet and real.

Maybe this was real. Maybe this wasn't a creation of her diseased mind.

The mouth moved again, making words Chaaya didn't understand. It wouldn't go away, so Chaaya took a chance that maybe, just maybe, this was real. She asked, in her weak, little voice, "Who are you? How did you get in here?"

The mouth moved again, but she couldn't read the lips; the lips were wet and real and pink. Chaaya had only seen maybe ten or twelve naked mouths in her whole lifetime, not counting Nani's poster. Only two in the light, and neither of those had been talking, only kissing, and all of them belonged to people she knew. "Who are you? What are you doing here?" she asked again.

The mouth moved closer, flashing pink lips, with a redder inside, and cream colored teeth. It talked faster.

"Stop," Chaaya said. She was wet and cold and her breath came fast as she tried to sit up in her heavy, dumb body. "Go away. Go away."

Closer. Closer. Chaaya tried to breathe, but could only cough. "Don't come any closer," she coughed. "Stop."

The mouth stopped. Teeth chewed the pink and red bottom lip, then a wormy tongue brushed the bite. The chin came into focus. It bobbed twice. *OK. OK.*

Chaaya panted and coughed. Her mask was wet. Her back was wet. She was really cold. "OK."

The pretty girl couldn't be real. There was no way

she could have gotten inside. Even the scavengers, hungry and desperate, couldn't get inside.

And there was nothing anyone would want. There was no food, nothing of value. Nothing to eat or drink or trade.

Except the gun.

Chaaya touched the gun briefly. It was under the pillow where she kept it. It was cold and real.

Chaaya was cold and real. Each breath let out more of Chaaya's heat. All the heat was slipping from her, escaping out into the world. Her voice beaded and ran down surfaces.

The mouth moved closer again.

"Don't move," Chaaya said. Her mask whistled with effort; the filter was sopping wet. But the mouth kept coming. An elfin ear, a slice of long neck. Then the mouth again, closer, closer. Chaaya tried to stand up, but the pretty girl used her hands to grab Chaaya.

"... Hello," the mouth said. Chaaya could suddenly understand a few words. It sounded far away. "Look... brother."

Chaaya tried to pull away, but the hands held on like clips, pinching her skin. She looked at the hands. Pink and small and wet and real, one smeared with blue ink.

"I can't understand what you are saying. How did you get in here?" Chaaya asked.

"My name is...you hurt?" the woman repeated, but Chaaya couldn't understand her. All Chaaya saw was the pretty fleshy mouth; all she heard were faraway words.

"Stop," Chaaya said. The mouth wouldn't stop. The hands pinched her skin. One dark eye peered at her. Then the mouth, lips flapping. "Stop. Please stop."

"You hurt?" the mouth asked. The chin tilted. The hand clips released Chaaya, but then they pinched at her face.

"Stop, stop, stop." Chaaya could smell her pretty girl smell, taste her fingers digging around, sour ink, and feel them loosen the loops over her ears.

Chaaya gagged, pushed her heavy feet on the mat-

tress. She needed air. Air. Her mouth was opening beneath
her mask and she was screaming, kicking, tangled in the
coverlet. Fighting, pushing, fighting, pushing, then she was
back against the headboard. She grabbed at pillows until
her hand landed on the gun.

Chaaya had the gun. She leveled it as best as she
could at the tiny pink mouth. Then she squeezed. Then
she shot.

⏮ ⏸ ⏭

Chaaya stood over the girl's body. She didn't know
how long she stood there, didn't know how long it took
someone to die, how long it took for blood to soak
through a queen sized memory foam mattress and drip to
the floor. Chaaya recited prime numbers—she knew the
first 500—but kept losing her place.

She didn't stand there long; she might have stood
there for hours.

There was nothing outside her body. Just breathing,
heart beating, moving her blood through and around, and
numbers, *73, 79, 83, 89, 97, 101.* She scratched at places
where blood and brain dried on her skin.

The scene was like something Nani painted. Splat-
ters of red and burgundy, thick in some places, a mere
wash in others. Bone and teeth, fragments in white and
dove grey. Her Nani was famous for her brutal accuracy of
color, the authenticity of texture, painstaking trompe-
l'oeils pulling viewers inside each grisly scene. But even
Nani's most famous pieces, the most convincing of her
canvases, were best guesses, simulacra, nothing like the
actuality of death. Of murder.

It was ugly.

Chaaya hadn't heard the girl come in. The door had
opened and the girl came inside, and Chaaya heard none
of it. The door opened now, and someone else stood there.

He filled the space, blocking the light, darkening the
scene like a curtain falling. Chaaya looked at him: he was
saying something she couldn't understand. But she wasn't

afraid. He belonged there. It was right, perfect.

He was so tall, his brown eyes bright above his plain brown mask, his arms—wide as legs—reaching out to her.

Chaaya was weak and exhausted and very glad to see him. His wide arms reaching. She was weak and exhausted, so she dropped. She dropped the gun. She dropped to him.

He caught her, righted her, his hands on her shoulders. "Can you hear me?" he asked and she could. "Do you understand me?" and she did. She nodded. He held Chaaya up like a doll and still so he could look at her. He held her up but could have just as easily pushed her to the ground.

She'd forgotten his hands. Flat calluses on his fingers scraped the fabric of her shirt. "Look at me," he said.

And she did.

"What happened?" he asked. She tried to answer. Her mouth wouldn't work, her brain was too slow. He looked at her like no one else had ever looked at her, like he was trying to decide what to do with her.

She didn't know how long he held her up. It might have been a long time; it could have been minutes. He finally folded her over his arm and dragged her into the living room. Behind his mask, she could tell, he was breathing hard with the effort. Chaaya was a big girl, a big, empty girl. Her skin was wet but her mouth was dry. Very dry.

He was close to her, his eyes making tiny flicking movements like he was trying to take in her entire face. "Hey, girl. Are you in there?" he asked.

She tried to nod. *Yes. I am.*

"What happened?"

|◀ ‖ ▶|

Earlier that morning, Chaaya opened her eyes as dawn broke full and cold and orange, thick though the blinds. She looked at the light for a few minutes and realized she was awake. She was hungry. She had to go to the bathroom.

Chaaya lay quietly and tried to ignore being hungry and having to pee, but it was like trying to ignore a house fire. She pulled her knees to her chest and rolled upright, waiting for the dizziness to pass through her before she stood up. That dizziness had worsened over the past week, as she shit more and more bots—and, usually, only bots.

The dawn light blinded her. She maneuvered through silhouette and shadow: Nani's rose damask fainting couch, the side table gilt in nickel silver and inlaid with carnelian cabochons, her gameset, two empty cans. Chaaya felt for the lamp plug, then followed the cord to the wall. She jiggled it into the outlet with a spark until it flashed. There was electricity today. She was grateful and blinked away floaters. The bathroom was cold.

Nani had loved the apartment. She loved the view of Lake Union, the old brick exterior and solid wood doors with green-brass turn locks. She loved the expensive and quaint electric appliances and the interesting people who also loved the view and brick and electricity. Nani loved those interesting people. She considered herself an interesting person. Maybe she had been. Toussaint lived upstairs; he could barely afford the place on a tech's salary, but only electricity gave electric guitars an authentic sound, he explained to Chaaya once, strumming the strings, the scrape of skin against wire.

Chaaya hated the place. She'd wanted a sleek and modern place, solar efficient and rife with amenities. Toussaint crashed around upstairs, practicing guitar jumps and kept her awake at night. She locked herself out, the heavy door swinging shut behind her.

But now, she loved the building too. As much as Nani had, maybe more, but for different reasons. It was safe from scavengers. The first and only time they tried to break in, they kicked the solid doors, which didn't budge; banged the doorknobs and locks, but they held: built soundly, shut tightly, and locked securely. Instead, all they could do was crush the glass and crystalline silicon back-up solar panels beneath their feet in frustration. And so, without solar power, Chaaya learned to love the stove and heater and lights that plugged into the wall. The electricity hummed, a friendly ghost.

Chaaya remembered the night of that first break in. She sat in the dark, clutching her mother's gun. Nani never knew Chaaya had the gun, that she kept it as a memento of her mother, who taught her to shoot, hands over hands — *Breathe, wait a moment, squeeze the trigger, meri jaan, don't jerk it.* They lived in the country then, Chaaya and her Maa and Baap, and Maa told her knowing how to shoot a gun could one day save her life. Chaaya held the gun and recited pi, *3 point 14159265358979323846264338 32795028* until the scavengers withdrew in disgust.

This morning, Chaaya used the bathroom, then went back to bed. She was exhausted from starvation. She closed her eyes just as the Protesters started their daily chants. Their voices washed in waves, loud then receding. Chaaya couldn't tell if she was sleeping or passing out. She tried to motivate herself to get up and get out, to search for food, but she would drift off again for minutes, hours. It was hard to tell.

The protest songs were familiar. They reminded her of Nani.

No one ever knew what the Protesters protested. They started showing up in groups of two or three. Nani brought them sandwiches and cold water. They loved her.

Twice, her Nani'd politely joined the Protesters, at their request, in some ritual. They smeared mud on themselves and then on her, then they all danced. Chaaya watched her Nani awkwardly sway with them both times from the window, her eyebrows pulled as low as she could manage it. Her Nani could see her and shrugged back from across the street, partially embarrassed, partially as if to say, "Who's it going to hurt?"

Chaaya fumed at her both times. The first time, she said, "You're fucking encouraging them."

And Nani replied, "Watch your mouth," or something like it. Nani's words were always muffled. She never did learn to speak up or put enough gesture in her eyes.

The second time, Nani brought in a hand-sewn charm, a gift from a Protester. Nani held it out to Chaaya and the tiny bell on the end tinkled. "It's a little elephant," she said. "For good fortune and blessings and protection and whatnot."

"It's filthy," Chaaya answered. "Throw it away."

"It's Ganesha," her Nani said. "The Lord of Infinite Compassion."

"You don't believe in that shit," Chaaya said.

"And you need as much compassion as you can." Nani shook her head. "You were a sweet girl once, herding your goats like a *Gopi* with a taste for sweets."

Her Nani tried to press the Ganesha into her hand, but she let it drop to the floor, wouldn't pick it up, wouldn't even talk again to her Nani until she doused the charm in diluted bleach and then took a shower, scrubbing herself twice, once with soap, once with baking soda. Her Nani had showered, and then dragged the heavy-ass Durga statue out from the back closet, into the living room. She made an altar, with folded paper flowers and broken jewelry, and the stupid little elephant toy.

Nani kept Durga out for weeks, sitting in front of her as if to prove some kind of a point, like she did believe in that shit. But then, a few weeks later, Nani quietly stored it away and didn't mention it again.

The Protesters restarted their song. It filtered in and out of Chaaya's dreams, across time and space. She was a child and her parents were alive: she held onto Pie, her brindled fainting goat, and listened to Pie breathe and bleat with pleasure; she peeled back sheets of salty smelling crabgrass to reveal black mud and worms, her Maa checking up on her though the small porthole of a window that faced their yard. Their house, painted purple and red and mauve like a cookie from her father's bakery. Her father pulled down the long driveway, the backseat stacked with long white boxes from the *Jin Ha Masissneun Bakery,* and she ran after the car, knowing her father would open the door and hand her a treat—a lotus root and red bean *ho-tteok,* a crumbly yellow almond moon, or fried honey flowers. Her mother would complain he was ruining Chaaya for her dessert, boiled milk custard or rice in rosewater.

Chaaya was a child surrounded by plenty. As long as she brushed her teeth, her parents allowed her the two desserts.

Chaaya was dreaming of sweets when the girl came in. Then she woke up. Then she killed her. Then Toussaint filled the doorway.

◄◄ ❚❚ ►►

Toussaint placed her—like a doll in his big, rough hands—onto the rose damask fainting couch. Chaaya dug her face into the couch, rubbing the upholstery across her cheek. It felt like a beard.

"There's electricity," Toussaint said. "And water. That's good."

She felt something warm on her face; he was holding a mug of something to her. "It's coffee," he explained. "With sugar."

With sugar. Like sweets. Sweets. She loved sweets.

"It's actually more sugar than coffee," he explained, as if an apology was necessary. Toussaint held the coffee cup up for her, and politely looked away as he nudged up her mask. He'd seen her lips before. She'd seen his. It was strange that he was being polite. She thought she must look terrible. The coffee was lukewarm, weakly smoky, powdery and wet. But it was sweet. He fed her sips and she lapped at it like a kitten.

Revival came in a rush. The sugar hit her blood-stream and she was in the moment. Aware, like a great camera shifting into focus, fast forward. Her thoughts were clear and solid and entire, one after another. She tried to speak, but everything wanted to come out of her all at once: *Girl, body, girl, killed, you, shot, girl.* Instead, nothing came out. Her voice had been strange; now it was gone.

Toussaint held out a plate to her. They were Nani's

ornately painted holiday plates. They used them only for special occasions and company. Heaped on the plate were chunks of cut-up fruit, striped dark green and lime and orange.

"Tomatoes. They're OK," he said. He balanced the plate on her lap. "I ate two earlier and I'm OK."

She didn't care. She shoved the slices in her mouth, into her cheeks, as quickly as she could. Her mask was wet again, with tomato seeds. She didn't care. She tasted salt. Pepper, maybe. Fruit glucose. She tried to make herself slow down and chew. Her blood hummed like the electricity in the walls. Her leg bobbed up and down.

"Jesus," he said. "That's better. You've got some color again." He sat back down on the floor and held a packet out to her. "You need a seeding, badly. Don't you?" He wasn't really waiting for an answer. "I'll prep some for you. Where's Nani?"

Again, everything wanted to come out at once. *Girl, killed, Nani gone.* She felt like she was going to explode if she didn't find her voice.

"Nani?" he asked.

Chaaya started counting Fibonacci numbers to herself: *1, 1, 2, 3, 5, 8, 13, 21, 34, 55.*

"Are you counting?" Toussaint asked.

She nodded, and then he was close to her again. He wrapped his huge hands around her shoulders again. "I'm sorry." A tear delicately held to his lashes. She always liked his eyes. He had the longest eyelashes she'd ever seen. They brushed his cheeks as he blinked. Decorative, ornate, like fringe on an evening skirt. He pulled her to his chest and she could smell him. The outside was strange, but from his skin, as it always was. Sharpened pencils and tarnished copper. She felt a bite on her shoulder.

"Just a seeding," he said.

The injection site felt warm inside. Her leg started bobbing and she relaxed into Toussaint. *Killed, gone.* The words came through her head slowly.

She might have fallen asleep. The sun moved from her thigh to her knee. He rubbed his leg, which must have fallen asleep, and kept his face in her hair.

She didn't blame him. Her strength was returning exponentially, and, awake now, Chaaya felt the girl seemed to be everywhere. Rain puddles of blood and the smell: sweet and rotten, like eggs and ammonia, but primitive. Chaaya was sure even if she didn't know what the smell was, that she would know what the smell was. "My fucking god," she whispered.

Toussaint squeezed her arm then stood up. He went to the bed and finally gazed down at the body. "Jesus, Yaya," he said. "You shot her in the face."

She sat up. And the plate slid off her lap and bounced on the carpet. A blob of wet tomato seeds shone like a jewel, shiny and beautiful, next to the dulling blood. "I hate it when you call me Yaya." Her voice was stringy, but stronger than she expected.

"Jesus, Ya—. Chaaya. Jesus."

"How did you get in, Toussaint?" she asked. She couldn't modulate her volume, and it came out soft. She repeated it louder. "How did you get in?"

"The door was open," Toussaint said. He wiped his brows and then looked at her. "What happened here, Yaya? Who's the dead girl?"

"The door was open?" Chaaya asked. It didn't seem possible.

"Wide open," Toussaint said. "I gave you back your key years ago." He pressed the back of his hand against his forehead and turned from the body. "Who is she?"

Chaaya didn't answer him. She didn't know. *Killed. Gone.*

He seemed to understand that meant she didn't know, and he smacked himself once on the head, to give himself courage, she figured, and bent down over the girl.

Toussaint gingerly looked through her pockets. "No wallet. No ID." But he pulled out a small paper journal from a cargo pocket by the girl's left knee. "A book, though." He slid the journal into his own pocket, then said, "We can't stay here. We've got to get you cleaned up. Then get the fuck out of here."

Chaaya nodded, but she needed him to tell her again about the door. "Tell me again. The door was open?"

Toussaint blinked his long lashes. "You must have left it open." He sounded annoyed. He didn't understand why this was important. "Come on. We've got to get out of here."

"I didn't leave it open," she said. "I haven't been any-where." She shivered. "I have not left the apartment in days. It was locked. Tight."

"I guess you thought wrong," Toussaint said. "Jesus, Yaya. Is that the most important thing here?"

"It is important," she said. "Very. What about the outside door?"

"It was closed. But unlocked." He motioned to her. "Look at yourself. Is the shower working?"

"It was," she said. She gripped the edge of the sofa. "Why was it unlocked?"

He shrugged. "We can't stay here," he repeated. "Can you move?"

"I think so."

He pulled her to her feet, walked her down the hall to the bathroom. She let him lead, like they were dancing. "Do you need my help?"

She swayed a little at the knees. "No." But he came in anyway, ran the shower, turned it off and went to kick the water heater. Then he ran the shower again and jiggled the window's HEPA filter.

"I can do this," she told him. "I'm not sick."

"Of course," he said. "Of course not." But he left the door open a bit anyway.

Chaaya tossed her mask onto the floor and stood in the shower with all her clothes still on. The water didn't get hotter than warm, and it cooled quickly. As soon as she shut the faucet, Toussaint was there with a towel. "Found this in the closet," he said. He wrapped her in the towel and marched her into her room, away from the dead girl. "Get dressed," he said. "And pack some things. Things you'll need."

Chaaya nodded. She looked at all her things neatly

folded, hung, stacked, and felt dizzy. She sank onto her bed. The comforter was cool and smooth. She wanted to lie down on it. "What did you give me?"

"Just some bots."

Chaaya let herself lie down. The bed felt so cold and wonderful. She did feel relaxed. "Toussie," she said. "Why are you here?"

"I hate when you call me Toussie."

Chaaya laughed at that. It came out like a cough.

"Come on," he said. "We need to get your stuff together."

"Why are you here?"

"I needed your help with something. And it seems like you needed mine." He started to pull her up. "Come on. Pack."

She didn't want to pack anything. She didn't want to leave. She wanted to go to sleep. She shook her head. "What did you need my help with?"

"It's not important now."

"Tell me," she said.

Instead, he reached into his pockets, rifling around. "I have something for you," he said. He held out a string of pink beads. "A gift."

She squinted at the beads, and reached out for them. She saw a smile start in his eyes. "Where did you get these?"

"I'm full of surprises," he answered. "Put them on."

Chaaya turned the beads over in her fingers for a few seconds them slipped them over her head, delicately avoiding her mask and then lifting her hair over them. The door couldn't have been open.

"Beautiful," he said. "Now pack."

Chaaya sighed, but turned back to her drawer. She weakly pawed through it. Everything looked the same, useless, mysterious and limp. She pulled out things, underwear, scarves, socks, and dropped them to the floor.

Toussaint caught them as they fell, picking them up, placing them into a plastic bag. She kept dropping things.

"Where are we going?" she asked. She dumped out

her drawer of masks. Everyday denim and cotton, a flannel plaid sleeping mask, a heavily embroidered one with beaded tassels, a pink satin one that had been a gift.

"Someplace else," he said. "Someplace safe."

She opened the next drawer, threw aside shirts, an old gameset. "Is any place safe?"

"I don't know," he said. "I hope so."

She caught something small that didn't belong in the drawer. It jingled. Chaaya pulled out the small Ganesha, the fabric fuzzy, threads weakened from bleach.

That stupid fucking elephant. She lost her breath and bent over, squeezing the charm inside her palm.

"This," she said, standing up. "This is the only thing I need." She looked past him. She thought to herself, someplace safe. But then she added, "And probably the gun."

Control, Alt, Delete

Book waited until he left Aberdeen and was mostly into Hoquiam before he pulled down his mask and lit a cigarette. He wasn't sure what tobacco was supposed to taste like, but this was dry and the end ignited with showy sparks.

The cigarettes were Shin's apology. Book asked for six bags; Shin could only get him three, the last of last of the human-sourced. Shin could get him powdered, and said he'd check other labs, but Book read that meant he was on his own.

Shin looked sincerely sad when he handed over the bags; he knew what Book was using the bags for and was personally sympathetic. The cigarettes were a gift from Shin's personal stash.

Book drove out of Aberdeen as fast as he could without attracting attention. Aberdeen spooked him. Aberdeen always spooked him. Aberdeen was the city in Grays Harbor, the closest thing to action until Olympia. As much time as he spent there, he never built up a tolerance. He couldn't imagine being Shin and living there.

The pandemic hadn't done anything noticeable to Aberdeen itself. It'd always been a crumbling, dumpy town of crazy folks, dying a protracted death for the past hundred or so years since the logging industry had filled the streams with silt, the paper mills pulled out, the nuclear power plant went dark, the cranberry bogs withered under some blight years ago, and the promises of biodiesel development lost funding. Once or twice, the city had tried to reinvent itself and artists had come, lured by its proximity to wild forests and wetlands and a quick drive to the beach, as well as ridiculously cheap real estate. But the artists left when they realized how far civilization had retreated from the bulk of the county, Or else they eventually gave in, gave out and blended in to the scary, deprived, empty-eyed residents watching their fat children listlessly playing in gardens knee-high with weeds or in tree houses built from wood and stone pillaged from public art installations.

He would never come to Aberdeen if not for Shin, research scientist and liaison into the thriving black market, a system of underground economics that long predated the current state of affairs.

Book took a draw off the cigarette and stifled a cough. Blood flooded his brain and he felt a little dizzy and very relaxed. He was beginning to see the appeal. He drove faster, more carelessly.

The Hoquiam checkpoint was unstaffed—not even a doll propped in the seat—so he drove straight through. Book knew he wouldn't be as lucky at the Ocean Shores turnoff. Usually, he tried to schedule his runs when one of the old guys was at the booth, anyone but Davey. But Shin had other buyers and dad was thin and pale and very confused. Scheduling was not on his side.

He'd have to lie to Davey. Again. He surveyed the lies he'd already told—weak shit about trading for vegetables, which he'd probably stick to again. Beets today. He'd tell Davey he had beets.

Being mnemonic was handy for lying. He wasn't very clever or creative with his lies, but he never slipped up. He wished he was an eidetic—being able to remember images and maps and floor plans would've served him well these days. Instead, he was blessed with a parietal cortex that lit up like fireworks as he spouted off facts he'd read or recited long digit spans, all handy for winning the occasional bet, wooing girls with classic poetry, and learning new percussion sequences when he played in a band.

And lying.

Book was diagnosed when he was ten. Everyone was really excited, even his sister, who perpetually had youngest child syndrome and was, by nature, rarely excited about anything having to do with him. His mother showed his MRI to anyone who stood still long enough. The doc himself encouraged Book to compete in the annual World Memory Championships, or, at least, get himself declared as a Grand Master of Memory. But he didn't do it. And now there were no bets to win and no time for girls impressed by poetry.

His mother, ever the optimist, called him a late bloomer.

If so, he was still waiting to bloom.

Beets, he rehearsed. *I've got beets in the trunk.*

⏮ ⏸ ⏭

Book lit another cigarette. He'd only ever seen people smoke and drive in really old movies. It felt naughty. Halfway home, he pulled up at a stoplight alongside a car of college girls in bikini tops sipping iced coffees from long straws poked through their masks.

Book honked and grinned at them with his whole bare face, exhaling smoke through his nose and mouth, and they squealed at the obscene danger of it all—OMG, *infected, maybe! Right there! OMG, lips!*—Exactly the reaction he wanted. He felt like Gregory Peck, like Brad Pitt, like Tray McTroy in "A Pocket Full of Stars." He winked at the girls, and one turned towards him, hooked her fingers beneath the ties by her ears, and flashed up her mask. She bared her teeth at him. Then they sped away.

He was raised to believe disease had been relegated to the misery of history, as history itself was the story of misery. No one documented good days, or even OK days where nothing much of consequence happened. It wasn't human nature. And in an age considered post-disease, aside from the occasional migraine or flash of diarrhea, disease was an abstract fact.

Book was good at abstract facts. He was good at history. Facts and figures. He knew the index cases for every major outbreak in history, the symptoms for every infectious and parasitic disease, beginning with the plagues in 430 BC, with Greek soldiers, returning home to their loved ones after years fighting the Peloponnesian War, wiping out at least half of Athens.

He'd have just enough time to finish the cigarette before town. There, he'd have to tie his mask back on—just about everyone left in Ocean Shores knew his parents, and he could hear his mother now: *Mrs. Rogers told me she saw my youngest boy sleep driving around, had to be!* Bare-faced— problem, of course, not being that his mother worried what the neighbors thought, but that someone like Mrs. Rogers or the McCarthys or Cassie from the Stop'n'smile would say it to her with sympathy, like he really was sick. His mother could stand lots of things, but not sympathy. Especially from the neighbors. She had enough of that over his dad's illness already, and besides, she called the year-rounders *campeneros*, although she herself had been one for nearly 40 years.

His dad's illness. He looked over his shoulder at the cooler. His dad's illness shouldn't be, should never have been. He hadn't finished being diagnosed and given correctly programmed MaGo before the first wave of shutdowns.

MaGo was hailed as the single greatest breakthrough in medical science, greater than the discovery of penicillin, better than the mapping of DNA, the x-ray, and tissue culturing combined. More precise than lasers, less toxic than chemotherapy. MaGo nanobots flying through the human circulatory system, little superheroes complete with capes, eating right through cancer cells, through antigenically shifted viruses, through bacteria bred for a trillion generations to resist antibiotics. Bashing parasites, extending telomeres. Lives were longer and more productive as long as you got a seeding.

He'd gotten his first dose at ten, just like everyone did. The whole Larsen-Gomez clan went for monthly seedings together as a family—all except his pop-pop and nana, who died of cancer and liver failure, respectively. They'd been too old to yield much, aside from that when they died they each had thick black hair and the majority of their own teeth.

Book threw the stub of his cigarette out the window, and then tucked his mask's elastics around his ears. Book could just about hear his mother reminding him that now more than ever it was stupid to take chances. He liked the feeling of air on his mouth and chin, though. It was freedom.

But his mother was right. This was not the time to rock the proverbial boat.

Half mile to the turnoff. Book thought about the young girl's pink mouth and was pleased. Eidetic or not, he could live on that image for a while. He tapped on the dashboard with his free hand, scattering cinders onto the upholstery. "Control, alt, delete," he sang. *Beets. I've got beets.*

Disease was history. Primitive history. Book was good at history. But even the experts forgot that history finds a way of repeating itself, in sneaky new asshole ways.

He watched the news blasts, just like everyone else. He saw the stories: an executive breaks in to the national headquarters, barricades himself into his corner office and staples closed his eyes, nose and mouth. A model— with nearly 300 international covers to her credit— knots a ten thousand dollar dress around her neck and strangles herself on the street. An honor student slits her wrists, painting, 'forgive me, forgive me, Alfredo' in blood on her parents' new Berber carpeting. He watched the parents beg the cameras for Alfredo to come forward. No one ever did.

He'd shook his head in brief detached pity at, as his mother called them, these poor souls, *pobrecitos.* Just like everyone else. But, like everyone else, he didn't really pay attention. There were always poor souls on the news, always had been.

But these were the index cases for the new pandemic: MaGo-initiated delirium. The MaGo themselves began living longer—and more productive lives—affixing themselves to the cerebral cortex, causing multifactorial failure of neurotransmitter circuits.

It'd knocked through Washington's flimsy Continuity of Operations plans like a house of crackers left in rain. Executive Order 13295 was reinstituted quickly, extending the hell out of the fed's quarantine powers, but it was everywhere and nowhere, depression, headaches, hallucinations, tremor. Aches, pains, nausea. Paranoia and psychosis. They closed schools, public offices, the museums and the libraries.

They closed down roads, the airports and bus stations. Logistics firms couldn't reliably access their data feeds, trucks stopped, production halted. Officials recommended private businesses shut doors, but it didn't take too much time before that happened naturally though sheer absenteeism, panic, and fear. The meteorologist on the evening news curled up like a fetus. A cross-town bus driver, crying, head buried in the lap of the neighborhood schizophrenic.

Towns burned through retirees, students, and the National Guard to fill seats to bury bodies. The economy crashed. Book didn't know how bad things had gotten in other places, but last he read, the Congressional Budget Office estimated an 8% decline in gross domestic product. Dysphoria, hopelessness, suicide ideation. Decimation in the classical sense, the delirium slapping down every tenth person, driving terror into the rest. The mayor of Seattle committing seppuku on a collectible sword. The last officially-sanctioned and paid guard at the Ocean Shores checkpoint resting his head on the barrel of his rifle.

Book slowed up as he approached the checkpoint and the silhouette of Davey's head.

Book and Davey'd gone to high school together. Davey took him to prom. *Beets.* He'd drifted away from his friends in the years between then and now, but he still hated lying to the guy.

Book cut the motor at the station. "Heya, dude," he said. "How are you?"

"Hey, man," Davey answered. "Nice to see you.

Where are you coming from?"

"Aberdeen," Book answered and made a face. He motioned at the back seat, hoping Davey wouldn't look too closely. "Traded some old wool blankets for beets."

"Nice," Davey answered. He yawned widely and excused himself. "Long day," he said.

Book nodded politely. "Beets. I have some beets."

Davey jotted down Book's name, time, license number, and cargo: beets.

"You need any beets?" Davey was an excellent cook, always had a gift with food. It'd seem weird not to offer, but he prayed Davey'd refuse.

He didn't. "Yeah," Davey said. "That could be nice. Come by the store later. I have some old cabs you can look at. Maybe a heavy merlot."

"That sounds cool, man," Book said. It didn't sound cool at all to Book. It sounded horrible. He hadn't been there since Davey moved into his parents' wine store after they ran into the woods to die. But he nodded his head.

"Nice." Davey said. "We could open a bottle and hang out, man. I'd like that." He looked at Book hopefully, like he really would like that.

"Definitely. Definitely. I should get home though now. My mom is expecting me with the beets."

"Yeah. Cool. I'll be at the store after 8. Come by anytime. Tell your mom 'hola.'"

Book turned the motor back on, held up his hand as he drove away. Book tried to remember the last time he sat and had a drink with someone his age, and couldn't. It had to be with Toussaint. They used to spend Friday nights drinking beers and talking shit about how anal sex was overrated and whether dolphins were smart, how much better British comedies were than American ones and how that had been true for the past hundred years.

Book drove down Ocean Lake Way, trying to figure out where he would actually get beets. Just past the Elks Club, he slammed on the brakes as something jumped out into the street. He pushed hard on the pedal with both feet and did a hard turn on the wheel. The tires spun out gravel as the car spun to a stop. The cooler slammed against the back of the driver seat and wedged itself open. He let out a long breath, and then a face popped up looking in the passenger side window. Her hair was hard and dull, like she'd been clumping mud into it. She must have, because below her small, red eyes, she'd drawn two lines in mud, like a football quarterback.

Fuck, he thought. He also yelled it. "Fuck!" It took Book a moment to register who it was—Cassie from the Stop'n'smile. He could just about see her somewhere inside that beast, she still had wide hips, small feet and a curve to her back. Cassie. God, she'd been a pretty girl, bad teeth and dead-end job and all.

This time he whispered it: "Fuck." She turned briefly towards him, and then stumbled into the thick woods. He held up his hand as if he were saying goodbye.

He waited a few moments before turning around and righting the cooler, straightening back the small box of dry ice, and settling the three bags of blood back on top and shutting the lid.

He thought about Cassie for a moment. His hands hammered out a simple beat before he realized he was doing it. He stilled them, then he started the car again. He straightened his mask. This really was a sonofabitch. *Control, alt, delete.*

⏮ ⏸ ⏭

Book couldn't get used to his mother looking old. *It wasn't that she looked old,* he silently corrected himself, *it was that she was looking her age.* He was used to aging happening imperceptibly, and between the pandemic and dad's illness, it ran to catch up. He gave her a kiss on the thin skin of her forehead and volunteered to set up the transfusion while she made two cups of tea.

It was hard to tell where the crumpled sheets and blankets ended and his crumpled father began. Book tucked one bag of blood carefully under his armpit to warm it and sat on the edge of the bed. "Hi, pop," he said.

"I have a present for you."

"Cookies?" his dad asked. "Tell me it's cookies. I was dreaming of cookies."

"Almost," Book said. "One 500 milliliter unit bag of CMV negative, leukoreduced, irradiated to 25 Gy, type A, grade A human blood."

"Excellent," his dad said, as Book hung the bag behind the bed. "Cookies would taste better."

Book could tell his father was smiling behind his modesty mask, so he patted his father's arm and went to work. He gave his father a pink diphenhydramine tablet, then tied the forearm tourniquet and started feeling for a vein. "Make a fist, *papi*. Give me something to work with," he said, then pulled the skin back and tight. He popped off the top of the needle catheter, and breathed out through his nose. He hated this part, although he would never admit it. He pushed, saying, "In quick," and felt the first pop—skin—the second—vein—then the flash of blood in the applicator.

He used to hate this part. He'd watched shows on phlebotomy procedures and practiced on an old garden hose. He did fine: better than his mother, never missed a vein yet, avoided major hematomas. But he never liked it and still didn't like it, although he would never let his father know. "Good." Then he fed in the catheter as he drew out the needle, yanked off the tourniquet and let it slap against the wall. He pushed down on the vein above the catheter, attached the IV line, and taped it down. "There," he said, as the drip began. "Lie back and relax."

His father's mask rippled. He was licking his lips. "My mouth tastes like soap," he said.

Book touched his father's shoulder. He always remembered his father as a big man—where he inherited his own bigness, the barrel chest, kneecaps big as antique globes. But under his hand, his father's clavicle felt light and delicate.

He went into the living room to let his father rest, sat down next to his mother. She placed a mug in front of him.

"Thank you for the tea," he said. It was awkward. He never knew exactly how to relax, what to say, after the drip started, but before they knew if anything was going to go wrong. There were delayed reactions, but the first 20 minutes were the most critical. They had to watch for fever, chills, signs of headache or chest pain, tachycardia, respiratory distress, swelling in the IV site. Anything that could indicate a hemolytic reaction. So far, there had never been anything, but every time they hooked up a new bag, Book cataloged everything that could go wrong. If the blood was mislabeled, incompatible. Or his father had developed antibodies that could react with transfused antigen having red cells, or alloantibodies in response to platelet antigens. The blood could've been mishandled, and they were feeding his father full of inflammatory mediators or burst, dead, useless, lysate cells.

He slapped his legs quietly and bobbed at the knees in time to the drip. He overlaid the beat, then overlaid rhythm.

His mother touched his leg. "Stop." Then she brought her teacup beneath her mask and sipped. She pointed to his tea. "Drink some and stop worrying."

"I'm not worrying." Book picked up the cup. He and his sister used to love when their mother made them tea, *niño*-style, heavy with milk and sugar.

His mother patted his knee. Across from them, his father's mask sagged and inflated with his snoring. "Ten minutes," she said, and glanced at the clock on the far wall. "Everything is going to be fine."

"Sure," he said. "Of course." They still had to watch for rash, fever, diarrhea, cytopenia, edema, shock. If nothing happened in 10 minutes, things were probably fine. Twenty minutes and they were in the clear, for, at least, another day. Book turned his cup around and around in his hands and tried to phrase the bad news for his mother. "The lab's out," he said. "I'm going to have to find a new source."

His mother didn't answer. They both watched the bag drip into his father. "OK," she said. "What does that mean?"

"I don't know," he admitted. He suddenly didn't want to think about it. He blew into his tea cup even though it'd already cooled down. "I need to figure out another plan, I guess. Shin told me he'd call labs, but I don't think that means very much."

His mother changed the subject. She always approached conversations sideways. "How was the rest of the trip?" she asked.

"Fine," he said. "I saw Davey. He invited me over."

"Oh." His mother brightened at that. "You should go. You should get away from us *gente vieja* for a little bit. If your sister were here, that'd be one thing, and I know you must miss your friend, Toussaint." She tapped his leg. "It can't be good for you not being around people your age."

He was 38 years old, he wanted to remind her, not a teenager. But instead he said, "I'd need beets to go. Do we have any beets?"

"Beets?" She looked confused.

"I told Davey I got beets in Aberdeen. He was at the guard house. I'm going to need to bring beets if I go."

"Beets from Aberdeen?" His mother burst into laughter. "*Hijo*, you are a terrible liar."

"Sasha was always the better liar," he agreed.

"Yes," she said. "Your sister could always pull one over." She stood up, shaking her head. "Aberdeen beets." She walked into the kitchen. "We have some carrots," she called. "Will carrots do?"

"I don't know." He shrugged. He didn't really care. He could just tell Davey he meant carrots. "Sure."

His mother came back and sat down next to him. "Is Davey living all on his own?"

Book nodded and his mother clicked her tongue and shook her head like Davey was a poor Victorian orphan. He wanted to remind her that Davey was also 38 years old. But, he laid down his tea cup and squinted at his father. He could see the blankets rise and fall, evenly. They were out of danger. "I almost hit Cassie with the car."

His mother looked up at him. "From the Stop'n'smile?"

He nodded. "Yes."

His mother sighed. "Was she—?"

"I think so," Book answered. "Yes. Definitely."

"*Que lastima*," she said. She looked uncomfortable and rubbed her temples. "I hope she's ok."

Book felt briefly guilty; he'd blurted out some sort of bad news again without giving his mother the proper build-up. "I'm sure she's OK," he lied. He rubbed his own temples. Control, alt, delete.

⏮ ⏸ ⏭

The wine store appeared to be sinking, the roof cocked like an eyebrow. It was part of a strip of barn-style stores developed on accreted land, borrowed from the ocean. And without stable management of the upriver dams and the southwest antiquated geotubes, the land was slowly creeping back out where it belonged.

In its heyday, the strip mall had also been anchored with the tourist-friendly staples upon which the town's economy pivoted, the extras and shit visitors had to have in order to prove they visited someplace IRL: souvenir shops selling fishermen carved from driftwood, shell-encrusted trinket boxes (manufactured in China), plastic sand dollar key chains, and other assorted replica flotsam. For a few years, there was also the kite shop, moped rentals, and the gelato shop where he worked for several summers, scooping with his left arm because he was irrationally afraid that the muscle development on his right would betray his frequent teenage masturbation.

Still, aside from its crookedness and the fact that the other stores were boarded up, if he squinted, the strip looked like any other time in the past, off-season, when tourists cleared out and the town hunkered down to muddle through the lean, quiet, grey winters.

Book banged on the wine shop door—it looked like Davey had fortified it with a few layers of cheap wood—

which gently exhaled rings of dusty particles in response. Something ruffled the blinds at the side window, so Book held up the carrots by their greens like a prize severed head.

"Davey," he called. "I brought over carrots."

The door pushed open, scraping the concrete, and Davey stood, eyes grinning full on and wide. "You came," he said, pleased and surprised.

"I said I would," Book answered, and stuck out his free hand for a shake. Davey grabbed it and warmly pulled him inside.

It had always been dark and cool in the wine shop to protect against oxidation. This evening it was almost too dark to see anything except Davey's white teeth.

"It takes a sec to get adjusted," Davey said, but he pulled Book's arm to lead him through the shelves to the back office, where Davey'd taken up permanent residence.

It was a shame. He remembered Davey's parents' house. It was one of those tall, four level jobs, ugly as sin, but with a great view of the ocean from the top two floors. He remembered Davey's parents—his pear-shaped mother with the orange hair and hairy legs, obsessed with grape production and fermentation recipes, and his leathery father in sandals with an air rifle strapped to his back.

Book stood still while Davey turned up a gas lamp, spreading cold orange light across the room, Davey's modest bedroll, and a stack of magazines. Book didn't want to look too closely at the kinds of magazines.

Davey swooped in and grabbed the carrots. "I thought you said beets."

Book swallowed. He couldn't believe Davey remembered, although he did say it like 30 times during the stop. "My mother took the beets," Book said. It sounded lame, and he tried to look like he didn't know how lame it sounded.

"That's fine. Carrots are great, too." Davey opened the back door that connected the office to the alley behind the shops and carried them outside, where a small fire pit was burning, and a camping style pot hung from a stand

over it. He squatted beside the pot, pulled out a pock-
etknife, and sliced the carrots. He threw them in the pot as
he worked, then pulled a wooden spoon out of his pants
pocket and started stirring.

"This is going to be awesome," he said.

The wind carried the aroma to him, through his
mask. Full bodied, savory, something delicious. "What is
it?" he asked.

"A quick stew of sorts," Davey answered, eyes smiling again, and then held up a hand. "You'll join me. It'll be
ready in a few."

Book leaned on a dumpster that now housed a
healthy collection of firewood and watched Davey stir.

Davey served them heaping plates of venison
braised in wine, the carrots, and some bitter dandelion
greens. Davey explained how he shot the deer down by
Duck Lake. "But I think this is my last for a while," he said.
"The lake's getting crazy."

Book thought of Cassie, caked in mud. But then he
thought about killing a deer, butchering it, everything it
took to get the meat onto the plate. He'd never thought
about it before, and tried to imagine his friend doing it.
"Did your father teach you to hunt?"

"My mother," he said, then beckoned Book to come
inside. Davey spread his bedroll across the office floor,
then popped open a bottle of wine and unwrapped long
straws for each of them. Book settled in uneasily next to
him and they began to eat.

"My mother was a good shot. My father *thought* he
was a good shot," he said.

Book balanced the plate on his knees so he could eat
and hold his mask. He felt shy suddenly, and had to
remind himself that Davey knew very well what was
underneath his mask. And this wasn't a date. It was dinner.
He took a sip of the wine. "It's so good."

"It's a German Riesling *auslese* to go with the venison," Davey explained. "Mom always used to pair a sweet
white with game." He bowed his head as he ate, and Book
looked at his scalp, just starting to show through at the

pate. It would be another year, maybe two, and then Davey would be all scalp. He sensed Book looking at his head, and took a long pull off his wine bottle, saying, "Race you to the bottom."

They drank themselves warm and tired, laid down on the blanket, hands tucked behind their heads. Drunk, in the flickering light, they could be anything—hunters in a cabin awaiting first light, soldiers hunkered down safe under cover, little kids at camp telling stories. Davey opened two more bottles and they talked, lips swollen and loose with wine until they were just volleying grunts and sounds back and forth and laughing. It was prom all over again, only with less making out and no dancing. He didn't feel shy anymore.

Book opened his eyes. He must have dozed off although he swore he hadn't, could swear no time had passed, but the lamp was down to just casting long shadows and Davey snored slow and steady through his mask.

Book sat up. The entire crown of his head hurt from the sulfites and tannins and dehydration. He winced, then pushed himself to standing, brushed off his pants, and looked down at Davey hugging a pillow into his stomach. Book smiled at him, and then started to feel his way out of the office through the front of the store. He touched shelves, furry with dust, and bottles, the glass cold and smooth. He tucked a bottle beneath his arm and pushed the front door open and closed over the cracked concrete.

He missed the days when MaGo would've precluded a hangover well before it happened. He drove home and then sat in the car. He watched the sun start to come up, all purple and blue and orange, and he tried to breathe deeply against this headache, in rhythm with the hushed ocean roar, the croaking of horny herons, the hum of the crickets.

It was all very beautiful. And he felt like shit. He thought for a moment about turning the car back on, backing out, hitting the main road, and then flooring it someplace, anyplace. He knew he wouldn't, and he watched the sun rise completely before climbing out of the car, wine bottle in hand. He muffled the door slam as best as he can and went inside.

Control, alt, delete.

Peak Serum Levels

The King of Seattle never had to put down Beluga Grace. Even now, he didn't *have* to put him down. But Beluga Grace was caught in a loop, talking and waving his hands, and the King needed to think.

Beluga Grace was not particularly good at delivering bad news. He'd panicked and stammered and told the story in a far more abstract way and with more gestures than were useful, and, at the end of it all, the King of Seattle still didn't know exactly who was coming to get him, only that someone was.

And he needed a minute of quiet to figure it all out.

The King looked at Beluga, who was as worried for the King as he would be his own life. Beluga Grace was a sound second, a perfect choice for Chamberlain, considering his only other choices would have to be either Toby or Joaquin. Probably they thought, quite rightly, that one or both of them should wear mantle.

And they were the ones, the King thought, most likely to come and get him. One or both.

Toby and Joaquin had always tried to come and get him, in one way or another.

They wanted whatever the King of Seattle had, never seeming to understand that if the King had it, then they had it too. The King of Seattle shared everything with his close friends—he even gave them songwriting credit even though neither Toby nor Joaquin had contributed anything to Figurehead's discography since the band's first release.

But Book should have been the King's second. If Book were here, the King might not even know Beluga Grace. Beluga would just be one the King's admirers, one of his subjects he knew by face, but not by name. Book would always be the King's true second. Even if Book had wanted nothing to do with this whole scheme to begin with. Even if Book was in Ocean Shores taking care of his father.

Beluga just about leaped from foot to foot as he waited for the King to say something. This would never do. He needed quiet to determine his next move. So he sighed and told Beluga to come to him. The King prepared a seeding of some of the last bots coded for somnolence. He looked at the love in Beluga's eyes, magnified through his thick glasses. The King wanted to pet Beluga's head; he hoped someone would take care of Beluga after he was gone. It didn't occur to him that Beluga could take care of himself.

The King always wanted a pet. A puppy. But the King's mother would tell him that even the most beloved pets bite, and that they will obey any master. She didn't seem to think these were good traits. She wouldn't have liked Beluga; she would have wanted to slap him for his weakness. But the King didn't think Beluga weak. He loved the King like the King needed to be loved: selflessly and unconditionally.

That was what Toby and Joaquin wanted. No one loved them like that. On three different occasions, they'd tried to fire him from the band even though he was the band and Book would have none of it. The King wrote the music, the lyrics, played lead guitar and sang. Book carried the rhythm section himself. They couldn't fire them.

The King loaded the seeding shell into the air syringe. "One, two," he counted, held it to Beluga's arm, and squeezed the trigger.

The King listened to the speed of Beluga's words, waiting for them to slow. He needed to think.

"I don't think you understand, sire," Beluga repeated, or so the King thought. Each time he actually listened to what Beluga was saying, all Beluga said was how the King didn't understand that this was a big deal. That the King was in danger.

"This is a big fucking deal," Beluga said. "You don't understand what they're saying. They're talking about killing you. I don't think you understand, sire. This is a big deal."

The loop was exhausting; it was probably a kind thing the King was doing by putting Beluga down. Beluga looked exhausted; he could use a good, long nap. The King checked his watch; it didn't actually keep the current time, but he only watched the minute hand anyway. These somnolence bots were good ones. The King figured that proved his gratitude to Beluga—he'd only dream of giving Beluga high-quality bots, ones he would seed himself with if necessary.

And these bots were quick-acting ones, with sugar husks for fast metabolizing. Although peak serum level usually took an hour, given Beluga's height, weight and time since last seeding, the King expected 15 minutes at the most.

But Beluga was talking faster. He wanted to get his point across before the bots took him down: *important, serious, danger, big deal.*

The King picked at some invisible lint on his pants and waited for Beluga to take a breath.

"They're coming for you, sire. You don't see what's happening. This is a big deal."

The King stood from the throne and held up his hands. He moved forward and Beluga took a step back.

"They're talking about killing you," Beluga said.

The King took Beluga's arm and led him to the throne. But Beluga wouldn't sit, even as the King moved closer to force him down. Beluga swayed above the throne to keep from falling into it. "They're coming soon," he repeated helplessly to the King.

"Sit down."

Beluga looked from the King to the throne, then back to the King.

The King nodded. "Yes, in the throne."

"I couldn't."

"Sit down, Beluga."

Beluga flopped down, but collected himself. He sat straight, pinched and nervous as if the throne was on fire.

"Relax," the King said. "Get comfortable, for christs-sake." He leaned on the wide armrest.

Beluga scooted back, tried to fit himself into the chair, which overwhelmed him like a visual gag. He draped his other arm onto the free armrest, and in a last ditch effort to look manly, spread his legs a bit. The throne wasn't designed for comfortable sitting: it had wide, low arms and a hard plywood back, made for effect. In fact, when he had the Enterprise's captain's chair dragged over from the Science Fiction Museum, it was because he imagined himself playing Kirk, with Book as Bones (even though, realistically, with his perfect recall of facts and figures and his inability to keep his knowledge of facts and figures quiet, Book was really more of a Spock). Toby would have made a fine Hikaru Sulu, and Joaquin, Scotty. Instead, he was sitting there with Chekov.

"There," he said to Beluga. "That's better. Lean back. It isn't going to break." He kicked the side lightly. "This was built to last, you know. Shatner's stand in used to tell stories about Bill tipping it over. But there's not even a chip in the paint."

Beluga's chin lowered and his glasses slipped down his nose. "I'm trying to protect you," he said, sleepily.

"Tell me again which your favorite song was. Which was the best show?" he asked.

"I liked them all." Beluga yawned. "Maybe 'In your Armageddon.' No, the Ashley song. 'Goodbye to Ashley.' That one."

"I wrote those," the King said.

Beluga bobbed his head heavily. "I liked them all."

"I know you did. Now stop fighting it and just relax. For me." The King stroked Beluga's arm reassuringly. "This chair can take it all right. I don't remember Shatner's stand-in's name. Book would know." He looked at Beluga, who was getting looser and looser, sinking deeper into the awkward chair and letting out a fart. The King patted his second's arm again. He petted his pet, then stretched. Now he could think.

He looked at the long line of guitars propped in stands across the wall. He wanted his guitar, even though it was a crappy fossil compared to all the others he'd brought over from the collections at the Music Project. He brought his guitar case to the window, sat down on a pillow and unlocked the case's clasps, carefully pulling out the guitar by its mahogany neck. He held it on his lap as he rifled through the sheet music tucked in the lid pocket.

Beluga snored loudly.

The music was all handwritten, fading, and he had to squint to find what he wanted. He set the music across the floor, over his feet.

He stooped over the guitar and quietly picked the strings, singing under his breath. He looked over at the Chamberlain. He didn't move, so the King strummed a little louder. The song didn't sound the same without the effects, but the lyrics held up: "*In your arms, I'd fall asleep without a care, through the thousand natural shocks to which the flesh is heir, Ash-ley.*"

⏮ ⏸ ⏭

The King of Seattle wasn't originally from Seattle, once upon a time. The King of Seattle was from northern California, a small town on the edge of the Central Valley, a town of research laboratories and vineyards and ranches between Sacramento and Marin County. Once upon a time, the King of Seattle moved from Livermore to Seattle for a woman.

That relationship didn't work out, but the King of Seattle didn't regret it for too long. It was just one small story, he would say to other women, later, of how people heroically, desperately, blindingly cast their lots with love. The King's mother used to say that no one could cook a gourmet meal or fall in love without breaking something, and this, tempered with a fear that he never had anything to lose, had always allowed him to weather heartache. The King of Seattle had been in love enough times to know that the end doesn't hurt forever, and enough times to consider himself unlucky in it.

Moving up to Seattle wound up being a good decision, although he wouldn't know it for many years, long after the woman he moved for had run off with a bull rider from British Columbia. He worked his way up from hospital orderly to certified technician with the help of a state grant and an attractive health care expansion program and found moderate success as singer/songwriter/lead guitarist in Figurehead.

How the King of Seattle became the King of Seattle was a complicated and messy matter, dirty pool if considered in certain terms, but simple in its execution—as were most stratospheric rises to power. There was no operating manual on establishing a monarchy, especially in a west coast seaport that had, in better times, prided itself on liberal values, civic responsibility, and environmental progressivism. There were, of course, a few examples of elected monarchs from history: the appointment of the new Pope by a Council of Cardinals, the eleventh century Irish *rí* chieftains, *szlachta* electing the kings of Poland, the Swedish *Vasa*. The King had enjoyed watching history shows growing up, especially the last few years before he moved to Seattle, living above his mother's garage in Livermore, California.

He also liked playing games, and there was no shortage of games where one could practice exerting will over scattered and broken individuals in apocalyptic scenarios. However, these examples, while parallel, were hardly analogous.

It probably began with the tattoo on his bicep. It read, "THE KING OF SEATTLE." It was going to be a song lyric, but he could never fit it in anywhere. It was a joke, a lark, a play on King County. A tip to his ego, his rock star persona.

Not that he hadn't been ambitious or known how to

seize an opportunity when he saw one. His mother paraphrased Virgil at him, saying fortune favors the bold (reminding him, most often, coincidentally, when he was sitting around watching history shows or playing games, and she wanted him up and out of the house). Figurehead was not his first band, although it was the most successful: at their best, they were successful enough to release a few albums to indie critical success and go on a few national live and gameset shows at middle-sized clubs; and, at their worst, they were successful enough to give them one big, dedicated fan (male, Beluga) and to keep the King flush with opportunities to be unlucky in love.

The King knew how to use what he had: his brown eyes fringed with long, thick lashes. What the King's mother didn't know was that all that time watching history shows and playing games taught him more than her mangled Virgil quote about fortune. Fortune favors those in control, and control was power.

Control the food, control the booze, the fuel, the love and the hope, and power was yours.

And while the King didn't have any of those things, he did have the knowledge of, and access to, cocktails of MaGo bots. He had the ability to program the bots so that anyone he seeded would feel as protected as they would with food, booze, fuel, love, and hope.

And thus, his Kingdom was born.

◄◄ ❙❙ ►►

The King heard a small noise and shook his hair off his face. Eliza sat cross legged, quietly, watching him. He raised his chin at her.

"Don't let me disturb you," she said.

Eliza Ocean had been with him since the very beginning. When they met, she was just a teenage stripper hanging out at Harborview. She really didn't do anything except be pretty and young—which, sometimes, was more than enough. She was also completely in love with him, and he'd had enough experience being unlucky in love to identify damaged goods, and Eliza was as damaged as was humanly possible.

"You aren't disturbing me," he replied, and slapped a chord. "I was just trying to think." The King stilled the strings with a palm, then laid the guitar down in his lap and looked at her. She'd taken up recently with Toby. Toby had asked the King's permission and for his blessing, and the King gladly gave it. Toby wasn't having fun unless his life was filled with damage. He told Toby to have at her.

Eliza sat quietly. Toby underestimated the power of the love of a damaged girl for an unconsummated ideal. The King placed his guitar back into the case, but left it open. He scooted his pillow around to face her.

"What were you playing?" she asked.

"It's called 'Goodbye to Ashley'," he answered.

"Is it a love song?"

The King thought about it. "They're all love songs."

"Is it about a real girl?" Eliza asked.

"Yeah," he said. "It's about a real girl." He considered telling her the story, but didn't.

"Do you want to fuck?" she asked.

He stood. "Did Toby send you?"

She shook her head. "No. Do you want to fuck?"

"Thank you, but no."

"Did he tell you?" she asked, gesturing towards the sleeping Beluga. "Toby and Joaquin are going to kill you?"

"Yeah," he said. "It's not the first time. They tried to kick me out of my own band a few times, too."

"This isn't kicking you out of the band," Eliza said. "This is murdering you. Like, dead."

"Yeah," the King replied. He couldn't explain to her that kicking him out of Figurehead would've been the same thing.

Eliza crossed her arms in front of her, squeezing her breasts up and together. "Well?" she asked.

Behind his mask, he smiled to himself. He stood up and then offered her his hand and helped her to her feet. He led her to the windows to look out. "How long 'til they make the move?"

"Not long."

The King of Seattle stared at the window. He looked at the superimposition of the city and his own face. Then, he looked at Eliza's face, reflected in the glass.

"Take me with you," Eliza said.

"I don't think that's a good idea," he said.

"Please?"

He didn't answer. They both watched the city rotate by. Once upon a time, this view was legendary. Tourists lined up to take the high speed elevator up and gape. If it was clear out, you could see beyond the city, a full sweep from the Olympics to the Cascades, the bay and the lakes. If it was raining, you could still see most of the city, downtown and Queen Anne hill, the west side of Capitol Hill, and north just to the University District.

The view was still quite beautiful, only now with grey empty waters, hills green with grass and brown with ruins, red with sirens, searchlights, and wildfires.

Toby would take care of Eliza. If she left the room now, he might never know this conversation even happened. "Go to Toby," he said.

"Where will you go?" she asked.

"I think," he said, "I'm going to the real Ashley's."

Eliza looked like he hit her. "I'll be your Ashley," Eliza said. "Take me with you. I love you. I wouldn't be a problem, I swear."

"I know you wouldn't," he said.

"Then you will?" Her eyes were huge and did the begging for her. "Can't I be Ashley?

"No, Eliza." He made himself sound sadder than he was. It was his gift to her. "You can't go with me. You can't be her." He turned away from her but took her hand and squeezed. She squeezed him back with more force than he expected. "It's really kind of pretty out there, isn't it?"

⏮ ⏸ ⏭

The King of Seattle packed his cargo pockets full of whatever he could: tea bags, packets of sugar, salt, some wrapped candy, vitamin pills, crackers, and relish. He hung a pouch off his belt to hold an air syringe and enough MaGo shells to hold a family for a year, and fit a knife and bandana in his back pocket. He thought of packing a backpack full, but that would invite scavengers, as good as a sign around his neck.

He looked longingly at the collection of guitars and his own, worn guitar case. He'd have to leave them behind. He stood up straight; he was good at being heartbroken. He slipped his favorite pick, as well his four-hole, eight-note Little Lady harmonica—the same model played aboard Gemini VI, Book had once told him—into his other side pocket. Those would have to do.

The King had to leave at once. He didn't have the luxury of waiting until morning, and by the sun, he estimated he had maybe 2 hours left of good light. Travelling in the dark was fine, if you were suicidal. And once upon a time, walking home from the Space Needle along the lakefront would, at most, take that 2 hours. But no sane person would race darkness along that route now. It was lined with the truly sick and the truly desperate.

That meant walking along the old monorail tracks, cutting through downtown, and onto the old Interstate. That would be much longer, far less direct, take him until tomorrow if he hid out the night. But it was safer, and *shit*, he figured, *I've got nothing but time.*

The monorail tracks were long abandoned. Built a hundred years ago for the World's Fair, once upon a time, the monorail tracks whisked tourists between the Westlake Center mall and the fairgrounds at Seattle Center. Now, the elevated concrete piers were crumbling, only twice as wide as one boot and high enough to kill you if you fell.

But, walking the tracks was the safest way downtown because you were above downtown. They were also the most dangerous because you were above downtown. The trick was to watch your feet but not look down or to either side.

The King walked carefully, singing under his breath to keep himself calm and focused. He was relieved when he made it to Westlake. The controlled movements stressed out his bad knee, and somehow he'd managed to sing and clench his jaw hard enough that a knot throbbed in his neck. He looked around to be sure he hadn't been followed, then decided to stop by the Pike Place Market for a few moments; he didn't know if he'd ever have another chance.

The waterfront market had always been one of his favorite places. Once upon a time, the vendors stood in clean stalls selling fresh fish, fruit, and flowers, produce and souvenirs and crafts. These days, it was more of a swap meet – the contents of looted homes and warehouses, cans and bits and trinkets and trash spread out on blankets and mats. He wandered and looked at wares. He haggled down the price of a pocket crank flashlight to 25 catsup packets, and even splurged on a pretty pink plastic pearl choker that would look especially spectacular around Chaaya's neck. He shelled out full price (12 packets of mustard and 20 single serving baggies of oyster crackers) for it.

Outside the market, downtown was relatively still and quiet. As the King walked along Olive Street, he only passed a few people, all sick: one sitting silently with his back against an office building, crying and blowing his nose into his dirty necktie; the other, a woman stripped down into mismatched bra and underpants, lighting matches and extinguishing them against the white skin of her belly. In the lot of an old car dealership, a family sat on a blanket heaped with lumpy heirloom tomatoes, and he traded a fistful of candy for two tomatoes, slightly green, but sweet, the wife assured him. He sat back on his heels, sprinkled the tomatoes with salt and pepper packets from his pocket, and ate one. The juice ran down his chin and onto his mask and coveralls, and he looked into the setting sun, trying to make both the tomato and the light last. When he was done, he loaded the syringe with a half dose of endurance bots. He was already getting tired and he'd only just begun.

He sat too long. The family watched him for a while

before getting up, rolling the rest of their tomatoes into the blanket, and moving off. That made him briefly sad, but he understood how anything, especially a man in plain grey coveralls enjoying tomatoes in the sunset, closing his eyes, as if he were sleeping and had no place else to go, could be something to fear. He stood up and wiped his face, wrapped the second tomato into his bandanna, and hung it from his belt. It was a short cutover across torn up concrete onto an onramp to the old Interstate.

Once upon a time, I-5 had stretched from Canada all the way to southernmost California. Tales of traffic were mythical. But now, the foot traffic and tent settlements on the shoulder and median far outnumbered the cars that occasionally drove through.

The King liked walking on the freeway. A hundred years of car tires wore smooth grooves in the concrete, and here and there the sun caught on reflectors bezel-set in tar. He walked along the line, built-up with layer after layer of paint, until he found a settlement that advertised sleeping quarters, and after arguing that he was not sick and haggling the price down to all his remaining tea bags and most of his salt packets, he settled down in the back of a broken-down Jeep to get some rest. He placed his tomato on the dashboard where it wouldn't get squished and rolled down the window to let in some air; the wind was coming from the west, carrying the smell of salt, fish, and tannins in from the Sound. He shifted around. It was impossible to stretch out. He loaded another half dose— this one of the same type he'd given to Beluga that afternoon. He shot them into his chest, something he would never do to anyone else, but for himself, it'd take the peak serum level down from an hour to a quarter hour.

He folded himself up best he could, his arms behind his head and waited for sleep to come. Outside the rear windshield, he could see the unmistakable black silhouette of the Space Needle, the gangly insect legs, the flat lenses at the knees and the top. It'd been so easy to take it. By the time the King had rounded up 20 followers, they'd just walked in. Security had padlocked a few doors before they'd abandoned the place, but Toby was good at kicking off padlocks, always had been. They'd even left the generators alone.

But now, here he was, cramped into a rusty old car, completely unprepared for what lay ahead. He looked at his watch. Two minutes had passed.

The enormity of the situation suddenly hit him with a wave of anxiety. His left pocket felt too empty for the beginning of what would be a long trip. First he'd go home. He'd get his Ashley. Then, they'd what? Walk? Ocean Shores was, he remembered, about two hours by car, so about 120 miles. If he walked between 3 and 5 miles per hour, it'd take them 30 hours or thereabout in total. They could do it in 2 or 3 days, walking well into the darkness. And on cue, his left knee began to hurt.

For the first time in a long time, he felt completely alone. He missed his mother. He missed Book. He wished he'd fucked Eliza before he left. He thought about other women he'd loved: Meggan, for whom he'd moved to Seattle in the first place; and Allison, who'd given him her underpants folded into a rose while he was on stage one night; Kim and Alana; Zan, Naomi, Sara, Viv; and then, finally, his Ashley— Chaaya Gopal Lee. In fact, he was less than a mile from Chaaya right now; he figured if he stood up and could see through the high concrete walls that had once acted as noise reducers when cars would actually drive along it, he'd be able to see the roof of the apartment building. He thought of *Nani* Gopal, Chaaya's grandmother, and her plates of fried *chaat* and rice *dosa*. She'd been an artist and she liked to talk about music, and he'd play her a song to pay her back for the snacks she'd bring. Toby and Joaquin would tease him that Nani Gopal was trying to marry off her fat-assed, sullen-eyed granddaughter, by bribing him with delicacies. Marriage never came up, and he and Yaya were together, for a difficult and intoxicating three months.

She was his Ashley. He didn't know it when he wrote the song, but he knew it now.

He reached for the tomato. Chaaya was fat and firm

beneath his hands in the same way. He loved cupping her ass like that. His thoughts finally began to drift, soft edged and disjointed, when suddenly, a small face popped in at him. A child, a little girl, maybe 7 or 8, her face too close for him to focus on clearly. "Hello," he said, but the little girl didn't answer. He rolled over and tried to ignore her, but taking the sedating bots made everything feel fuzzy and meaningful so he finally dug around in his pockets and offered her a packet of sweet pickle relish so she would go away. She grabbed it, tucked it under her mask and scampered into the darkness.

He didn't remember falling asleep, but, within what felt like moments, blades of light sliced through the wind-shield shade and made the Jeep unbearably warm. He opened the door and stretched his legs, one at a time. His left knee still hurt and he'd slept funny on his neck and it pulled gently to the side.

He checked the tomato. Safe. He tied it onto his belt, next to the MaGo pouch.

He blinked to get adjusted to the sun, but he made out the shape of the little girl from the night before. Then she came into focus and he realized, stupidly, that she wasn't a child, but a tiny, wizened old woman. Her mask sank in where her teeth had been.

He was shocked by her. She was natural old, with sharp, deep wrinkles and a body shrunk unevenly with osteoporosis. He'd seen photos of people that got old like that, but never in person. She didn't have her dosing inter-rupted; she looked like the old people before MaGo was even invented. "Good morning," he said to the old woman.

"Good morning, too," she answered. She seemed to be able to read his face, and it gave her pleasure to make him so uncomfortable. She bobbed her head at him and he could see the pink of her scalp through her thin, cot-tony hairs. "You're looking at my oldness. I wasn't always old. I spent my girlhood in a church. A church against those blood robots. Never had 'em. Never will."

He tried to nod at her, calmly, like it didn't really matter to him. "I have a friend like that. It was sort of cute.

And strange. I was always having to remind her to get a seeding. And she never did quite get what was going on with the rogue bot pandemic." He didn't know why he was saying all this and wondered if it made any sense. He couldn't tell if the old woman understood him at all. "My friend," he added. "She grew up in a cult."

The old woman centered her face at him. He could swear he saw her milky blue eyes flash. "Christian Science," she said. "Ain't a cult."

"Of course not." He wished he hadn't said anything at all.

"We believe that God heals. And only God heals. Folks get old. They supposed to get old." She was shaking —the King couldn't tell if it was age or anger. "Are you some sort of a doctor?"

"No," he said. "I'm not." He decided not to mention that he was a nano technician.

She seemed genuinely relieved to hear that he wasn't a doctor. She waved her skeletal hand, marked with brown spots, to signify the argument was over. Her nails ridged and pitted and yellow in the light. "Thank you for the pickle last night. I used to have a wicked sweet tooth, way before you were born. When I had teeth to be sweet." She motioned behind her. "There's water for a wash. Been heated through three times. Safe as anything's gonna get."

"That's great," he said.

He splashed his face and forearms. In his peripheral vision, he saw her watching him. He turned to give her a friendly look, but as he did, she pulled up the corner of her mask to spit on the ground.

He was horrified again, but also fascinated. It was completely indecent. She was so naturally old and withered, plus, now she spit. It was like she threw her skirt up over her head, squatted on the ground, and pinched out a shit in front of him. His heartbeat. He wanted to run away, but his hands seemed to move on their own, washing, washing.

She heaved herself down with a heavy groan, down on the ground next to where she'd spit. "You're a nice boy," she said. "Where you headed?"

He tried not to look at the glossy wad of spit. He couldn't think of a lie so he told her the truth. "I'm going home," he said, a little surprised at himself. He hadn't realized he'd actually decided until he said it. "I'm going home to see a friend of mine and her grandmother. Then, we're heading for the coast."

"Very good. I love the coast," she said. "Do you have any more of that sweet relish?"

He wiped his hands dry on the front of his pants. He could hear all the little packets crinkle in his pocket. "I don't."

"You're lying," she said. "I bet you have a whole fistful of pickle relish in those pants." Then she cackled. "If you come back this way, come stay. You're a nice boy. I'll make sure my daughter will give you the van, same price. You just bring some more relish." She closed her eyes. "That relish sure tasted good."

He stood up. He'd need to give himself another shot, but he'd wait until he was in the neighborhood, where he could sit underneath a tree and rest before going on to the apartment. "I will save you the relish."

The old lady started to collect some more saliva to spit again. But before she did, she said, "You have a nice trip, now, nice boy. Be careful out there."

He'd find a tree and maybe he'd eat that second perfect tomato. He'd give himself a shot, then he'd go to the apartment and get Chaaya. He knew those plastic pearl beads would look really striking against her smooth brown skin. "Thanks," he said to her. "I'll sure try."

Anoneira
Part I

There were cats everywhere, mewling from treetops, alleyways, garages, hollowed out beach logs—skinny, starving, confused cats of every variation, size, and temperament. Sasha started taking them home, one at a time, wrapped in a towel, sad sacks of screaming and claws. There didn't seem to be anyone else to take care of the cats.

Eventually, the cats started showing up on their own. Whether guided by pheromones or some mysterious kitty underground railroad—or, more likely, the growing stench of canned fish steaming from the house—cats would show up, stand off to the side of the yard looking as uncomfortable and casual as parents at a high school keg party, then eventually blending in. They were tripping over cats, sliding on hairballs; Sasha couldn't turn them away.

Now, Didi had a house full of cats.

At first, Sasha had tried to name each and every one of the cats, after people she admired, then people they knew, then by any characteristic markings on their fur. But soon it was impossible to keep them straight. So, Didi suggested that they name them Ira.

"What about the girls?" Sasha had asked.

"This isn't a household concerned with traditional gender constraints," Didi answered. "We know lots of girls with boy names."

They did. Timmie the bartender at the Honey Pot,

Magnificent Todd the drag king, and butchy Alan, with the goat farm who always managed to spare a little milk and a little cheese after things got tight, because she always had a crush on petite, tender-hearted Sasha.

"The Magnificent Todd is a stage name," Sasha protested. "Her real name is Kieko. And I think Alan's legal name is Alanis." But then Sasha shrugged. "OK." She turned to one of the cats sniffing a pan on the kitchen counter. "Get down, Ira," she said. The cat immediately jumped down and scuttled off.

That night, Sasha and Didi laughed and cuddled on the couch, Ira on Sasha's lap and Ira at Didi's feet, Ira and Ira dozing together like a yin-yang, an Ira at each window, and 3 Iras jockeying for the warm spot near the wood-burning stove.

Now, Didi had a house full of cats named Ira. All except one: Mrs. Lopez. She was the sole exception, an ancient, half-blind cat with a club foot, a Buddha face and a belly that dragged on the ground when she walked, attesting for the fact that she probably sat somewhere towards the top of the Ira family tree. She'd arrived at the house with a beatific, half-blind look on her face, a pink rhinestone collar, and a note that simply said, "Mrs. Lopez." Didi loved Mrs. Lopez immediately. She didn't mind mashing up Mrs. Lopez a special plate of food—even adding a few drops of their precious goat-milk. Didi beamed at Mrs. Lopez as she heartily gummed the plate, then gave a little burp that stank. "She's like one of my clients," Didi had said, and Sasha had agreed.

So, these days, it was Didi, 30 plus Iras, and Mrs. Lopez. She couldn't believe Sasha was gone.

She should have been angry. She tried to be angry. She'd lie on the bed and stare at the ceiling and try to hate Sasha, try and feel anything but sad. It made her feel weak to be sad, silly to be sad. She was shocked at how romantic she was, that the last few mornings surprised her, as if she couldn't really believe the sun would or could rise without Sasha right next to her.

But eventually, Ira would come and jump on her

chest, kneading the fat around her middle and mewling something about breakfast. Then Ira would join them, butting his head against her arm, while Ira stretched against the bedpost and Ira began sharpening his claws on the throw rug. Eventually, if Didi held out long enough, Mrs. Lopez would drag herself into the room and stare at her with one milky eye, wheeze, and then vomit ceremoniously across the hardwood.

That got Didi up in the morning, like it or not, Sasha or no Sasha.

Once she was up, she was OK. She'd set water for herself on the wood stove, then dole out food for the Iras and Mrs. Lopez on 20 plates, she and Sasha's entire wedding set, then fill up 20 bowls of fresh water. This would take at least 15 minutes, take her over the hump between asleep and awake, and by then, her water would be ready for the instant coffee and a glass of oatmeal. She'd watch the cats eat while she did, then spend another 15 minutes washing the whole brood's dishes and dousing out the high, sharp stink of the ten boxes and pan of dirt that served as litter. Then she'd splash some water onto her face, force herself into shorts and onto the backyard court for a workout.

Once she was up, she could make herself OK. She stretched and looked over to the house. From the yard, she could pretend Sasha was there, using up all the hot water. Even when there was regular electricity, Didi never minded a cold shower. She strapped on a gameset, to run a drill, chose an intermediate combo, rubbed her thighs and knees, then sprinted back and forth to the free throw line. After 4 or 5 drills, she speed dribbled down the court and shot a left-handed lay-up. Then she bent over and tried to catch her breath. When she was younger, she could have drilled like this for hours. She did drill like this for hours. Then she'd play ten games a month, half of them on the road. Her left knee, as if on cue, began to throb.

"That was a long time ago, fat girl," she muttered to herself.

Didi understood aging well now. Her clients

mourned for their youthful bodies, when they could run and jump and dance without worry, without pain. For a few years, it seemed as though science had finally explained that equation, encouraging cell regeneration, toxin removal, extending the lifespan of nuclear telomeres. The MaGo was a miracle.

Didi shut off the gameset and picked up a basketball from a nest of weeds. She dribbled to the end of the driveway, then held the ball above her head and tried for a half court throw into the hoop on the side of the house. No gameset program compared to a real throw. She missed, as she expected, and the ball rolled out into the long grass by an Ira, lazing in the morning sun. He didn't even move, just gazed at the ball as it rolled to a stop, and then yawned.

There was a small pile on the front stoop. The jammy remains of a banana slug and three moths, two of them big as a half dollar and the third, bigger than that, missing a wing. Didi would have missed them, except one of the freckled Iras, plopped next to the pile, who, as she approached, began licking one of his paws, stealing glances at her out of one olive-green eye.

"Thank you, great hunter Ira," she said. She scritched his head. "We'll eat great tonight."

She opened the door and he slunk in proudly. Once he had rejoined the herd, Didi scraped the bodies off the porch by the side of the house with her foot.

She laid the gameset down on the kitchen table and took her cold shower. She looked up into the spray, squeezing her eyes until she saw little lights. She tried to pretend that Sasha was in the living room, reading watching the morning news, boiling up another pot of water for coffee—but she couldn't muster enough to believe it. Instead she thought about how this shower would probably fill the greywater tank and that she'd have to remember to empty it out into the garden this weekend. She bundled herself in a towel and opened the bathroom window, pushed out the screen, and shook her scrubs vigorously to loosen up some of the embedded cat hair—30 cats' worth.

In a beam of light sparkling with dust and cat dander, Didi caught a glimpse of herself. She looked tired. Tired, but OK. She always looked tired—it was one of the side effects of her injury, never getting past delta sleep into dreams. The tired, well, the tired was to be expected. What she didn't expect was to be this sad.

Sasha refused to believe that Didi didn't dream. "Dreamers always dream, even if they can't remember," she'd say, and trace down Didi's long cheekbones with her fingertips. The doctor had told her cessation of dreaming was neither common nor uncommon when an injury such as hers occurred. Didi remembered falling. Her feet slipped out from under her on the smooth wood floor. She landed kneeling, but the back of her head cracked down hard. Didi wound up with a bad knee, a cracked vertebra prominens, a bruise shaped like her sports bra, and potentially permanent damage in her inferior media occipital lobe.

"It's called *anoneira*," Didi explained. A few days later, Sasha handed her a strange, lumpy fruit. She told Didi to slice it in half, and eat the sweet, milky flesh. "That's cherimoya," she told Didi. "A custard apple. In Portuguese, *anoneira*." She dabbed at Didi's mouth with a napkin. "Delicious, yes? That's *anoneira*."

The sun rose every morning and Didi woke up from dreamless sleep. She fed the cats, she did her drills. The world turned and fell apart, then the sun set. The stars had seemed to multiply as more houses stayed dark at night, and the moon seemed colder. But she could still taste the fruit.

And everything moved forward without Sasha there, if not in a straight line.

The Iras were sufficiently wounded by Sasha's leaving. They'd already stopped watching the door for Sasha. Why couldn't Didi?

Didi clenched a fist and breathed out, then slung her bag across her shoulders and wheeled her bicycle towards the door. "OK, Ira," she called behind her. "If you guys aren't too busy today, I left a chore list." The Iras looked at her blankly, then went back to cleaning themselves and setting themselves up in their respective napping positions. Mrs. Lopez padded out to see Didi off, as she had done each morning since she arrived. Didi reached down and scritched the old cat behind the ears, then she pushed the door with her front tire and headed out to the office.

|◄◄ ❚❚ ▶▶|

Riding into the wind made Didi squint. When she squinted, everything looked, almost, like it did before— houses carefully cultivated for island shabbiness, not abandoned or wrecked. Wild spaces looked overgrown and fresh, not full of sinister chaos and manic brambles. When she squinted, it was hard to tell if boats were overturned or seaworthy, and she could convince herself the air blasting through her mask smelled pleasantly of autumn, not decay, of homey wood burning stoves, not fire. Of leathery scented sea salt, not stagnant standing water.

She always tried to bike into the wind.

She biked to the office, the hard work making her sweat beneath her jacket. Blood rose to the surface of her skin and her muscles were still loose from her workout, but she noted how much harder it was to petal, even more than yesterday, noting her own body's age and weakness incrementally, hyperaware that each day she could do a little less with more effort.

She leaned her bike outside the office and knocked a few times on the window to warn Bob she was coming in. At one time, they'd been a receptionist, a full staff, CNAs, but Didi could barely remember any of them.

One was frizzy, another tall and rectangular. One had family just over on Camano Island, another no family at all. Didi remembered people answering the phone, clicking at keyboards, complaining about whoever drank the last of the coffee without the common courtesy to start the next pot. Then she saw Bob and knocked again. He'd officially moved into the office a month ago after his wife and son leaped from the lower deck of the 11:10am ferry and he just couldn't stand to sleep in their house. He waved at her through the window and opened the door for her.

"There was power for a bit," he said, holding up a mug. "There's hot coffee. Make you a cup, kiddo?"

Didi nodded and Bob looked pleased.

It'd been months since things ran as a business, although Bob offered Didi whatever he could. She usually refused, even as she and the Iras and Mrs. Lopez and Sasha grew a little desperate. She knew where such compensation came from and she couldn't get comfortable with it, even though she knew what Bob told her was right—that for many years, he'd helped these clients live independent lives and that they would want it this way. It would all go to waste without family to claim it, which was, increasingly, the case.

She sat next to Bob and they drank their coffee. He kept bobbing his leg, which meant he had something to tell her, but Didi knew he would tell her in his time. His time turned out to be a moment later. He carefully laid down his mug and reached beneath his desk. "I have something for you," he said. He didn't meet her eyes and he pushed something folded towards her, the formality of receiving the folded flag off a military coffin.

In her hands, the fabric was worn and soft, faded prints, and through her mask, over the top of note of disinfecting spray, Didi smelled Mrs. Hamilton's house: artificial rosewater, scorched pans, and wine. It was the Hamilton wedding quilt, remembered Mrs. Hamilton slapping her hand when Didi accidentally dropped some of the oatmeal she was feeding her onto it. *Been in my family for over a hundred years,* she snapped, pointed out the scraps that had once been nightgowns and shirts worn through at the elbow, of cocktail napkins, prom dresses, and christening blankets.

"I went over there last night," Bob said. "She would have wanted you to have it."

Didi dug her fingers into the quilt, thought about Mrs. Hamilton, skin the yellow of an apple core with eyes so mean she was all iris and no white.

"No, she wouldn't," Didi said. "She would want her daughter to have it."

"Yes, her daughter." Bob shook his head at her. "I wouldn't know where to find Mrs. Hamilton's daughter, even if I wanted to." He was bitter; months before the quarantines, Mrs. Hamilton's daughter played some games with her mother's fees, stopping payment, sending expired paper credits.

But Bob chose to have his staff continue caring for the old lady, even though Didi reported she grew difficult, then impossible as her body collapsed, dried up, deprived of the weekly shots of MaGo. Didi tried to be patient with her, trying to imagine what it was like to have to suddenly meet death, but it was hard. Didi pushed the quilt away, towards Bob. "I won't take it."

"Put it in your office," Bob said. "It's getting cold and you may change your mind."

Didi's office was the old conference/supply room. The strip mall seemed to get more regular electricity, and Bob gave Didi the biggest room in the office because he wanted Didi and Sasha to move in there, so he could watch over them, so he wouldn't be alone.

It's practical, he said, and it was, except that she never mentioned the Iras or Mrs. Lopez to him—first, because it hadn't seemed like that big a deal. Then, Sasha had left, and Didi couldn't seem to tell Bob that either, partially because she was afraid he would empathize and sympathize too much, and then, because she was afraid he would resent her because Sasha left, but Sasha was not dead.

Didi went into her office. For some reason she couldn't explain, the quilt made her want to cry. Instead, she placed it underneath her chair and looked instead at the rest of Mrs. Hamilton's things Bob left for her. He was generous, as usual. Cans of corn and red beans, white hominy and instant iced tea, two cast iron pans seasoned with rust, two large throw pillows, a plaid wool blanket that smelled like camphor and benzene, a stack of towels worn bald to velvet. She'd take it all, except the quilt. "It's all lovely," she called to Bob, then she went to the supply closet, still filled with portable sets of masks, gloves, and disinfectant. She started to grab a kit for each of her clients, realizing that with Hamilton gone, she only needed two for the DeVotos. She took two and ticked the rest back. She put the kits in her backpack, along with a can of corn and one of the blankets. "Bob," Didi said. "I'll have to come back with another bag to take it all home. After my rounds."

"Just the DeVotos today?" Bob called. "Then dinner, here, 7 o'clock?"

"Yes," Didi said. "Sounds good."

⏮ ⏸ ⏭

Didi pedaled up and down the DeVotos' street until the ache in her legs turned hot and numb and her tears dried to crusts. The quilt had fucked her up. The responsibility of memories. She laid her bike down on the lawn like a child, and sat down until her knees quit being rubbery.

Mr. DeVoto was nearing 95, his wife 15 years younger. A May-December marriage, both now December, although still spry. In the best of times, they paid for Didi's companionship and some light marital refereeing, and in the worst of times, for her to them cook some meals, run a sponge over everything, and then pack out the compost and recycling. Like all her clients, they'd both slowed down since the pandemic—not sleeping made them too afraid to leave the house for their nano shots, then, there was no more nano to be had. The slowing hadn't been gradual. It didn't take long for Mr. DeVoto to become brittle as a bar of toffee and Mrs. DeVoto to lose fine motor memory. They were dying; they were her favorites. Didi tried to keep Mrs. Hamilton out of her mind.

A man stopped her at the front door. He was big,

filled the whole door frame, blue pants and shirt, black belt, sunglasses. Policeman clothing, but not quite right—a neighbor, a handyman? The man held up his hand, palm forward. "Sorry," he said. "No one comes in unless they're a relative. You a relative?"

"No," Didi said. "Sort of. What happened?"

The man stepped forward, forcing Didi down a porch step. "You are or are not a relative?"

"I'm their caregiver," she answered. "From the agency."

"The CIA?" he asked.

She laughed, but then she realized he was legitimately asking. "I'm the closest, I guess. To a relative. Their son Walter was killed in Afghanistan a long time ago."

The man stepped forward again and closed the front door behind him. He took a pad out of a pouch on his belt. "OK, then," he said, opening the pad and tapping it with a finger. "Can you give me some kind of a statement?"

"Who are you?" she asked. "What happened?"

"I'm Lieutenant Tom Trailer," he said. "And it's not pretty in there."

Didi breathed in sharply. The DeVotos. "I didn't know there were any officers left on the Island."

"I'm not Island. I'm Anacortes. Helping," Lieutenant Tom Trailer said. He muttered something Didi couldn't quite hear, then asked her name.

Didi wondered if Lieutenant Tom Trailer was actually a cop or just a crazy person. A neighbor, a handyman. He waited for her answer with a hand on his hip like a cop, and the pad looked like it was sheathed in navy blue leather, something official and expensive. She wondered if she should ask to see his badge. "Didi Van Ness," she said. He looked the part, and that would have to suffice. These days, you had to start taking people at their word.

Lieutenant Tom Trailer tapped the pad like he was writing it down. He didn't have a pen. "Is Didi short for Deirdre?"

"No, Boudicca." she said. "Do you want a pen? I may

have one."

He ignored that. "Boo-dick-ca," he repeated, slowly.

Didi thought she should spell it, but then wondered whether she should bother. Cop or crazy. "Yes."

"Unusual." Trailer looked at her. "What kind of name is that?"

Didi was starting to feel a little sick, but she recited as she had, so many other times, "Boudicca was a Celtic warrior who led a revolt against the Romans," then she looked into Lieutenant Tom Trailer's sunglasses. "Can I see them?"

"The Romans?" he asked.

Crazy. "No," she said. "The DeVotos."

"If you want," he said. "Are you Irish, then?"

"No," she answered. "My family, maybe, some-where." The sick was starting to grow into full-blown nausea.

"But Van Ness is Dutch, isn't it? It means—" Lieu-tenant Tom Trailer chewed on the edge of the notepad, then continued, "—of the peninsula. Or something like that." He looked at her. "You don't look Irish or Dutch."

Didi almost automatically shot out her other usual canned response: *Haven't you ever heard of the Black Irish?* which she occasionally followed up with a reminder about the Boers in South Africa. Instead she said, "You don't look like a cop."

Tom Trailer shook his head as if he couldn't believe that.

She felt like she was going to cry or laugh, couldn't tell which. They sometimes felt the same: both pushed up hot behind her eyes and nose. If she let herself, she couldn't have been sure which would have come out at Lieutenant Tom Trailer. "What happened? Can I see the DeVotos?"

"If you'd like," Lieutenant Tom Trailer answered and stepped aside. He muttered to himself, "DeVoto, now that's Italian, I think. Sounds like devoted, though. I won-der. That would be a nice name."

Didi stepped into the house, Lieutenant Tom

Trailer behind her. He steered her into the kitchen, made her wash her hands in the basin in the kitchen. "It's not much, but it's something. Gotta hold onto some kind of procedure." He slid the pad back onto his belt. Didi noticed he didn't have a gun.

Everything looked pretty normal. A few dishes in the sink, a bowl half full of swollen oatmeal. Mrs. DeVoto didn't like oatmeal, but it was easy for Mr. DeVoto to prepare and they had a lot of it in the pantry. Sunlight streamed through the east-facing kitchen window, illuminating a fine layer of dust—today would have been a wiping surface day. Didi rinsed her hands in the basin, and then dried them on the thighs of her pants.

Lieutenant Tom Trailer nodded at her. "Now, Trailer," he said. "That's Anglo-Saxon—" and he said something else, but Didi couldn't hear him again. Inside the DeVoto's bedroom, he interrupted his muttering and said clearly, "Looks like he smothered her in his sleep. Broke his own back in the process."

The bedroom was quiet. Dust sparkled in the air. Mrs. DeVoto lay bunched in the covers, head beneath a pillow, her feet bare and fat as an infants' but the wrong shade of pink. Mr. DeVoto was collapsed across her, his middle soft and deflated, separated hips to trunk.

Didi stared, while Lieutenant Tom Trailer said, "This either proves or disproves 'devoted.'"

She couldn't look anymore and spun around into Lieutenant Tom Trailer. He put his hands on her shoulders. "It's OK," he said. "It doesn't look like they suffered."

Didi knew he was trying to be kind. She also knew he was wrong. So, she turned and fled.

She ran out of the bedroom, out into the hall, down the stairs, and over her bike. She ran up East Harbor, past the fire station and the row of mailboxes. Her legs hurt, a cramp stabbed into her gut and she thought she would vomit, but she ran through it until she could smell fresh salt blowing in from Holmes Harbor. She ran through her panting, through the salt and cold, until she was on

Saratoga and she couldn't feel anything anymore. She ran until she was back into the silence of her body, a game, up and down the court, one goal. She ran past the turn off to the Bales' place, her first clients, the house abandoned, past the goat pasture filled with alpacas, until Saratoga turned to 2nd Avenue back in Langley. She ran until she couldn't see Mrs. DeVoto's feet, the color of rare meat, or Mr. DeVoto, slung soft and boneless across his wife. Didi ran and ran until she got home.

She sat down on the floor of her house and started to cry. Didi was never a graceful weeper. Some women were quite beautiful when they cried. Sasha was beautiful when she cried. Capillaries in her cheeks bloomed pink and her tears drew delicate, shiny streaks down the sides of her nose, dangling from her lashes like crystals. When Didi wept, she honked like a goose through her mouth, and her nose grew large and red while her eyes swelled shut. Sasha wept with her face; Didi's whole, long, awkward body sobbed. But today, she didn't care. She cried and cried, for all of it, for herself and the Iras, who scattered around her like they weren't quite sure what to do. She pulled a cushion off the sofa and hugged it to herself, but there was no comfort in it. Mrs. Lopez forced herself onto Didi's lap and she stroked the ugly cat and cried herself empty, until she couldn't keep her eyes open another second and she fell into a deep and dreamless sleep.

One Master

Rumi VanRijn's second act as an adult was to re-name himself Rumi VanRijn.

His third act was to leave behind the small farm, his Hard Luck Dad and his Hard Drinking Dad, his boyhood bedroom overlooking tangled vineyards and nearly everything he owned, including his birth name.

He took only one small suitcase of clothes, a framed poster, and his third-hand gameset.

His dads were good people. Loving people. He'd been birth-named after them.

So, when he renamed himself, leaving behind their names, he took names that honored them.

Hard Luck Dad was a romantic who answered his son's questions about sex with a double feature of old vampire flicks and a volume of Rumi in translation. The former confused him; the latter confused and moved him.

Hard Drinking Dad once gave him a Rembrandt self-portrait print partially because of the resemblance—like the artist in 1630 and like Hard Drinking Dad, Rumi was fuzzy haired, wide nosed and thick lipped with a natural expression that suggested he'd seen some sort of monster—but also because Hard Drinking Dad attributed his favorite quote to Rembrandt VanRijn: "Choose only one master—nature."

Hard Luck Dad and Hard Drinking Dad had a fundamental disagreement with Rumi about how to exactly define nature. Both dads were naturalists, raised without bots. Arguments began when Rumi VanRijn, not yet calling himself Rumi VanRijn, took himself to the clinic on his 18th birthday for his first shot.

That'd been his first act as an adult. An infusion of bots

His dads always said they'd wanted him to make his own decisions about religion, sexuality, and bots, but he could tell they were surprised when he did.

Rumi's acne scars and eczema would fade, and he'd lose his slight gluten intolerance and allergies to ragweed and dander. His eyes improved enough to get a non-commercial pilot license, but his metabolism was untouchable; bots couldn't stroke his fires high enough for the slim build he needed to be an astronaut.

Rumi didn't hate his dads for giving him their bodies, barrel-chested and large, but he swore to himself all kids could be astronauts, if they wanted.

So he left home to study nanotechnology design and programming, on a scholarship awarded to Rumi VanRijn.

Hard Drinking Dad would drink and rage at Rumi, long-distance, over gameset. Then, Hard Luck Dad would take the screen using a voice heartbreakingly, manipulatively, passive-aggressively soft. Rumi fought with his dads on a regular schedule. But the distance helped. The family always made up, taking turns dialing back whoever disconnected first.

When Rumi was in his last year of school, Hard Drinking Dad died. Within a month, Hard Luck Dad fell ill.

Rumi was so close to finishing, as afraid of losing the precious scholarship as he was of losing both his fathers, so moved his Hard Luck Dad into his dorm room.

Hard Luck Dad slept in a hospital bed borrowed from Rumi's internship, pushed beneath the Rembrandt self-portrait. Rumi rubbed bio-oil on Hard Luck Dad's skin, which had gone thin as flakey as pastry.

Hard Luck Dad watched him study. In the end, he was amazed at how much Rumi had learned, had to know. Techs had as much training as a physician, and had to memorize twice as much: functions, cross functions, contraindications. Doctors diagnosed, but Rumi had to know applications, chemistry, how to read medical records and common external symptoms.

Rumi asked Hard Luck Dad exactly once if he wanted Rumi to try and save his life. His dad said no.

Rumi programmed the bots anyway, telling himself he had the stones to inject his dad against his wishes.

But Rumi didn't. Hard Luck Dad grew small and his hair fell out. When he died, his hand was light and dry as a cracker in Rumi's fat, wet hand.

Scholarship or not, Rumi took leave for the rest of the semester. He buried his sadness by learning to fly. Rumi's vision had settled and while he'd never get to space, landing a sea plane on the smooth lake was alien and challenging. He finished school over the summer semester and was awarded three things: a glittering holographic diploma, a full time job as head clinician at the hospital, and a beautiful girlfriend, Roxana.

Roxana was a rock climber, paid to scale exhibitions, faces, and cliffs in distant lands. She was a bottle blonde, with a tiny upturned nose and a massive collection of Sherlock Holmes memorabilia. Moves Rumi'd gleaned from Hard Luck Dad's vampire films and Muslim dervish poetry worked well on Roxana.

Rumi loved how Roxana's hair would turn the colors of a flame when she was overdue for a bleaching, how it marked the passage of time. She also had a birthmark on her thigh that reminded Rumi of an old-time smallpox vaccination scar, which for some reason turned him on.

Roxana loved how Rumi loved her. She also loved his dads' little farm, the little suburban town around it, and spent wads of her climbing credits on local wines and antiques from the local shops. They flew back and forth in his seaplane and fucked regularly, Rumi's finger on Roxana's birthmark like a button.

One day, after they were together for six months, Roxana showed him jpegs of her as a little girl, before her regular bot infusions. She was awkward and oily-looking, with weak muscle development and thin hair. This, in his mind, validated, again, his career path. Every child could be an astronaut, or a rock climber, or anything they wanted.

Rumi promised Roxana one day they'd move to his dads' farm, one day when the dust didn't always settle into the shapes of his dads and when he could stand again the smell of grapes rotting on the vines and filthy wild goats.

But they never did.

|◄◄ ❚❚ ►►|

Rumi was building an anniversary present for Roxana, bots designed to reduce immune response during post-exercise muscle recovery, when one of the docs came down to the clinic for a consult. The doc was one he respected, Lex Green; Green had gone through clinic tech training before his MD, and was now a brilliant, over-achieving, and talented diagnostician who only saw patients for whom all other avenues had been exhausted.

The fact that Green was stumped by a case was extraordinary; the fact that he came to Rumi for a consult was flattering.

He had a case, Green explained, involving an ordin-arily healthy 25 year old woman who started exhibiting sudden onset of severe, chronic schizophrenia.

That wasn't weird. What was weird was that the woman showed no physiological or genetic markers for schizophrenia. They'd scanned her thoroughly and found absolutely no abnormalities in her brain. No ventricle enlargement. Normal levels of frontal lobe activity. "But I did find these guys," Green said, handing Rumi a sample vial. "Hanging like barnacles off her brainstem. Check them out."

Rumi slid over to a free scope and fed in the sample. The blood was saturated with a pack of what had to be bots, but no bots Rumi had ever seen: at first glance, they appeared nearly spherical in shape, but then you could just see they were truncated icosahedrons with 60 vertices and 32 faces. They shone like burnished silver.

"They look like Fullerenes, right?" Green said.

"That's what I was going to say," Rumi answered even though it wasn't; he didn't know what Fullerenes were. He thought they looked like magnetic desk toys acquaintances and colleagues gave one another for holiday gifts. He moved on. "Where did she get these?"

"That's part of the fucking mystery," Green said. He leaned over Rumi's desk and poked at some numbers on the main clinic set, waving open a file. "There're her records. She's only ever gotten bots here. Since she was a kid."

Rumi watched the bots. "Black market? Designer?"

"Has to be, right? But the mother swears her daughter would never, could never. Honor student, *magna cum laude*, devoted to Christ, the whole package." Green sighed. "But people lie." He clapped a hand on Rumi's shoulder. "Think you can take a closer look at these and suss out what we're dealing with, VanRijn? I wouldn't bring this to anyone else."

Rumi flushed under the additional flattery. It proved Green's genius—few things, aside from money and sex, were as motivating as flattery. That and a good mystery. He really had never seen anything like these and couldn't figure out what they were designed to do. "Absolutely."

Green left him to it, and Rumi left the clinic's schedule to Toussaint, his easily distracted but extremely talented assistant.

Rumi did the usual: inspected them for a maker's mark, analyzed the components, pulled out strings of code like fortunes from a cookie. He was at it for less than 2 hours when Green knocked again, with a second sample from a 50 year old male displaying all the symptoms of delirium, with no acetylcholine involvement—but a forest of the same pentagonal bots rooted in the base of his spine. He mouthed the word "coincidence," but Rumi could tell he was spooked.

"Only takes 23 people to get a 50% probability one shares your birthday," Green said, placing the sample next to Rumi's hand. "Thirty people and you get 77%."

"Right," Rumi answered. Rumi didn't know that for certain, but he moved on. "Another?"

Green nodded and slid him the sample. "The birthday problem. We underestimate probability."

He delivered sample number three an hour after that. One of Hawk Montel's patients, a kid this time. Green's eyebrows were set in a straight line. He rubbed the bridge of his nose. "This is big shit, VanRijn."

Roxana was climbing in Switzerland for the rest of the week, so Rumi decided to stay late. He inspected, analyzed, decoded. He added blanks into the mix and watched as the mystery bots sniffed at them like squirrels offered a peanut. He spun them out and sliced at them, blew them open with lasers. He finally fell asleep in his lab chair at 4 in the morning, dreaming of desk toys and monsters.

⏮ ⏸ ⏭

There was nothing to be done. They had a full blown, man-made pandemic on their hands. They could make people comfortable and try and keep them from hurting themselves or others. No researcher, clinician or doc could crack the "Fucky balls," as the bots came to be known.

Rumi had since looked up Fullerenes and R. Buckminster Fuller, and finally understood the joke. He'd also run the numbers on the birthday probabilities and hung to those implausible numbers like a life raft.

He also put the anniversary muscle recovery bot project on a back shelf and, instead, bought Roxana a string of pink South Sea pearls.

Rumi came in every day and reviewed the facts:

Fact: The bots acted together, coordinating their movements, each individual part carrying a bit of code. MaGo, on the other hand, were programmed to be discrete, each one containing all the information needed to complete a job.

Fact: They went for the brain and the brain only.

Throw in any other type of tissue and the bots ignored them like cool cheerleaders do fat girls.

Fact: They also ignored all other bots, except ones programmed to attack or ones perceived as a menace. Those were swiftly dispatched, ruptured like they were soap bubbles, their materials stacked in carefully tended piles where they were reassembled in the Fucky ball's own image.

Fact: Transmission was random. Unlike MaGo, who needed to be directly transfused within 30 minutes of activation, the Fucky balls survived anywhere for any length of time, but some people, even after prolonged direct contact—including Rumi himself—seemed unaffected. Countless hours of research concentrated on isolating genetic, hormonal or chemical patterns immunity factors, only to conclude that all environmental factors had to be positive for infection—although no one would be quoted enumerating these positive factors.

Fact: They made people crazy. The continuums of symptoms were wide, from mild depression to full blown auditory and visual hallucinations. Suicides were up 400% in the city alone.

And fact: These bots were not originally man made. The connotation of this was not something Rumi, nor any other clinician, tech or researcher, was ready to say out loud.

After reviewing these, Rumi'd skim the news and academic lists, looking for new facts. He took long bike rides to think and to work off the banana milkshakes he indulged in daily as comfort food. When his ass ached from the bicycle seat he took long walks instead, coming home with blisters that glistened like Roxana's anniversary pearls. He didn't sleep; he collapsed next to Roxana. Sometimes, he would wake up and find her stroking his hair. He would think to himself about proposing and moving to the farm, but never managed to say anything about it.

One day, Green didn't come in to the hospital. He didn't come in the next day, or the day after that. A few weeks later, Rumi was sure he saw a man that looked just like Alexander Green yelling at a brick wall a few blocks from the clinic.

Rumi didn't stop to check. He rushed to the clinic. And when he got there, Rumi cried. He cried for Green, he cried for his dads who raised him right and loved him well and then let him go. He cried from stress and exhaustion and frustration, and then he went back to work.

Rumi rarely saw patients. He overworked Toussaint and could see it cracking around the tech's eyes as he gave Rumi daily reports.

Rumi promised himself when this was all over, he'd recommend Toussaint for a major promotion, or at least a hefty raise. And he always hoped the tech was sleeping better at night than he was.

|◀ II ▶|

One morning, five months later, Rumi came into the lab and found that the Fucky balls in the first sample Green had given him were dead, their shells no longer shiny. He shone lights at them, raised the temperature, and increased the oxygenation. He picked up the sample and shook it, the bots clacking together like ball bearings. He even tossed in a small slice of brain tissue, but they were motionless.

Dead.

He jumped on the net and could barely call up the academic lists because of shaking hands. *Has anyone found a dead sample? My first sample's dead.* And he waited with his heart beating harder than even when he was on a serious bike ride as other clinicians piped in answers, all no, until one yes, a Dutch doctor clinician who had two dead samples but feared they were some sort of fluke.

Rumi compared findings with the Dutchman, Horstadt, whose own samples had died three weeks ago. No commonalities in number, atmosphere, or additives. Even the patients were as different as two members of the same species could be.

Then Horstadt asked when Rumi's sample was harvested. Rumi pulled up the records and Horstadt calculated the dates.

Six months. Horstadt said. *All our samples died at six months.*

And like that, Rumi added a new fact: The bots die. With no other bots present to allow them the raw materials for reproduction, the bots just grow old and they die. He and Horstadt started composing their report and the simple solution. *Withhold bots infusions and seedings and starve the fuckers out.*

Rumi and Horstadt were nearly done feeding each other their data when Roxana broke through on the main gameset. "Please come home," she said. Her eyes looked red, but it could have been the signal. He said he'd be right there. He'd tell her the news in person.

⏮ ⏸ ⏭

Strands of Roxana's white blonde hair stuck in her gummy eye makeup. She wore only one shoe.

She looked like the final girl in a horror movie.

Climbing made her arms muscular, but he was always surprised by her strong grip. She held his hands now, tightly, and when she let go, he realized his hands were wet. Roxana had picked open her cuticles, and each finger was wet with blood, diluted with lymph and clear plasma. He sat her down on the sofa and brought in a clean towel from the kitchen to clean her hands.

She was quiet at first; let him wipe each finger clean, not even wincing as he brushed at the shiny, sensitive patches she'd picked. When he was finished, she cleared her throat. She looked right at him as she spoke, but he got the feeling she was very far away.

"Everywhere I go, everything is dancing," she said. "Dancing and turning and leaping. It should be happy but it's not. It's not happy dancing." She put her left index finger in her mouth and bit off a strip of skin, pulling it down and off like a pull tab. Blood started flowing again, and Rumi tried to catch her finger with the towel.

"I read a book once about people who danced themselves to death in medieval France," she said. "The crops were bad, there was terrible drought, and so people danced to appease the Lord. They danced and danced, without stopping, without music, until they danced holes in their shoes. Then they danced until they wore holes through their stockings, their skin and muscle to the bone. They danced their feet off." She stopped and sucked the blood off her finger, and then as if she'd just realized it, said, "That's how the world is dancing. Right to the bone. The bone."

Rumi didn't know what else to do but hold her. He didn't tell her about his discovery, but instead used it as a source of strength, strength he needed to get his athletic girlfriend to stay on the sofa, in his arms, until she finally fell asleep. He looked at the pink of her scalp and the pink of her battered cuticles. He listened as she repeated the word "Bone...bone...bone..." and then as her breathing grew slow and even. And even as his arm cramped up, Rumi fell asleep, holding the infected Roxana all night long.

When he woke up, his first thought was of how stiff he was, until he remembered they'd slept sitting up. Roxana was not next to him, and the indentation left on the overly soft sofa was cold to touch.

He suddenly felt a little sick, but convinced himself she was in the bathroom, or had moved into bed, and he pushed himself up to standing with a few cracks of his back and knees.

Roxana was in neither room, nor the kitchen, which, along with the living room, was the entirety of their tiny little house. He realized she must have slipped out before dawn. He slipped on his shoes, kicked off during the night, and went for his bicycle, to do, at least, a cursory search of the neighborhood.

But his bike was gone. Roxana must have taken off on it, which seemed odd because his bike frame was altogether too large for her. But, he reasoned, she was not herself, so anything was possible.

He opened the front door and morning sunshine stung his eyes, still bleary with sticky sleep. He stretched and waddled into the front yard. His bike lay on its side at the end of the drive, where, he reasoned, Roxana must have dumped it after being unable to ride without bruising her pelvis.

Years later, he still wouldn't understand what compelled him to look back at the house instead of walking forward. But he did. He turned around.

And saw Roxana dangling from the topmost portion of the roof. While Rumi slept, Roxana scaled the side wall of the house and, with his bike chain attached to a climbing-ready carabiner, hanged herself.

⏮ ⏸ ⏭

Rumi went into the lab one more time. He met Toussaint there, after hours, for a farewell party of sorts. Toussaint showed up with a six-pack of mismatched beers. They turned on the filtration system and ditched their masks.

The beers filled the spaces when neither man knew what to say.

Rumi asked Toussaint about his tattoo. He'd seen it when it was new, a few years back, but never asked his assistant why he'd gotten "The King of Seattle" etched on his arm.

"It's not literal," Toussaint answered.

"But if someone offered you the job?"

"I think that's the sort of job you just take." Toussaint handed Rumi another beer. "So, you're really going to farm and milk goats and keep bees and shit?"

"Yeah, all that," Rumi said. "I can't stay here. Roxana always wanted to move to the farm. And there, maybe I can keep a few people isolated and see if the bots really die."

"Back to nature," Toussaint said. He purposely didn't mention Rumi's harebrained idea that the bots had a life expectancy, an idea which was skewered all over the tech lists. He also didn't mention anything about his new gig as the interim head of the department, even though Rumi himself put Toussaint up for the gig.

Rumi swallowed the last of his bottle in one long gulp. "Nature is the master."

He shook his assistant's hand and Toussaint pulled him in for a hug. Then Toussaint arranged his mask back onto his face and left Rumi to close the lab one more time.

By then, many samples had died. Rumi pulled Green's sample from the stack and looked inside at the inert bots, then cracked open the sample lid. In death, the bots bonded to one another, congealing into a bumpy lump of dull metal. He pulled the lump out of the blood sample with his bare fingers, and held it up, looking at the enemy for the first time, face to face. Then he placed the hunk gently onto the hard tile floor, by the drain.

With a look like he'd just seen a monster, Rumi stepped on the bots, crushing them under the heel of his shoe.

Then he locked down the lab, went to the plane, and took off for the farm.

Ashley

Sonja Smith-Wicket, MSW, explained Eliza Ocean's options using simple words; Eliza's file indicated the girl's last year of formal education was at age 13, when Eliza's mother moved then into a Hagaan ashram. The file itself was thin, pending results of facial recognition tests, which were bottlenecked, routed through main lab. Until then, Ms. Smith-Wicket went with simple words.

She genuinely wanted to like and help Eliza. Ms. Smith-Wicket found this an effective approach—clients wanted to listen to and please counselors who wanted to like and help them.

First step was to get the girl out of the sex industry. Ms. Smith-Wicket estimated the thin girl at 16, maybe 17, because of her freckles.

"I've uploaded job training information for you. There are lots of legitimate opportunities available for a girl like you," she said to Eliza. "I've included information on a number of entry-level positions. I'd like you to read them carefully and decide which interests you."

Sonja Smith-Wicket's sweater was greasy from wear, the chairs were greasy from wear. Everything in the office was greasy and wet. Except her lips. I bet her lips were chapped beneath her mask.

I tried to sit still and listen to Sonja Smith-Wicket talk about job training, but I picked at the greasy cushions. I thought about Patricia, elevating her feet between dances, waving around the classifieds. Patricia had gone to

college, even did a year abroad in Tokyo and Nagano, sup-
porting herself as a club hostess. Blondes did very well in
Japan, she said, and the money spoiled her for any other
career. But she looked for jobs anyway. Patricia wanted to
have a legitimate opportunity, but every opportunity
seemed like a short-cut to greasy offices and chapped lips.

That's what I thought of as I sat there: Patricia read-
ing those classified ads out loud to anyone who listened,
even sometimes when no one listened: "Housekeeper."
"Bicycle messenger." "Phone sales, office clerk, product
sampling." "Minimum wage." "Customer service." "Min-
imum wage." "Mail room." "Minimum wage."

Eliza nodded and picked at the chair cushions.

"Do you understand?" she asked Eliza.

"I'm sorry," Eliza said. "I've never been very good at
sitting still." She looked at Ms. Smith-Wicket, who wanted
to like her and help her, and her mouth kept talking
without meaning to: "In the ashram we were supposed to
sit still during chanting, during meditation, during lessons
from the guru, during *darshan*. It was more sitting still
than I ever had to do and when I couldn't, the *acharyas*
rolled me long ways inside a rug and beat me with sticks."
She looked surprised at herself—she hadn't said that many
words, true words even, all at once in a long time—and
she clapped her hand over her mask as if she could shut
herself up.

Instead, she shut herself down.

"Where was your mother?" Ms. Smith-Wicket
asked.

Eliza went dead-eyed and quiet. She held the pause
for a long time, not for dramatic effect, but to try not to
answer. Finally, she said, "I don't know."

Ms. Smith-Wicket studied the girl in front of her,
ginger-haired and so delicate, possibly from a lack of
adequate nutrition. She looked for a hint of hurt from the
girl, of pain, of distress or anguish or anxiety, but saw
nothing. The girl was looking at her cuticles with quiet
disinterest. She looked back at the girl's file.

Ms. Smith-Wicket tried another approach. "Eliza Ocean," she said. "What a pretty, unusual name."

Eliza picked at a finger, and then wiped it on her shirt. "Thank you," she said. "I chose it myself."

When I was 14, Srirajanan Hoffman grabbed me behind the meditation hut. He pushed me down to the ground and shoved his cock in my mouth. I fought him a little, but he was larger than I was and close to the guru. Instead I became aware of a sharp stick under my back, a scrape on my arm, the bright smell of melting winter. I let it happen, and I let go, filling myself with all the calm and the stillness the acharyas tried to beat into me. I became a splash of water, cold and impossible to hold or hurt. I sank into the ground like a creek, flowing away from him and his cock and the meditation hut, picking up speed and strength as I went.

Water takes the shape of whatever it is poured in, deceptively deeper or shallower than it appears: creamy and clean, yielding and dangerous, buoying boats, bestowing abundance or death on my own command.

I left in the night.

In the grand tradition of runaways before me, I rushed towards the west coast. I had no skills aside from being young and fluid, so I showed up at open call. They checked me for track marks and C-section scars, explained stage fees and mandatory drug tests and gym membership—then they asked me my name.

I didn't say I couldn't remember who I'd been or that all the women of the Ashram shared one. I thought of a name I liked and what I was and said, "Eliza Ocean."

And so I was. "Three shifts a week, 6 hours each. Tips are yours, Eliza Ocean."

Ms. Smith-Wicket handed Eliza a cup of coffee and watched her load it with 6 sugars and dilute it half milk, exactly how Ms. Smith-Wicket had taken it when she was a teenager. She was seized with tenderness towards the girl. She wished she could just take the girl home, give her a curfew and teach her how to drive and yell at her for wearing too much makeup and then talk about boys over a balanced meal. This surprised her enough to lose her composure and so, instead, she said, "I think I'm also going to give you a referral for some counseling," she said.

Eliza blew at her coffee, even though the milk had cooled it down. "You think I'm crazy," she said. She dipped the finger she'd been picking into the coffee and stirred it around.

"No," Ms. Smith-Wicket said. "Not at all. I think you've been through some extraordinary hardships, though. More than you're telling me."

"Maybe I am," Eliza said. "Crazy, I mean."

Ms. Smith-Wicket wanted to reach out for the freckled hand and hold it, but she looked at her desk. "You've been through more than many people experience in a lifetime." She wanted to say more, but knew that to be an unproductive approach—while clients wanted counselors to like them, they didn't react well to counselors who felt *too* much compassion towards them. "I'm not a psychologist, but I believe you are suffering from post-traumatic stress disorder, Eliza. PTSD. Do you know what that is?"

Eliza probably didn't, but she nodded anyway.

"There's a program at Harborview I think can help you," Ms. Smith-Wicket said. "The information is in the packet, where to go, who to ask for. Do you have any other questions?"

The girl shook her head.

"I'll see you same time, next week." There was no reason for a second visit that soon, but Ms. Smith-Wicket wanted to keep an eye on the girl. "That's the 12th. You'll read everything carefully by then."

"Yes, ma'am," Eliza said. She left her coffee cup on Ms. Smith-Wicket's desk.

The other girls watched me carefully for two weeks. I'd showed up without a gear bag, in everyday clothes. They called me a runaway like it was a dirty name, then a tourist like it was dirtier. But soon, I was just another girl, just like them.

I watched Debbie pluck stray hairs off her inner thighs. Debbie wasn't as smart as Patricia, but she had three children and usually called me honey or sweetheart or something else nice. "Do you think I have PTSD?" I asked her.

"I don't know what that is." She winced at a deep hair. "Is it a sexual disease?"

"No," I said. "My counselor says I have it and I have to go to the hospital."

Graciela laid down a few sheets of paper towel down on the bench next to me before sitting down. "I know what it is," she said. "It means you're crazy."

"I'm not crazy." I never liked Graciela. She was tall with a face that looked cinched shut by a drawstring.

"The counselor thinks you are, girl."

"She said I wasn't crazy."

"Do you ever tell a crazy person they're crazy?" Graciela said.

"No," Debbie piped in.

"No." Graciela zipped up her sweatshirt in satisfaction.

I was annoyed. I hadn't asked Graciela. "It more means that something bad happened to you and that you're broken because of it," I said to Debbie.

"Well, shit. That describes every single person I know." Graciela shivered dramatically and wrapped her arms around herself. "Why do they keep it so cold back here? They know we're naked."

I shrugged. I was wearing a wool skirt and vest. I'd started coming out in a schoolgirl uniform on Patricia's advice. "If you look sixteen," she said to me, "you may as well play it up." She helped me find the right kind of skirt because I'd never been to in-person school.

Debbie slapped her leg and stood up. "You should go to the hospital, cupcake. Maybe they'll give you good drugs."

I didn't want drugs. I liked the idea of working

hard, living clean, being the sort of girl for whom there were legitimate opportunities. I did want that.

The next day off she had, Eliza went up to the hospital on the hill. But once she was inside, all she did was sit in a waiting room wondering why she did come.

She came back the next day. The next after that. And so on. First she told herself it was that she wanted the help, but she never made it inside the office. There was something else, something she liked about the place. It was warm and dry and more comfortable than the library, and, among the sick, she felt important and anonymous. The cafeteria served French fries a la carte and the gift shop had racks of cheap jewelry she liked to look at. The same-day surgery waiting room gave away little cups of free coffee, no limit, and the candy machines by the south elevators took both slugs and Canadian coins. But Eliza liked best the little lounge by the seeding clinic. It was done up like a living room or a study, with leather padded chairs and individual reading lamps, and she could sit there for hours.

Eliza began to recognize people, even if most of them didn't recognize her. Asking if she needed help or was waiting for someone, sometimes twice in the same day. Only one man from Seeding, nametag "G. Toussaint, CRT" recognized Eliza. He was tall and handsome with almond shaped eyes.

The first day, he asked if she was waiting for someone.

She almost didn't hear him. She was looking at his throat, the skin pale with black dots of stubble, stretched finely over his Adam's apple. She wanted to reach out and touch it. "My sister," she lied.

G. Toussaint, CRT saw her again, the next day in the cafeteria. She didn't see him until he was already towering over her, her book, her tray of fries and milky coffee. He sat down across from her and asked what she was reading.

Then, she saw him almost every day. Eliza didn't know if she was looking for him or whether it was the other way around. She learned his days off were Tuesdays and Thursdays, so she traded her weekend nights for day shifts. Then she stopped showing up at work at all.

After the first week, Toussaint stopped asking about my sister. We sat in same-day surgery and drank coffee and talked about the books I read; he never heard of a single one, but listened intently as I described them. We had excellent conversations. He told me about his band and his job, and I watched his eyelashes rise and fall for emphasis over his liquid brown eyes. I wondered what his mouth looked like.

He asked me what I was doing there, and I told him, "My counselor thought I had PTSD, but I don't. Then I liked it here. It's warmer than my room, and less lonely, and I like French fries. Now I come to see you."

He seemed to like that answer.

We wrapped ourselves up in each other. Without even touching me, Toussaint filled secret crevices and nooks inside me like water, and I let him in without any hesitation.

My mother used to tell me I was a stupid, stupid girl.

Toussaint and I went on dates around the hospital on his breaks: lunch at the cafeteria, laughing in the pediatric playground. We didn't see anything but each other; that must have been how we missed all the signs.

One day, we were squeezed out of same-day surgery —there weren't two chairs open next to one another. We moved to the lounge by Seeding, and when that filled up, we tried telemetry, then the birth center. By the end of two weeks, we'd sat in every waiting room in Harborview. It became harder for him to get away from the Seeding window, and then, he couldn't get away at all.

Sonja Smith-Wicket, MSW, read the stats on Mallory Jacobs three times. Her date of birth made her barely 15 years of age. Last residence was the ashram, a 'John Doe' father on her birth certificate. The only child of one

Mary Louise Jacobs, raised up and down the east coast. Mallory'd been described as an extraordinarily bright but troubled young lady with a record of poor attendance, late sign-ins, and behavioral problems in school, but also, as noted by her teachers, exceedingly sophisticated work. Ms. Smith-Wicket waved through the vid of a 12 year old Mallory presenting a report on Kierkegaard and the source of human anxiety, and paused on a close-up of the girl's freckled face, light from the room illuminating stray red hairs floating above her head like sparks of fire.

Such a small, delicate girl.

Mallory Jacobs, alias Eliza Ocean, was a minor of interest in the mass carbon dioxide poisoning of residents at the Hagaan ashram in Wheeling, West Virginia, where she'd moved with her mother just a year past the date stamp of the vid.

The deaths were suspected as foul play; the doors of the sleeping huts had been nailed shut from the outside after the diesel generators were set to maximum. One victim, Harold Hoffman, 42, appeared to have been strangled beforehand. Mallory Jacobs, the only known survivor, disappeared from the scene before police had obtained the presence of a guardian *ad litem* to question her.

"I don't have an address for her. She missed her appointment. She never showed up at the PTSD clinic either," Ms. Smith-Wicket said. "I wish I knew more."

"I know, Sonia," the detective answered. He'd known Sonia Smith-Wicket professionally for nearly ten years. "She hasn't been at the club, either. Not a surprise. Plus, according to the owner, lots of girls have been staying home sick. He was already thinking of shutting when I slapped corruption of a minor and child prostitution charges on him. "

"I had no idea," Sonia said. "How could she do these things?"

"How could you know? She's such teensy girl, right? Five feet nothing." The detective squinted at the video still. "Eliza Ocean. Pretty."

"She chose it herself," said Ms. Smith-Wicket.

I recognized him in the main lobby, picking his way through the crowd. He was trying not to be noticed, which is exactly why I noticed him. I didn't know his name but for weeks, I'd seen him going in and out of same-day surgery in full shield and disposable booties. He'd nodded a few times at Toussaint and me as he poured himself coffee from the waiting area. Now, he was in street clothes holding a briefcase, weaving towards the exit when a woman grabbed him and shouted something about being a doctor. He looked anywhere but back at her, even catching my eye for a second until he saw that I knew who he was. Then he shouted back at the woman, "No, I'm not. Sorry," holding his briefcase against his chest to help him push through the crowd.

"Hey!" I shouted after him, but he was out the door, into the sunlight, and if he knew what was good for him, at a full on run. I cursed a bit and Toussaint looked at me. "The doctors are leaving," I told him. "One just ran out the door."

"Yeah," he answered. He was out of breath, but it sounded sexy. "Nurses too. Anyone with medical skills is overwhelmed by now. They just keep coming." His sleeves were rolled up. He had a tattoo on his forearm. Letters. I tried to read what they were. I hoped they were my name.

I looked around at all the people. Where had they all come from? Some were sitting quietly, but some were jumping up and down, others screaming. One woman appeared to be conducting an orchestra that only she could see or hear. "No, no," she said. "C major. C major."

"The doctors are just going to leave them here?" I asked. "Isn't there a code?"

"Not all of them are leaving. And we won't leave," He flicked his long eyelashes to emphasize he meant it. He was dedicated to his work. To the people. I wanted to run my hands up and down his arms. But then he was close, not to kiss me, but to make sure I heard. "I need your help" He handed an air syringe. "You load the shell here," and pointed to the top. "Then you shake it. Just once or twice." He tapped the syringe against his other hand.

"Then just point and shoot." He pointed at my shoulder.

"Stop," I said.

"You probably need a seeding, too."

"I had one earlier," I lied. "Ronan," I said, meaning his coworker, "Ronan gave it to me."

I didn't tell him I didn't have bots.

He nodded at me. "Can you do this, then?"

Of course I would. "Of course I would."

We topped off people all day. I got used to the recoil of the air syringe, and could dose almost as fast as Ronan, who was half as fast as Toussaint. We topped all day. I felt like a good person when people thanked me, better than being on stage. We topped until the clinic ran out of primaries, then Toussaint gave me some other shells to use. When my fingers couldn't pull the syringe trigger anymore, we snuck away into the basement. Toussaint rubbed my hand and we slept among the bodies.

In the morning, I woke before he did. He started to open his eyes, sleepily. Before he could react, I flipped up my mask with one hand and pulled his collar towards me with my other hand. As I went in, I pushed his mask aside with my lips, over a rough patch of black stubble, shot through with silver, and kissed him, as hard as I could. He didn't kiss me back.

I didn't worry about it. I was young and fluid. Given enough time, water moves mountains and wears them down to pebbles. We were in it together.

Mary Louise Jacobs never had MaGo installed in her daughter. Eliza only remembered her mother in snatches, as if it'd been longer than 8 months since she stood over her. She remembered how her mother would twist hair at the back of her head when she was lost in thought. She remembered how her mother squeaked when she yawned. She remembered how she could see, although she always lost count, each of her mother's vertebra as she prostrated to gurus: first one that had revived Rajaneesh, then one where the guru was kind and told all the children they were made of the same exact material as stars. Then her mother converted them to Haga, and that would be the last, for both of them. All the sects were so very different from one another. At the first, Eliza was always hungry. At the second, she was never hungry. At the third, she was both. They were different, but they had some things in common: they took Mary Louise's money and they prohibited the installation of new bots in the young, and the seeding of bots in the adults who had them when they came in.

Eliza avoided the subject with Toussaint. She hoped he would stop asking her about seeding. He'd stopped asking her about her sister, about where she'd come from and where she wanted to go.

She didn't like the serenity and relaxation in the subjects' faces, and the ease with which consensus was reached after dosing. She and Toussaint spent nearly every second of every day working in concert—it seemed like as soon as they completed a cycle, the duration was up, the bots died off, and they had to begin again. And even though they worked next to each other and slept next to each other, he never crossed over and touched her—something she was sure would change when one day, he'd look at her and see the fever with which she dedicated herself to his dream, how tenderly she nursed the growing flock.

They'd started with twenty from the hospital. The Space Needle made them higher profile, and Toussaint brought Toby Bennett and Joaquin Dentin and Beluga Grace. Eliza didn't like any of them: Joaquin was condescending, Beluga breathed through his mouth, and Toby eyed her all the time, once or twice even flashing her his mouth, licking his lips, like he knew something she did not.

I lined up with the subjects for the nighttime dose, for appearances, but I always drifted away before my turn would come.

One by one, the Kingdom was pulled down into the loose, deep sleep of the freshly seeded, bots circling around inside, picking off viruses and bacteria, doing whatever else they were programmed to do.

Toussaint was still awake, somewhere. I laid next to his bedroll and listened for him. I tossed and turned and waited. It was quiet and still. I wanted to sit up and scream.

Then he was on me, pinning me down. Toby. He dug his knees into my chest, his hands locked around my arms. His eyes glittered from the inside, lighting up his face, teeth glowing white inside his naked mouth. Then he moved his face close to mine. "I've waited for this," he hissed into my ear. "I've been very patient."

I struggled a little, but he was larger than I was and close to Toussaint. I struggled a bit, but then I let it happen, and as it did, as he moved above me, flashing eyes and teeth, I was still and quiet. I felt the tile under my back, a cramp in my leg, stale air and cinnamon on his breath.

When water is very still and quiet, it will show you your true reflection.

Toby wrapped his arms around me afterward to hold me, hold the moment of stillness. But it was gone. I shook him off.

When water moves, that reflection is shown to be nothing but light, light bending across its moving surfaces. Toby looked at his face in mine and shifted his weight.

"You think the King of Seattle loves you," Toby said.

"Bad things happened to the last man who did this to me."

"He doesn't love you," he said.

"The last man who did this died," I whispered.

"The man who did this or the one who gave him permission?" he asked. "Who do you think told me to have at you?"

"Died," I repeated. The tile was cold against my cheek. He loosened his grip on my arms. "He doesn't love you. I do. If you have to make a choice, make the right one." Then he rolled away into the dark.

She didn't see it before. She hadn't been watching anything but Toussaint. That must have been how she missed all the signs.

Toby offered her the juice from his canned peaches, saved a cushion for her to sit on. The King of Seattle said, "I thought you two would make a good couple."

She settled her bedroll next to Toby and let him massage her neck. He has big strong hands. He told her about how he'd gotten a baseball scholarship, then something about how he screwed it all up. He liked to hit baseballs off the observation deck out into the air, then watching with binoculars to see where they landed. Showed Eliza how to hold his bat, even though she could barely wrap her hands all the way around the handle. He taught her to swing and when she hit a few balls off the observation deck, Toby whistled through his teeth like he was impressed. In the evenings, she would lie on his chest and let him ask her questions. He asked about her mother, where she had come from and where she wanted to go.

The King of Seattle asked her if she needed a seeding.

Toby said he loved her eyes. The King of Seattle looked over her, through her, at a spot on the wall.

One night, she looked at Toby thinking he loved her, and her mouth began talking. She told him how when she was a little girl, before her mother moved them to the first ashram, they lived in a little house in Staunton, Virginia. There was a little boy who lived next door and she thought he looked like an angel, blonde haired with deeply set blue eyes. The angelic little boy tortured and killed small animals. The little boy's parents and the couple who owned the little house to the left of them all blamed the dead squirrels and white-footed mice and red breasted robins on Eliza's cat, Grady, but one day, the little boy pulled Grady's head away from his neck and killed him. That was the only time the little boy ever invited Eliza into his house, to see her dead cat. He asked her to come over and then took her to the basement and showed her Grady lying on the cold cement floor. He looked like he was sleeping, but Eliza knew by the look on the little boy's face that Grady was not sleeping. The little boy's face wanted to see Eliza's face when she realized that her cat was dead. Then Eliza stopped telling Toby the story. She said even more words than she had to Sonja Smith-Wicket, MSW.

"Oh-em-gee," Toby said. He squeezed her hand. "Did you tell on him?"

Eliza could tell by Toby's face that he thought that was the right answer.

"Of course I did," she said. "A few weeks later we moved to Maryland to live with the Rajaneesh."

"I want to hear more," Toby said. "I want to know everything about you." Then he told her to take all the time she needed. He said they had nothing if not time. Eliza thought they didn't have nearly as much as he thought.

I did threaten to tell on James. That was his name. James. He took me by the hand into his house and then through the airy yellow kitchen to the basement. He held my hand, but only to lead me.

The light in the basement was blue. It smelled strange, a smell I would always remember but only later know was mildew and wine. At the bottom of the stairs, Grady lay on the floor, his head propped on his paws, exactly as he liked to sleep. Only I could feel the cold floor through the bottoms of my sneakers and knew that Grady would never lie on anything so cold. Grady liked to lie on the stove after my mother heated dinner, liked to wedge himself almost completely inside the heating vents. If the floor was too cold and he had to walk over it, he would run to get it over quickly or goosestep like a tiny robot soldier.

"What did you do to him?" I asked James. I could tell he was smiling by his eyebrows, arched over his eyes. James looked like a doll to me. Over the strange smell of his basement, I smelled him. He smelled like candy.

We stood over Grady and just looked. James waited for me to say or do something, so I finally nudged at

Grady's rear with the toe of my sneaker. "Can I take him home?"

James finally spoke. "I'm not done with him yet. You can have him back when I'm done." He looked at me with his tight brows and his blue eyes, so blue they looked painted in. "He's dead. I killed him."

"Uh-huh," I said.

"Want to know what I'm going to do to him?"

I waited for him to tell me and he waited for me to ask. "Not really," I said. "Can I go home now?"

His brows wavered, but just for a second. "Aren't you going to cry?"

"No," I said. "I'm going home now," and started up the stairs.

James pushed in front of me and blocked my way. "You going home to cry?"

"No." I climbed the next stair, which forced him up one, then another. "Let me know when I can take him home."

"Cry," he commanded.

But I took another step up and forced him to do the same. "Get out of my way." I went up, then he did, again, then once more. We balanced at top of the stairs. "Get out of my way or I'll tell."

James grabbed my wrist and pinched. His hands were soft and warm and a little wet. "Cry," he demanded again. "Cry for your dead kitty."

I raised my arm so I could reach his hand gripping my wrist. His eyebrows were straight lines. I brought my arm as high as I could, pushed aside my mask and licked the back of his hand.

He made a high pitched sound of surprise as he fell down the stairs. Then he was quiet. Before I ran back home, I arranged his arms under his head like I imagined he liked to sleep.

Eliza Ocean sat down on the floor a few feet from the King of Seattle and listened to him play his guitar and sing quietly. She wanted to see him one last time. She wanted to give him one last chance to love her.

Toussaint sensed something then saw her. His hair fell into his face and she wanted to go over and sweep it away from his eyes, tuck it behind his ears, but she forced herself to keep still. "I'm going to have to leave," he said. "Have you heard?"

"Yes," she said. It was easy to start the rumor about a planned murder plot. She'd kept it vague and let the details fill themselves in.

Beluga Grace was curled up on the throne, snoring though his mouth. She gestured towards him. "Beluga said something?"

"Yeah," he said. "He said I couldn't trust anyone. He said they were coming to kick me out or maybe even kill me." He sighed. "I'm just going to leave. Not going to fight." He briefly looked around. "Nothing here to fight for."

Eliza swallowed at that. *Nothing?* she thought, but said, instead, "I liked the song you were playing."

"Yeah," he said. "It's one of my favorites."

"Does it have a name?"

"We called it 'Goodbye to Ashley'," he said. "It's a love song." He stood tall above her, as if making a point.

"Was she one of your favorites?"

"Huh?" The King of Seattle grabbed Eliza's wrist to help her up.

"Ashley."

"Ashley wasn't anybody," he said. "She was a lot of people. She was an ideal. I guess."

Eliza Ocean and the King of Seattle looked out the window. "The kind," he said. "The kind you can't help but love."

The afternoon sun seemed to sink in quick time. She took a breath. "Do you love me?" Eliza asked.

He looked over her shoulder, considering. He was quiet.

"I love you," she said.

He turned back towards the window. The sky was strange and ominous, shades of lavender and pink and peach. Below it, the water was grey and choppy. "It's so pretty outside."

She put her hand on his shoulder and rubbed it in small circles.

"They sent you, didn't they?" he asked. She assumed he meant Toby. She imagined bitterness in his voice. She thought it was too late for that. "No," she said. "This is all me." She rubbed the circles harder. "We should be together," she said. "Take me with you. Please."

"No," he said.

"I love you," she repeated.

"You said that."

"Haven't I been here for you? Haven't I always done what you asked?"

"You have."

"Take me with you. We can leave together."

"No, Eliza. You can't go with me," he said. "You just can't." And then he looked like he was going to say something else, but decided against it.

I cried. Toby tried to comfort me in his big, clumsy arms, holding me against his big, clumsy stomach. He was pleased to hold me because he thought it brought us closer. But if we were closer, he would have known I never cry. But now, I cried until I was empty. He brought me a glass of water and I drank it greedily. He brought me another and was so happy to do so.

I was on Toby's lap drinking water when Joaquin came in. He looked at me and rolled his eyes as if I said something stupid. Then he asked Toby, "Have you seen Toussaint?"

"Not since this morning," Toby answered. He rubbed my back with gentle little circles. "Have you seen him, Eliza?" he asked me in a quiet voice, as to not upset me more.

"She doesn't know anything about anything," Joaquin said. "If you see him, tell him I need him."

Then he was gone. I let Toby pet my hair and kiss my nose. I let him lay me down and while he grunted and groaned above me, I worked his belt out of the waistband of his jeans.

He closed his eyes.

"I'll be right back," I whispered.

The bat was up against the door of the observation deck. Toby taught me to swing, that the power came from my legs, my shoulders the follow-through. In my hands, it felt solid.

It'll take one swing to get him to tell me all the places Toussaint would go.

Then another swing would bash in Toby's big head.

Joaquin would get two swings, just because.

As I walked back to where Toby lay, I started thinking about what I'd call myself next. I wanted something good, something better. Something pure and legitimate.

Ashley was on the top of the list.

Horrible Ways to Die

"Jin and I found a house. The house," Lily said.

To a stranger, her voice would have sounded detached, or, at worst, a little annoyed. Avinashi knew that meant Lily was excited.

"It's close to the beach, close to downtown," Lily continued. "Three bedrooms and a yard for Chaaya and the goats."

"Goats?"

"Yes, Maa. Goats. I told you about raising goats."

"You want to raise goats?" This was the first Avinashi had heard of that.

Lily sniffed into the phone. That meant she was a little annoyed.

Avinashi continued, "Of course, the goats, *betee*."

The affectionate term softened her daughter's voice back to its happy, disinterested tone. "You'd love it, Maa. The previous owners have it purple, pink, and maroon. Jin doesn't love the combination, but it's perfect for one of those painted lady Victorians."

Avinashi smiled and looked down at her robe, which was, albeit faded from use, a demanding green and orange paisley. She tried to imagine her pretty, understated daughter herding goats and her chubby daughter alongside a garishly painted house. "I love those colors."

"Always, Maa, the more obnoxious, the better. Chaaya likes it too. She calls it 'cookie house.'"

"So, where is this goat farm?" It had to be way out there to get beach and yard. "Edmonds? Mukilteo?"

"No. We drove by it first when Chaaya had to go bathroom when we were on that weekend trip around the peninsula a few months ago. It's in Port Townshend."

Avinashi was quiet, so her daughter mistakenly thought she was trying to place the town. "It's north. Up the Straight," Lily said. "Across from Whidbey and—"

"I know where Port Townshend is. I can even picture the kind of house. I spent time there as a girl."

"You did? You never mentioned it."

"It just never came up," Avinashi said. "It's where your *nani* wrote the code."

⏮ ⏸ ⏭

The winter after Avinashi Gopal turned 13, she read a book that listed all the worst possible ways someone had died.

Her parents rented the first floor of a converted Army barracks on a converted fort that had been converted into a state park. Off season, it was quiet and mainly deserted, aside from the park ranger and a couple of European students who would spend a few nights in the hostel down the other side of the park. Her parents chose it because it was so quiet and deserted: her father had a dissertation to finish and her mother had a contract to finish a program which Avinashi didn't understand at the time.

They didn't seem to think about the fact that Avinashi herself would have nothing to do except study, which she'd do as quickly as possible and report to her father who was to be her teacher for the time (she'd hold her netbook up at him at lunch and say, "Baap, I did my maths/English essay on *Animal Farm*/research on coastal tidal pools already.").

Her father piled his notes on the kitchen table. Her mother set up her workstation all across the living room. There was no place for Avinashi to be, except to sit on her bed with her school netbook or stare at herself in the bathroom mirror, so she'd get her schoolwork done and then spend the rest of the day climbing the crumbly dunes down to the beach, tossing rocks, worn smooth as eggs, into the waves, too cold to swim in, until the wind chilled her through her heaviest sweatshirt and the salt spray made her eyes feel small. She'd try and draw the black California gulls or the tumbling strait, but the sketches were never very good.

There was a perfect, tiny castle right in the middle of the park. A lovesick Episcopalian minister had it built for his Scottish fiancée in the 1880s, but by the time it was finished, she'd apparently married someone else and he sold it to the military. *It was still romantic,* Avinashi thought, and she loved its miniature proportions, the high turret which was originally supposed to both gather rainwater and give the lovers an incomparable view of Discovery Bay and the Strait of Juan de Fuca, as well as the Olympic mountains – when they weren't trying to masquerade as clouds. Alexander's Castle was rented on and off during their stay, and Avinashi was too chicken-shit to try the doors when it was unoccupied.

Breaking into the castle was the sort of thing you'd do with friends. And she didn't have any.

A few days a week, she walked the few miles along the rocky beach to downtown and ambled around to Water Street. She'd get a cocoa or a bubble tea, then look in the shops which only sold crappy souvenirs masquerading as artisan crafts: hand-felted pirate hats and scrap tin mermaids.

The shop keeps were always polite and happy to see her, even though they knew she wasn't there to buy; they were as bored as she was in the off season. The bead store lady complimented her skin and hair a hundred times and then gave her a weird curved pendant made of bone ("It's a traditional Hawaiian fishing hook," the bead store lady explained, even though Avinashi, who had been fishing once or twice in her life, couldn't see the practicality of the ornate curves) and she wore the hook around her neck on a leather thong.

Two times, she bummed a few cigarettes from one

of the French students at the hostel, but stopped doing it because her mother could smell it on her even after she brushed her teeth and splashed on rosewater and because the second time, when she showed the French students the bone fishhook, one of them tried to grab her breasts.

By the end of the first month, she'd done everything a bored 13 year old could possibly do during the stay, except take the walking tour of the historic Victorian painted lady style homes, which sounded horrible.

Then she would do it all again.

She even considered going back to the hostel, not for a cigarette, but to see if what it would be like if she let the French student actually hold her breast. Maybe she'd like it better when she was prepared.

Nights were better. Her parents would go to bed at 8pm, and in the quiet, she'd pretend the converted barracks was her very own house. In the dark, she could imagine it her weekend cottage, a swanky loft, a flat in the city. She'd stand in front of the refrigerator with the door wide open and let the cold blow over her, just looking at the food.

If she stood like that at home or when her parents were awake, her mother would snap that the motor would burn out. Avinashi would remind her that fridges no longer had motors and hadn't for at least 20 years, and her mother would pause, then wave a thin hand around and say, "*Meri jaan*, it still isn't good for it," and her father would tell her to listen to her mother, then they would both tell her to go wash her hands, which is what they both always told her when they didn't know what else to say or didn't feel like talking to her anymore, which, in both cases, was more often than they would admit.

So, at night, she was as alone as during the day, but she could pretend she wasn't or that she was glad to be. She'd stare inside the open refrigerator, then move around the kitchen and living room, picking up and putting down her father's notes, turning on and off her mother's monitors, as well as all the other things that came with the converted barracks, including a number of curiosities the

Gopals' did not have in their home: a full set of bar ware, including a smooth chrome jigger and blown glass swizzle sticks; creamy marbled guest soaps scented with cucumber and green tea in the shape of conch shells and seahorses, carved wooden bowls of *papier-mâché* fruit and vegetables or blown glass fishing floats; models of ships with masts as delicate as toothpicks; and books—thin volumes by local poets, a biography of jazz clarinetist Buddy DeFranco, a business book called "The Closed Sale is Open: Zen and the Active Prospect," and "Really Horrible Ways To Die, As if There Is a Really Good One."

Avinashi would take a martini glass from the bar ware, fill it with apple juice and pad around the wood floor in her bare feet practicing how to sip gracefully from the wide glass and toss her hair. That winter, she became good at drinking from martini glasses and tossing her hair to show off her long brown neck—skills which would serve her well later in her life. Then she would wrap herself in quilts and sit on the small porch with an old flashlight, and read bad poetry and about hash snorting beatniks, about generating solid leads and closing techniques, and then, almost exclusively, about the most gruesome and horrible ways to die.

She'd tell her parents about what she read: keelhauling, marooning, flaying, electrocution, immolation, garroting, defenestration, disembowelment, dismemberment.

She would rather have told friends, but all she had were her parents. So, she described gassing, hanging, impaling, drowning, asphyxiation, poisoning, starvation, dehydration. Her mother drew the line at scaphism, which Avinashi described over a dinner of apples, cheese, and salami: "It's when you are tied up and forced to eat so much honey that you have honey diarrhea and get covered in insects which eat your flesh and you die."

"I swear," her mother said. "I'm taking you to a doctor when we get home."

"OK, then..." Avinashi thought for a few seconds. "How about spontaneous combustion?"

"*Betee*," Her father said. "Go wash your hands now,

kripaya."

The winter was a successful one. Her father finished his dissertation. Her mother wrote the 10,000 lines of code which helped perfect nanotechnology's first widespread application: reversing DHT follicle miniaturization that caused male pattern baldness. Avinashi stopped mentioning the most horrible ways to die and her mother never took her to a doctor. But, she remained haunted by the morbid images which would become her first and most famous painting series.

Her mother died from an aneurism at age 50. Only her father would live to see her series: by then, he was in a wheelchair and hardly knew who she was or what he was looking at (she wheeled him in front of one of her favorites and explained to him, "Baap, it's someone getting decapitated by an elevator."), but he had the most lovely, lustrous head of hair.

|◀ ❚❚ ▶|

"What about the bakery?" she asked Lily.

"We haven't decided," Lily said. "We could hire a manager and Jin could go in a few days a week. Or, we could sell it and find a place here. Or a commercial kitchen. Sell on the web. We haven't decided yet."

"Port Townshend is still pretty white, *meri jaan.*" Avinashi thought of the bead store lady fussing over her exotic hair and skin, and wondered what happened to that necklace.

"What do you mean?"

"I mean, do you think there's enough business there for lotus and bean cakes?"

"Maa, you know Jin can bake other things. He's a pastry chef. Besides, no place is really that white anymore."

"Yes, *meri jaan.* Everything your husband makes is delicious. Speaking of which, let me say a quick hello."

|◀ ❚❚ ▶|

The summer Avinashi Gopal turned 30, she gave birth to her daughter, Lily Reva Gopal.

Lily liked to hang on her mother's back as she worked. The smell of linseed oil and acrylic and acetone seemed to comfort her daughter as much as it did Avinashi, one of the two things that reminded Avinashi that Lily was, indeed, hers and not a changeling or an alien: her skin, the same milky tea brown as Avinashi's, and the fact that cold studios and their rich, chemical smells made her smile. If not for these, Lily would always have remained strange to Avinashi—a bit too pretty, too doll faced and altogether too relaxed and languid, beautiful and strange. Like her own parents, Avinashi wasn't entirely sure what to do with her little girl, but it wasn't for the same reasons, not at all she would tell herself over and over, it was that she was accustomed, simply, to creating her creations with single-minded attention and reverence, then releasing them: to galleries, buyers, whatever. She was used to finishing, then moving on to the next. Lily would never be finished. She would always be a work in progress.

But Lily was hers and Avinashi painted with Lily, swaddled in fleece against the cold of the rented studios, strapped firmly to her back. Lily was restful everyplace else, but there, there she would settle against Avinashi's spine and blow and burp the warm baby breath of sleep.

Avinashi did what she considered her greatest work with the warm weight of her daughter against her back. That series, done while Lily was an infant, was less critically and commercially successful than her first series, "Horrible Ways to Die," but she herself preferred the gentle hopefulness of "Terrible Disasters."

Avinashi did this until Lily was simply too big, until her long legs (she must have inherited her father's legs) waggled ridiculously out of every carrier, like bell clappers.

Avinashi never took Lily to the converted Army barracks on a converted fort that had been converted into a state park. She took Lily to New York and LA, to London and Tokyo and Taipei, and on more than one occasion to her family's homeland. But she knew these places had the same effect on Lily that Port Townsend had on her—she was boring and warping her daughter as her parents did to her, and now she realized, her grandparents had done to her parents. Avinashi would look at her beautiful, languid daughter and wonder which place, what thing would be her defining break. She thought sometimes it would have something to do with the fact that Lily was hardly ever physically around other children; Lily attended school online, which made it simple for them to travel to Avinashi's openings. It was the dominant trend anyway. Online schools started picking up steam when she was a girl, and now over half the world's children attended virtual schools.

And even around other children, Lily was better around adults. She had good posture and a serious demeanor, and by 4 years old, could politely converse in English, Mandarin, Hindi and Italian.

But Avinashi knew she could have sacrificed, bought a home someplace uncomplicated and with good weather and given Lily her own bedroom and allowed her to attend a school instead of flying to San Francisco and Miami, Prague and Rio, sleeping in hotel suites next to her mother. She kept the small loft in Seattle, but it was a way station, a place to receive packages. A place to keep the few important things that she couldn't carry in a suitcase. The weaving loom and Durga statue, family heirlooms that her own mother had hauled from India, and the clothes that Lily would outgrow and, then, the clothes Avinashi would pick out for her that Lily would wrinkle her beautiful, strange nose at, even as she smiled politely at her and accepted them.

Avinashi knew it could be something smaller, something randomly fated to cross her path, something that would appear harmless, instead of the most obvious ways and things. It could be anyplace, anything—for her it was a winter in a state park with no friends but a paperback on death.

Avinashi watched Lily grow. Her face changed, her reach extending, and her heavy breasts appearing out of nowhere (again, her father's side). Motherhood was like being on a speeding train. Nothing seemed to change moment to moment, but when she would look up, and everything was speeding by—Lily walking, Lily talking, Lily walking a block ahead or behind her mother in supreme embarrassment, Lily flirting, Lily graduating high school and announcing she was taking a scholarship at Seattle University. Avinashi could only glimpse these changing seasons and scenery for an instant before they were already gone and they were on to something, someplace else. Lily in a muted *chogori* and a long, flowing *chima* at her wedding, becoming Mrs. Gopal Lee. Lily swollen with Chaaya. It all happened too quickly.

She never discovered what or where her daughter's scars were.

⏮ ⏸ ⏭

"Hello, mom." Jin's deep voice buzzed a little. "Lily told you about the house?"

Avinashi loved her son-in-law. She'd never seen her daughter smile as much as she did around Jin. "She did."

"It's a monstrosity. We love it. The paint job made us think of you."

"So Lily says." The first time she met Jin, his huge hands enveloped hers, made them seem small as a girl's. Strong hands, a maker's hands, hands Lily loved, in which she saw potential, hands she put through cooking school. And those hands made the most delicate and exotic sweets, filled with beans and persimmons, pine nuts and candied chrysanthemums. Avinashi never developed a taste for eggy Korean pastry, but she could never deny his artistry.

"There's a third bedroom just for you. Whenever you want," Jin said. He had an easy way of flirting with her that she also appreciated.

Avinashi tossed her hair back over her neck and giggled. "I'm thrilled for you. I really am." She heard her granddaughter yelping in the background.

"Want to talk to the monkey? She's jumping for the phone."

"Yes," she answered. "*Kripaya*, yes."

|◀ ‖ ▶|

The spring Avinashi Gopal was 53, she nearly died from the flu. It took her nearly a month to recover.

She didn't remember much, just snippets from her fever: a thin arm that could only be Lily's, handing her water; a hulking silhouette in a rocking chair, shaped like her new son-in-law, Jin; her baby granddaughter curled up beside her, fat and smooth to touch, her tiny face mask a slash of pink across her cheeks.

In and out of dreams, she was at a crowded opening in an airless studio. Her paintings hung on the walls, bloated with insistent colors that felt smothering: vermillion and carmine, antimony and Hansa yellows, Payne grey. Blood and fire and smoke.

She didn't want to look at them, so she looked at the crowd. The only face she recognized was Lily's father. He cocked his long index finger at her to follow. She tried, but trapped inside her heavy body, she sweated from the effort. One step took hours, days, but she followed him to a balcony, where he started to wave his arms. He was angry that she never told him about Lily. He called her a stupid girl, which didn't feel like the terrible insult his face meant for it to be.

It was cooler on the balcony. She tried to enjoy it. But he wouldn't let her, leaned in closer and closer and demanded to know something—what did he want to know?—about Lily, about how she carried Lily in secret, never told anyone who her father was, not even Lily herself. Avinashi tried to explain, how Lily might have been a shared idea, but he was no collaborator, but other words came out of her mouth instead. So he pushed her, and she fell, through the cool air. She didn't even care that she fell; she smiled at the breeze and her growing distance from him.

"Mom's smiling. Lily! Lily, get in here."
"Maa? Maa? Can you hear me?"
"The fever's broken."
"You're OK, Maa. It's all going to be OK."

Everything slowly came back into focus. To a stranger, Lily's beautiful torpid eyes, above a tasteful plaid facemask, would have looked bored or a little sleepy. Avinashi knew that meant she was worried.

"Hello, *meri jaan*," she said. "I had the strangest dreams."

Lily sat at the edge of the bed and told Avinashi that she'd had the flu, a bad one, with a fever of 104, but that she was going to be fine, that she was at her and Jin's apartment. Avinashi struggled to understand her daughter's words, muffled behind the mask.

Avinashi tried to sort out her thoughts. The flu. The flu was dangerous, spread quickly. Deadly. Her granddaughter. A child. It killed children and the elderly. She wasn't elderly, yet, but. She told her daughter that she should have taken her to the hospital.

"Maa." Lily furrowed her eyebrows. To a stranger, it would look like her daughter was thinking, but Avinashi knew it meant she already had thought. "You were in the hospital. For a few days. But then you were OK to move once—" Lily pressed on her mother's chest a bit to prevent her to move. "Once we all got the bots. The bots saved you. The bots killed the virus. The bots protected us."

The bots.

Avinashi felt nauseated. Suddenly, she could feel them swim in her, restless guppies in an aquarium of blood. The bots, microscopic nanobots, called MaGo bots in honor of the woman who wrote the code that allowed for the bots to take their programming from the body— from hormones and neurotransmitters, from immune response and nutrient levels— all those years ago, one winter in Port Townshend, her mother, Malaya Gopal. Her mother.

Since their first function reversing male pattern baldness, an entire industry exploded developing new applications for the MaGo bots, funded by hair money. Avinashi flexed her hands.

She never wanted those. She had told her daughter that. Now she was frozen this age. And Lily and Jin. And what about Chaaya?

Lily had looked at her and said clearly, "You are not frozen at any age. Once the virus is eradicated, yes, the MaGo will work on some of your cells, but—"

"And Chaaya?"

"Chaaya will be fine, Maa. Cuts will heal faster. But they won't activate that way until she hits puberty." Lily moved her hand from Avinashi's chest to cover her hand, which Avinashi curled to a fist. "You would have died, Maa."

Avinashi tightened her fist below her daughter's long hand (like her father's). "Dying's not the worst thing that can ever happen. People die, *meri jaan*. People die."

|◀ II ▶|

"*Nani, Nani, Nani!*" Chaaya screamed into the phone.

"Hello, Muppet. I heard your Maa and Baap are putting you to pasture with some goats?"

Chaaya heard the word goats, and started babbling in a 6-year-old's excitement about goats and how one goat would be her goat, but that she wanted a dog more, no, a dog and a goat, "And I'll name him Pie."

"The goat or the dog, Muppet?"

Her granddaughter panted into the phone, thinking hard. "Both," she finally answered.

|◀ II ▶|

The fall after Avinashi Gopal turned 65, she held her granddaughter, Chaaya Gopal Lee, in her lap, even though the girl, at 13, was nearly the same size as her grandmother and twice as chubby.

Avinashi was trying to make the girl cry.

Chaaya had remained stone faced through the news, the recovery of her mother and father's bodies, through the funeral, through the packing of the house and its sale to the Port Townshend Historical Society. She turned her lips down a little bit when they dropped the goats off to their new owners, and gave Pie, the fainting goat she raised from a kid, and Cake and Cookie, Pie's own kids whom Chaaya had helped deliver, and long hugs where she buried her face into their necks. She watched Pie and Cake and Cookie, as well as the others, stiffen and go myotonic at the sound of Avinashi starting the motor, held her hand on the window, but only for a second. Then Chaaya turned around in her seat and looked straight ahead. They drove to Seattle in near silence; Avinashi pointing out the changing leaves to Chaaya, who grunted approval.

Autumn was like motherhood. Every year, Avinashi tried to look for it, but always she missed its arrival, noticing only after the leaves had already begun to fall.

But through everything, Chaaya hadn't actually shed a single tear.

Avinashi tried to change that by holding her granddaughter close and stroking her hair, like she'd done when the child was smaller.

Chaaya wriggled around on Avinashi's lap, then slid down her grandmother's legs to the floor in front of her. She picked at strands of the carpet. Avinashi held back telling Chaaya to stop picking, but she wanted her granddaughter to feel at home. This was her home now, and she wasn't sure if Chaaya picked the carpet at her parents' house, so she kept quiet and looked at her own hands, too smooth for her age. She rubbed her palms on her skirt.

"*Nani*, do you know the odds of being struck by lightning?" Chaaya asked, looking at a few furry strands she'd pulled from the carpet weave.

She didn't. She only knew it was a horrible way to die.

"In an average year, they say there are about 700 people who get struck by lightning, but only 10% get killed." Chaaya said. "Statistics I find say things like the reported odds of getting killed by lighting are about 1 in 750,000 and the odds that you know someone who was or will be struck, but may or may not be or have been killed are 1 in 625." She pointed out that wasn't very much. "You only need 50 people at a party for 2 of them to share a birthday. Like 99% probability."

As Chaaya talked, Avinashi panicked; she realized she knew so little about where Chaaya was in school. Did she learn these facts in school? Avinashi tried to think about what she learned in school. She was pretty sure she never learned about lightning strikes killing people in any grade. "Fifty people is a big party, little monkey."

Chaaya ignored that. She continued, "And there are between 10 and 36 ground strikes on the Olympic peninsula alone." She rolled the wooly carpet strands between her fingers and lamented that she wasn't old enough or smart enough to figure out what the odds were that two people would get struck by lightning on the peninsula and die. "But I will be." She nodded her head and lay back against Avinashi's legs.

The carpet strands uncurled themselves, writhing like small worms.

"I know you will be, *meri jaan*," Avinashi had said. "Now, be a good girl and go wash your hands."

Glasses Guy

Kristina meant most of her vows and she was really sorry about the one she couldn't keep. Sorry she still loved and cherished him, sorry she could overlook rich/poor, and sorry she could have and hold. She was sorry. Sorry enough for the sickness and in health and the for better and for worse—she stayed until the itching began, over the slim odds the itching would never begin—but not sorry enough to stay until death do they part.

She didn't even need to tell Beluga how sorry she was— although she did, every other sentence— he could read it in her face, in the careful way she packed her things that she was deeply, horribly sorry.

She could barely look at him, only for brief seconds when she met his eyes to prove her sincerity, and she folded each shirt, scarf, skirt, quilt corner to corner, as if they were precious and delicate to her even though that was not how she treated them in use.

Beluga wondered if she would have stayed if the itching never started. He didn't ask. It didn't really matter anyway.

"You'll be just fine," she repeated. That was every tenth thing she said, in and around the apologies. "Just fine."

Physically, he would be fine. The itching was progress, an essential component of healing. His docs warned him the itching would be unpleasant, but they buried it beneath explanations so detailed he could picture the nerves regenerating and bones knitting together; fresh pink ligaments and tendons trussing his joints; blood feeding new tissue. They didn't prepare him for the itching; if he thought to curse the med team, he brushed it away. They couldn't have possibly described it and it was best they hadn't tried.

He existed as itch. Unceasing, unremitting itch. It crawled and prickled, tingled and burned. He'd wake from fantasies where he scratched and gnawed at himself, grated right through the skin, tearing bloodless flesh away until he was nothing but gleaming white bone. He could live inside those dream horror shows; they gave him momentary respite from the itching, and from the other dreams he had, nightmares replaying the accident.

He thought at the chair. It responded, and wheeled him where he needed to go. Sometimes, he'd wheel himself near the edge of the dining room table or the back of the couch and blew into the armrest controls, flinging an arm against the edge for relief. He'd let himself droop down in the chair until he could chew on some part of himself. In and around the apologies and he'd-be-fines, Tina rubbed the creams on him, even used her nails. But there was no liberation to be had, no moment of satisfaction. The itch was under his skin.

All he could do was watch his wife pack her things. The itch superseded any emotion he had about it. He tried to care. He watched her spine bend and flex like a fish's beneath her thin shirt.

"I wish you wouldn't stare at me like that, Lou," she said.

"I can't do anything else, Tina," he said. "If I could, I would."

She turned to him. Sweat separated her bangs into thick curls. Her eyes were deep set and red with sorrow. She would apologize now. "I'm sorry," she said.

"I don't want to watch you leave me," he said. He didn't, although he would. He couldn't care, but he could focus and concentrate on watching her, get absorbed so the itching, which never ceased, would move to the back of his mind, like a phone continually ringing in the distance.

There was no way to truly ignore the itching.

Tina wiped her forehead with her hand, then wiped her hand on her shorts. "You want some music? How about you watch some music?"

It was a good idea. Better than watching her pack. "Yeah," he said. "Sure." He even tried pull up his eyebrows in a smile.

Tina's brows raised back, a gesture of relief. The music had always been her go-to move when Beluga was angry or stressed or moody or lost in thought, or when she just couldn't figure out what else to do. She said, "You'll be OK," and wheeled him into their bedroom—his bedroom now—and booted up a gameset. She clipped on the headphones and waved through files. "What do you want to see?"

Beluga had hundreds of music vids, one of every show he'd ever been to, and quite a few of shows he'd only seen on gameset. Tina had her hand on his shoulder. If only he could move, he could use the pressure on the itch. "Figurehead," he said. "Not a show you went to. One I saw alone." He didn't look at her face again, but sat expectantly, waiting for her to choose.

She snapped at one of the files, and it expanded. She snapped again to set it to play and stepped back. "I'm sorry, Lou."

⏮ ⏸ ⏭

Beluga watched the show twice through. He remembered the night: Toussaint broke two guitar strings in a row, and Joaquin was so drunk by the end of the show he'd pissed himself. Beluga hadn't started dating Tina yet, and he'd had to promise a favor to one of the guys he worked with at the factory to cover that night's pick-and-pack shift. Beluga was hell bent on a good concert, and Figurehead didn't disappoint. They didn't play 'Goodbye to Ashley' even though he and some other guy had yelled for it, but they did play an acoustic version of 'In your

Armageddon' and a fast version of 'Facing West.' Today, Beluga sang along with 'Facing West,' loudly. Tina always teased him about his off-key voice and he was usually self-conscious about it, especially when compared to a steely-soft voice like Figurehead's Toussaint, but at that moment, he just didn't care if Tina heard. She was leaving and that was that, and his singing wasn't going to convince her to stay nor drive her out the door faster. "The orange sun, the day is done, and you are gone. But somewhere, you still care, and we both face west together," Beluga sang, eyes closed. "The moon is hung, I am one and I am done. Somewhere, and I don't care, you'll face west alone." And when he opened them again, he saw Tina in his rear view mirror on his chair, looking struck.

"I'm going now, Lou," she said. "I'm sorry."

He wanted to say something. He wasn't trying to hurt her. He just wanted to remember a time before the itching, before the accident, before Tina. He wanted to remember how he lived, and that he, indeed, did live before and without any of them. Instead, he said, "Yeah. I know."

"I wish you'd reconsider," she said. She meant reconsider going into a facility once she was gone, just until he got movement again.

"I wish you'd reconsider," he said. He meant leaving their marriage. He didn't know any more if he meant it. But since he couldn't even think about it, much less throw things or smash things, this was all he had, and it would seem ruder to say or do nothing except flap around and try and scratch himself.

She kissed him on the forehead, and lingered there for a long second.

He didn't even know where she was going.

He knew it was going to hurt him soon, that he would handle it badly. She wasn't leaving him for someone else. She wasn't leaving him because they'd grown apart or even because of an argument. She was leaving him because having no one, having nothing, was still better than being married to the man who accidentally killed her sister.

"I'm sorry," Tina said. "You'll be all right." Then she was gone.

The show started again. He realized it would just replay and replay until the nurse came by in the morning. Until then he was alone with his itching and his music.

Beluga waited until he heard the front door close and lock. Then he said, "Fuck you, Tina."

⏮ ⏸ ⏭

Sometime in the night, he was able to move an arm. Not well or with any accuracy, but enough to slap his belly and thigh until they were hot and pink. It didn't stop the itch, but instead cloaked it in a different sensation, one that reminded him of being a bullied kid in tribal school.

Soon, he'd be able to scratch until the nurses bound his fingers with gauze to reduce the violence and depth of the digs and scrapes. Eventually, the itching would fade away entirely, and be replaced only with pain, but they could give him something to mute that, and he could busy himself with relearning to walk and wipe himself and maybe, one day, drive again. But for now, he slapped him- self and watched Figurehead and slipped into short, scrambled dreams about Tina and her wet bangs; Joe Hog, the school bully; playing on-stage with Figurehead; driv- ing the forklift at his college night job; and the long seconds when the car careened out of control, and Tatiana's last scream.

The morning nurse let herself in. The door woke Beluga up. For a second, he was confused and about to call for Tina, but the nurse popped her head into the room before he found the strength to conjure the word.

She had frizzled brown hair and one thick eyebrow. She introduced herself as Haregu, and was very excited to learn he'd been slapping himself. "You've got to stop," she said. "No good for you, but soon you can go." She made a gesture like she was jiggling a marionette.

She stood next to him and looked at the show. "You like music?" she asked, but didn't wait for an answer before waving it off and wheeling him into the kitchen. She held his hands and pinched his wrists each time he tried to slap an itch. "No good for you," she repeated. She made him a tall stack of pancakes, and while she was turning them, he managed to get in a slap or two.

Haregu sat down across from him in Tina's chair, cut the pancakes methodically into tiny bites and fed him the whole plate.

Pancakes, he thought, were a weirdly intimate food for a nurse to prepare. His father would make the family pancakes when work was good, which meant he was in a good mood, and Beluga would eat three portions as if he could literally absorb as much of his father's good mood as possible. Then, pancakes were what he prepared for women who spent the night. They were his specialty, a thank you of sorts to them for facing him, even though he was a thin, dorky half-breed, compete with an astigmatism too severe for MaGo treatment and a job in urban planning no one—not even Tina—quite understood or could muster up enthusiasm for.

He did wind up naked in Haregu's arms later that same afternoon, but only as she jiggled him like a marionette beneath the shower nozzle. The hot water briefly soothed the itching. She was stronger than she looked, and Beluga wondered how many men she jiggled under the shower.

She dried him off and explained she'd be back Wednesday, and that in-between he'd have a nurse named Oona, who was, according to Haregu, "Very nice, big arms," whatever that meant.

"Tomorrow, early," she said. "Tech tech will come and see you."

"Tech tech?" he asked.

She pulled her one brow down as she tried to think of the words. "Tech tech." She jiggled her hands again, then made a gun shape. "Tech tech," she repeated, then pantomimed shooting him in the arm.

A MaGo tech. "Ahh," he said and nodded.

Haregu looked pleased. "Tech tech. Then you can

go." She jiggled her imaginary puppet.

"Yes," he said. "I'd like that."

"Your wife will let him in?"

"Yes," he said. "Of course." If his docs knew he was staying alone, he'd get forced into a facility. He just wanted to sit and itch and slap himself in peace and privacy. "Of course."

"Good," Haregu said. She wheeled him back into the room, and on his request, waved on a different show, a Colossus show, one of his first when he moved to Seattle. "No slapping," she said to him, and then she left.

He listened for the door to close, then he said, "See you Wednesday, Haregu."

⏮ ⏸ ⏭

Beluga didn't feel sorry for surviving. He was glad to have lived. He wanted to live, even if now he didn't know exactly what he'd be living for.

He didn't compare and contrast himself to Tatiana, agonizing over whose life was more valuable, just as he didn't blame Tina not being ready to pick up her sister when she'd promised, for making him go to pick Tati up, any more than he blamed the malfunctioning stop light.

The accident was precisely that: an accident. Beluga could have refused his wife. He might have driven faster or slower, taken a different route, jerked the wheel with more force; there were a thousand tiny decisions that could have altered the course of the night with direct effects on its outcome. But it happened as it did.

No one could blame him, and he didn't blame himself.

That was what his wife found unforgiveable.

Tina didn't understand. And like the docs who couldn't describe the itching that came with healing and therefore didn't try, Beluga couldn't substantiate his reaction in any way that she'd understand and he couldn't be sorry that he was prepared for death in a way that made him unmoved by its injustice, randomness and sudden revelation.

Beluga'd never been given a sex talk, but he'd had several death talks by the time he was thirteen and received his gravestone, complete with his full name and date of birth, placed next to his mother's and his father's with a few feet leeway for his own husband or wife, and flanking his grandparents and great-grandparents, all the generations of Graces that lived on that same land back to the days when they were first given the name. You had to pass the cemetery to and from the house. It was one thing to know in the most abstract of ways, that everyone dies. It was another to picnic and play baseball on the land under which you'd spend your own eternity. He could picture his grave, the answer to a question not yet asked but on the tip of the tongue.

Tina couldn't understand. And she couldn't understand that while he was sad Tatiana had died, he was sad her family was sad, was sad she was sad, what he was the most sad about was this: when he was thirteen and presented with his gravestone, his father held his upper arm and told him there were two ways to meet death and both were bona fide means to measure the merits of a man. He could meet death fighting or with his heart and eyes wide open. Beluga blacked out at the moment of the accident and still didn't know what kind of man he was.

⏮ ⏸ ⏭

Beluga slapped and slapped the itches until he felt sunburned. The practice improved his aim, and he slapped off the Colossus show, slapped his hair down, and slapped free a few cookies off the kitchen counter. He was trying to slap open the refrigerator when the front door opened. He thought and wheeled himself around until a tall man in tech coveralls found him in the kitchen.

Beluga looked up at the guy. Even if he could stand, the tech would still top him by at least a head, maybe a head and a half. There was also something familiar about the guy, but Beluga couldn't place it.

"Mr. Grace?" the tech asked.

Beluga nodded and the tech smiled. "I'm Greystone," the tech said. "You know why I'm here today?"

"Time for a seeding," Beluga answered. Something tugged inside, like the itch. He knew this tech. He opened his mouth to say something about it, but closed his mouth again.

"Yes, that," Greystone said. "You also get some specialized bots to help accelerate your healing." He leaned in. "I've heard the itching is something awful."

"It is unbelievable," Beluga said.

Greystone wheeled him into the living room where he'd set his case and tablet when he entered. He turned Beluga towards the couch, then sat down directly opposite him.

Beluga studied Greystone. Seated, Greystone's knees reached his chest. He knew he knew him. He was sure of it, but the itch was taking up half his brain.

Greystone scrawled something onto the tablet, then unclipped the case. "Your first name is Beluga?" he asked.

"Like the whale," he answered. He's given that answer countless times before, but it never seemed to satisfy the asker. They always seemed to expect a different response, although Beluga couldn't imagine what it was.

The other man just nodded, however. Beluga figured Greystone fielded a lot of questions about his own name. He tried to place the name—he knew this guy, seemed like the name was familiar too.

"Folks tell me this load relieves some of the itch. The rest is just time." Greystone looked at him. "You know, you look really familiar to me."

Beluga let out a breath of relief. "I was thinking the same thing. In fact, it's driving me a little crazy already."

"I've probably given you a seeding sometime." Greystone loaded a shell into the air syringe. "I'll give you the special first, OK?"

"OK."

Greystone leaned towards Beluga and aimed the syringe at his leg. Beluga looked at the tech's hands, big and callused, and just as Greystone shot the bots, Beluga knew who he was. "Greystone Toussaint," he said, huffing in with the injection.

"Yes," he said, shaking the spent syringe.

"From Figurehead."

"Well now," Toussaint said, leaning back. "That's it. We know each other through the band. La-mao." He started loading up a second shell. "I should have recognized you. You're glasses guy."

Beluga didn't know whether it was the fact that Greystone Toussaint was his tech or that the specialized bots were already working, but the itch abated slightly and his heart was beating very loudly. "I'm a huge fan. I've been a huge fan forever. I listen to Figurehead all the time." Then he finally registered that Toussaint called him glasses guy. "Glasses guy?"

"Yeah," he said. "Glasses guy. You ready for a second?" He held up the syringe.

Beluga must have nodded because Toussaint leaned over and shot his shoulder, then continued. "Glasses guy. We'd look around for glasses guy in the audience and knew it'd be a good show." He leaned back. "You were like a good luck charm."

The itching was definitely better. Beluga flushed with relief and pleasure at being glasses guy. "I can't believe you noticed me."

"Of course we did. You were at more shows than you weren't." Toussaint scratched something else on the tablet then clipped closed his case. "It was the glasses, of course. I thought they looked cool." Toussaint squinted at Beluga and continued. "Now I see you need them. How come you haven't gotten your eyes treated?"

"It's a pretty severe astigmatism. Would take more bots and reshaping than—" he said, then paused. More than his parents could have afforded. Then, he just didn't bother, although he couldn't say why. "Besides, the glasses are distinctive."

Toussaint nodded. "Well, I'm glad you're going to be OK. Looks like it was a pretty serious scrape."

"My wife's sister died," Beluga said, then immediately regretted it. He wished he could just be cool.

"That's awful. I'm so sorry," he said and sighed.

"Me too," Beluga answered.

"You're well on your way to recovery, though," Toussaint said. "You'll probably only need one boost of the specialized bots, then you'll be back to normal. Expect some rapid heart rate and respiration for a few hours. Even a bit of adrenaline. You'll gain movement quickly but be pretty weak. That's all normal. Call your med team if anything uncomfortable or unusual happens. Call your med team if you develop a headache." He stood up. "Great to see you, glasses guy."

"My wife left me because of it," Beluga said. It sounded sadder and more desperate than he meant, and he looked at Toussaint. "This morning. I don't even know where she's gone."

Toussaint sat back down and looked over his knees. "She has other family? She's probably with them."

"I sang 'Facing West' as she was packing," Beluga said.

"Oh-em-gee," Toussaint said, amused. "That is cold." He tried to put a leg down into a more comfortable position, but couldn't. "I moved to Seattle for the girl that inspired that one."

"I didn't mean to hurt her." Beluga didn't know if he meant his wife or her sister. He supposed it didn't matter.

Toussaint stood up again. "I'm the last guy to ask about love. I'm unlucky in it," he said, edging towards the door.

"I didn't even try to stop her," Beluga said.

"You know you shouldn't be here alone," Toussaint said. He had his tablet under his arm and case in hand.

"Maybe you could check on me?" he asked.

"I don't know about that," Toussaint said. He looked again at Beluga. He must have seen something in his face, in his expression, so he came closer and continued. "I have to go now," He said. "I have more appointments I have to make. Been a lot of in-calls. Something going around." He leaned down and patted Beluga's arm, which barely itched anymore. "Yeah, I'll check on you. And you know, my boss is a real genius with bots. Maybe I can talk to him about your eyes. Although the glasses are great. Glasses guy. Beluga." He held up a hand in goodbye, then left.

Beluga waited until he heard the door lock click. Then he said, "I'm going to be OK."

Beautiful Words

Davey's mom was "oversalting the soup," as his dad would say. She ran a damp rag over the Shiraz rack again as the vacuum bumped Davey's leg.

"Remember what I said," she repeated. "No tastes, nips, samples, sips, swigs or swallows. Not even smells unless I am standing there."

"I know," Davey said. "I know." There was no soothing his mother from oversalting the soup, only enduring it.

She looked at the rag, which was coming up clean. She hooked it onto her belt and looked at her son with suspicion. "You look nice," she said. "Are you wearing your father's cologne?"

He was. "No," he lied. "Why would I do that?" His cheeks grew hot. His mother knew better, but she didn't know his reason: two of the most beautiful words in the English language. Rebecca King.

His mother reached out and picked a piece of lint from his sleeve. "Wash it off. It creeps me out." She walked off to redust the Malbecs. "Plus, it'll be distracting. Go wash. They'll be here soon."

Twenty minutes to be exact. Thirty six of his classmates, juniors and seniors, would be arriving for experience lab, the only time they were all officially together—except for dances, like the prom—even though they all lived in the same town. Davey had pushed hard for today's lab, on the history and science of fermented beverages, although he presented it to his parents as a favor to the school. He knew his mother would be thrilled to show off her sommelier training, even though she was both dubious—about presenting to a group that couldn't taste what she was talking about—and anxious about it spiraling out of control and into a teenage orgy. Davey was sure it wouldn't, although he would hardly object if it did. Especially with Rebecca King.

Willowy Rebecca King. She'd always been tall for her age, stuck in the back row with the boys for class pictures, and really skinny. But somewhere along the line, tall became sinuous and skinny became lithe, her thin legs punctuated by jutted knees that reminded him of a mare, but in a good way, like he wanted to put her knee in his mouth kind of way.

Rebecca King.

With a curtain of ginger hair and peridot-colored eyes, she was the loveliest girl he'd ever seen. And he seemed to be the only one who did see it. He'd batted her name as a contender onto the hot girl list, and the reception among the others was lukewarm, at best. He didn't mind. He'd simply found an undiscovered treasure.

Rebecca. King.

Today, he was definitely going to ask her to prom.

Probably.

He had the "home court advantage," as his dad would say. He had the money, earned over an entire sacrificed soccer season's worth of weekends sweeping the store, enough for a gas limo, an orchid and a beach-facing hotel room. He was a little sure she'd say yes. No one else had dibbed her for asking, and there was a way she said his name—always Dave, pronounced as little like "Dove," and never Davey—that made him suspect she took him seriously as a man.

The vacuum bumped his leg again. He was in too good of a mood to nudge it into the wall, something he liked to do, letting it bump itself a few times for good measure before it righted its bearings. Instead he patted it on the head like a friendly dog and went into the kitchen to check on his appetizers.

Even though no one in the class would be able to taste the wine, Davey wanted to make the experience as memorable—and romantic—as he could, so he prepared the dishes that would ordinarily be pared with the wines his mother would discuss. He washed his hands and started wrapping slivers of prosciutto around cantaloupe squares, then stabbing them through with picks. He'd already stuffed mushroom caps with caramelized onions and spooned eggy zabaglione (with 2 cups extra marsala his mom didn't know about) into tiny custard cups of bitter chocolate.

Whenever an adult asked him what he wanted to do with his life, Davey automatically answered "chef." He didn't know if that was truly what he wanted, though. He wasn't called to cook, necessarily, not like his mother was called to wine or his father to being a park ranger: like a religion. In fact, he could hear his mother back in the main room, standing at her pulpit reviewing her notes for her sermon.

He wasn't called to cook, but it calmed and focused him. As he speared the last of the melon—and oversalted his own soup, moving the appetizers around on their platters—he rehearsed one of the fifteen different scripts he'd composed to ask Rebecca King to the prom.

Which he was definitely, probably going to do today.

⏮ ⏸ ⏭

Everyone was on time. Labs, even though no one would cop to it, were almost everyone's favorite part of school, the only time school didn't feel quite like school. It felt more like a party, and everyone dressed for the occasion. Including Rebecca King.

Davey spotted her immediately. She was wearing a green sun dress, the same family of green as her eyes, and Davey immediately decided that every redhead everywhere should always wear green. She looked like she was just standing there, so he waved. But she didn't wave back, and when the crowd shifted position he saw that she was actually talking to tiny Sasha Gomez. Sasha was short and delicate, but looked even shorter and more delicate next to Rebecca. Davey realized he still had his hand in the air and felt stupid. He mingled around; talking to the same people he always did, working through them—Dallas Saunders, Nobuyuki Sören, Book Larsen, Marguerite Maldonado, and Janell Vang—getting closer each time to Rebecca, flashing green in his peripheral vision. He had managed to get on one side of Isaac Diaz, with Rebecca on Isaac's other side, when his mother started calling for attention and welcoming the class. Everyone sat down in the chairs he and his mother had set up, and she started her lecture.

"The history of wine is indistinguishable from the history of civilization itself," she began.

Davey knew this talk backwards and forwards. He tapped Isaac and motioned for him to lean forward. He complied, but with a dirty look. Isaac could be a real asshole when he wanted to be.

"Fermentation allowed nomadic hunters and gatherers to preserve fruits past their season in a form that was easy to carry with them," his mother continued.

Rebecca was leaning forward, listening. Davey reached around and tapped her gently on her freckled upper arm. Her arm was so warm and, he imagined, soft. She looked up.

"Hey," Davey said.

"Traces of tartaric acid, which gives grapes their characteristic taste, have been found on pottery as old as 8 thousand years BCE."

Rebecca jerked her chin at him. "Hey," she whispered back. Then she turned back to listen, and Isaac sat back in his chair with an asshole smirk.

"Wine established itself as an essential cultural component in Greek and Roman society, with cults rising to worship and honor the gods of wine, grapes, and the harvest: Dionysus and Bacchus."

Davey crossed his hands across his stomach. Rebecca was bent over her pad, typing notes. She was a good student. He couldn't distract her. Besides, Isaac wasn't going to make anything easier. Davey momentarily hated him, but then refigured his plan. He'd get her alone during break, when everyone was eating his appetizers. He'd casually drop in that he made all of them himself, and she would be impressed. He imagined feeding her a zabaglione, the chocolate melting slightly with his body heat, which she would suck off each of his fingers. He shifted slightly in his seat and tried to listen to his mother's lecture. It felt like they'd been there for an hour already, but she was just starting to get to medieval Europe.

"Wine production continued at a lively clip after the fall of the Roman Empire, due to increased demand for wine to be used at Catholic masses."

Davey tried to move his head so he could see at least some of Rebecca, but Isaac was everywhere. When he looked, all he could see was the giant pimple on Isaac's cheek, fat and white as a pearl. Nasty. He tried to refocus on his mother, concentrating on making the lecture go faster. The Industrial Revolution and Prohibition alone was 20 minutes worth of talk.

Then Isaac punched him lightly on the knee. "Dude," he whispered. "You fucking reek."

"Fuck you," Davey whispered back. "It's cologne. And at least I bathe, you filthy motherfucker."

Isaac snorted at that, loud enough to get his mother's attention. Even though Isaac was the one who made the noise, his mother shot him the death look before continuing.

"There are still a wide variety of vintages and blends made from those mission grapes, planted by the missionaries who followed the conquistadores to the southern and western coasts."

Just as Davey resigned himself to zone out, there was a rustling from Isaac's other side. Rebecca placed her pad on her chair, and eased herself down the row, ostensibly to the bathroom. However, just as she squeezed by Paul Croy on the end, she glanced at Davey with what could only be construed as meaning.

All the blood in his body rushed to his cheeks and

his groin and he felt hot and dizzy. Rebecca was surely, probably signaling to him, telling him with her eyes to follow, that she understood his "Hey," that she wanted to talk to him as much as he wanted to talk to her. He counted to 10 under his breath to make sure there was enough time between when she left and when he did for it to simply be a coincidence that they both had to go to the bathroom at the same time. Then it didn't seem like enough time, so he counted to 10 again, then one more time for good measure. Then he slid out the row the other direction, just having to squeeze by Janell, who had encouraged him on more than one occasion to go after Rebecca.

And this was his chance.

His heart was beating and his skin was damp as he headed down the hallway towards the restrooms. *She must be in the women's room, freshening up*, he thought, so he leaned his back against the wall and tried to get his head together. He absolutely couldn't remember any of the fifteen approaches he'd composed. He'd have to wing it.

Down the hall, he could hear the echo of his mother finally getting to the Twentieth Century. He wished Rebecca would hurry up. His mother would call for a break once she got past the rationing during the World Wars. But there was still no Rebecca. No Rebecca. He knocked a few times, quietly on the women's room door. No answer. Maybe he'd knocked too quietly. He opened the door slightly. "Rebecca?" he whispered.

Nothing. He opened the door the whole way. The restroom was empty. He checked the men's room just in case, and it was empty too. She must have gone outside. "Fuck," he whispered to himself as he crept towards the back door. He'd wasted time at the bathroom. He shoved the back door open and sunlight momentarily blinded him. "Rebecca?" he whispered again. He pushed the back door most of the way closed behind him.

Then he saw her. A strip of green against the dumpster, her red hair spilling down her back, luminous with light. She seemed to be bending down, her spine filigree pressed through her dress. But something was wrong. She wasn't standing right. Her mask was on the ground.

"Rebecca?" he called.

She looked up, behind her, saw him with unmistakable alarm. In front of Rebecca, back against the metal bin, was Sasha Gomez. Her small arms were plunged elbow deep down the front of Rebecca's dress, one foot hooked around the back of Rebecca's dappled calf. The two girls parted slightly, and then Sasha said something along the lines of "Hey, Davey." But he didn't really hear her. His stomach felt like it hit his feet. It was all he could do to get himself back in the door and slam it behind him.

He propped himself again against the wall, but this time because he absolutely didn't trust himself to stand on his own. He tried to process what he'd just seen, but couldn't. All he could think about was a wasted soccer season, an empty hotel room and a dead corsage.

Nobuyuki stuck his head into the storeroom. "Hey, dude," he said. "There you are. You need to come out. Your food is fucking amazing."

He let Nobuyuki lead him back into the main room. Everyone except Rebecca and Sasha was standing around with his little plates, talking and eating his melon and his mushrooms and his zabaglione. They were patting him on his back and arm, complimenting him, telling him how amazing it all was. Somewhere, he spotted his mother beaming at him. He looked at his platters of food and raged. This hadn't gone at all like it was supposed to. Not at all. The zabaglione was almost gone, Rebecca would miss it, but then he imagined her sucking chocolate off Sasha's little baby fingers. He grabbed the last two cups and shoved them in his mouth, barely tasting them.

No, this wasn't how it was supposed to go at all.

He swallowed the sweets and looked around at the blur of classmates and eating and dust hanging in the air. His mother hadn't even gotten all the dust, even with all her inane wiping and wiping and wiping. He hated the place, he hated everyone.

But especially Book. He spotted Book in a corner, eating mushroom caps and talking intently to Marguerite

Maldonado. He was as bulky as his sister was small, awkward and barrel-chested. He knew what was going on. And there he was, eating Davey's food, probably asking Marguerite, who was peeling the prosciutto off the melon, to the prom right that second. Davey pushed straight through to the corner, nearly knocking over Marguerite's plate of melon.

"What the fuck, man?" he said to Book, who looked dumbfounded.

"What, Davey?" he replied, eyes wide and innocent. Davey wanted immediately to punch him.

"Why does your sister have to be such a huge slut?" Davey asked.

Book excused them from Marguerite, who looked confused—but then again, Marguerite was never the smartest girl either. Then he grabbed Davey by the ear, and dragged him across the room into the back. Being dragged hurt, but he didn't feel it. Only anger turning into fury. A whole season wasted. A whole plan gone to shit.

"What the fuck are you saying about my sister?" Book hissed.

"I said she was a fucking slut," Davey said. "Are you fucking deaf?"

Book's face was gorged pink. He shoved Davey against the wall. Davey waited for the hit, but it didn't come. Fighting during school time was a suspendable offense. "What the fuck is your problem, man?" Book asked.

"You. Your whole fucking family." He didn't like how his voice cracked. Under ordinary circumstances, he'd be shaky. He wasn't very confrontational, and all in all, he liked Book.

"I'm not going to fight you right now."

"Then after. After lab. Out back. Unless you're fucking scared."

Book pushed Davey's shoulder in assent, then walked away, back to the main room.

The rest of the lecture felt high speed. Davey shifted around in his chair, but not from pleasure. Even Isaac sensed what was going on and left him alone.

The food was all gone, so students lingered long enough to thank Davey's mother and make plans for where they would meet up now. Once or twice Davey felt Rebecca trying to catch his attention, but he would stare straight ahead until the green sweep would move back out of sight.

He helped his mother stack the chairs so she could open for customers. He worked quickly enough so even his mother sensed something was amiss, amiss enough not to remark on it. As soon as the last chair was stacked and the load wheeled back into the storage closet, Davey was out the door.

As promised, Book was waiting for him, pacing back and forth. And Davey dove at him.

There was no sense or elegance to the fight. Davey hadn't been in a fight since he was a little kid, and he didn't remember Book getting into many fights either. He didn't know how to win, but he also didn't care. He punched and kicked, sometimes hitting Book, sometimes hitting the grass. He was too amped to feel the blows Book landed on him.

They flailed and rolled around until neither of them could catch their breath. Book got Davey on his back and sat on him, but only because he was bigger. He was panting as hard as Davey was. He held Davey down until he seemed convinced Davey was too exhausted to launch again, then collapsed next to him.

Davey felt the cold grass and mud under his back. He stared into the blue sky, listening to Book catching his breath. He wasn't angry anymore. He wasn't sad. He felt empty and calm. He just was.

And his cheek hurt a lot where Book must have nailed him. It felt hot as the bots rushed to repair any damage.

Book finally rolled over onto one elbow to look at Davey. "What the fuck was that all about?"

Davey blinked. "I'm sorry," he said. His voice was plain. "I shouldn't have taken this out on you. That was fucked up."

"It was my sister and Rebecca King, huh?"

Davey nodded his head, sliding it against the grass. "Yeah."

Book sat up and rubbed his knee. "You fucked me up good, man."

Davey sat up next to him. Calm and empty turned to sad. Pathetic. His face felt hot all over now, not just from the bots, but because he felt like he was going to cry. "I loved her, man. I quit soccer to work. I was going to ask her to prom. Now she's going with your sister."

"Hey, now." Book picked at the grass. "Doesn't mean she is going with my sister." He paused. "You were kind of right. My sister makes out with a lot of people." Then he threw the picked grass on Davey's leg. "But that doesn't make her a slut."

"Yeah," Davey said, although he wondered then what made one a slut if not that. "I know." He picked the grass off his leg and rubbed a few blades between his fingers. "Now I have a fucking hotel room and a limo and it's for nothing."

"You can still go to the prom," Book said.

"I have no one to go with."

Book picked more grass, rolled it between his fingers like Davey, and smelled the freshness. Davey liked the smell of grass, too. They sat in silence for a few minutes, then Book muttered something Davey didn't catch.

"What?" he asked.

"I said," Book said, loudly, then dropping in tone. "You could ask me."

"To prom?" Davey looked at Book. "You'd go with me?"

"I would," he answered.

"OK," Davey said. His cheeks began to cool down and he smiled behind his mask. "Go with me."

"Are you asking?"

"Do you want me to get on my knee?"

"Are you asking me to prom or to marry you?"

Davey punched Book's arm, but this time with

affection. "Fuck you, dude. To prom."

"Yeah," Book said. "I'd love to go with you."

Davey smiled behind his mask. Those sounded a little like the most beautiful words in the English language.

"But ditch that cologne," Book added. "It's pretty bad."

Room at the Bottom

The pills stuck in Toby Bennett's throat, melting hotly in the middle of his chest. Heartburn. He swallowed a few hard gulps of beer to wash them down or burp them up, but they just hung and burned.

Aside from that, he didn't feel anything else. So, he punched Joaquin in his elbow, and smiled at the bassist's yelp.

"Asshole," Joaquin said. "That was my funny bone."

"La-mao," Toby replied. "This isn't doing shit to me."

"Me neither," Joaquin said. "Fucking crazy old bitch."

"Me?"

"Yes, you." Joaquin rubbed his elbow. "No. The lady that sold me this shit. She said it was legit. She said the guy she got them from was a collector."

"They're ancient." Toby belched again and the pills moved down, finally. "I think they're expired." He turned to make a comment about how stupid Joaquin was for buying ancient drugs from a crazy old lady and to ask what kind of person collected antique medicines when Joaquin landed a punch on his elbow. "Fucker," he yelled.

"La-mao," Joaquin said. He danced around in victory and Toby had to laugh; Joaquin always thought he looked smooth when he danced, but to Toby, he looked like a little cartoon monkey with a ridiculous pencil mustache. It was a good thing he always had his heavy bass strapped to him on stage.

Toby sank down onto the shredded couch to watch Joaquin. There was always a shredded couch backstage—didn't matter the city or venue—a shredded, old couch baring its springs like teeth, a vestigial light fixture hanging from the ceiling and a mirror with a black chip off one corner. If there was a backstage at all, that is. Figurehead still played gigs where they holed up behind a curtain holding their instruments to their chest and tried not to breathe too hard. Toby actually liked those kinds of places; they attracted younger crowds who danced with stupid abandon like monkey man Joaquin, and he could stand and listen to the other bands instead of having to share the old couch with them and make bullshit conversations. But those gigs became rarer and rarer as Book got louder and louder bitching about sharing other bands' drum kits. Toby leaned his head against the back of the sofa and let the springs catch onto his hair. "What are these supposed to do, anyway?"

Joaquin flopped onto the couch next to him. "Make us motherfucking high." He pronounced it with three syllables: *hi-ii-gh*. He was such a little knob.

Joaquin laughed to himself, and Toby shook his head as Book walked in. "What's making who 'hi-ii-gh'?" he asked. He sat down on the couch arm rest next to Joaquin, the old wood creaking under his weight, and started slapping sets of three beats on his thighs—hi-*ii-gh, hi-ii-gh*—then changing to two on his leg and the third on the back of Joaquin's head.

For the few seconds before Joaquin finally ducked, it had to be the funniest fucking thing Toby had ever seen.

"Pills," Joaquin said, scooting uncomfortably close to Toby, out of Book's reach. "I got some pills."

Book stopped drumming. "Are you two fucking deficient?" He squinted his eyes at Joaquin, furious, and then looked at Toby. Toby shrugged. "WTF are you thinking? There's a fucking crowd out there."

Book looked like he was going to get an aneurysm. "Calm down," Toby told him. "They aren't doing anything anyway."

Book started to say something else, but then Toussaint came in, holding the hand of a totally blank looking girl of indeterminate age. She could have been anywhere between 16 and 36. Her face was totally blank. Toby itched to find a marker and draw something on her.

Maybe the pills were working. "They aren't doing anything anyway," he repeated.

"These two took pills," Book told Toussaint. "Pills."

Toussaint dropped the girl's hand. "What the fuck?" Toby noticed the blank girl continued to stand with her hand still clasped, as if she didn't realize Toussaint had let go. "Throw them up."

Joaquin sprang up. "Are you crazy?"

"Stick your fingers down your throats and throw them up or I will stick my fingers down your throats and..."

"Throw them up for us?" Joaquin finished. He looked satisfied, but then Book had him tucked under his arm. Toussaint grabbed Joaquin's feet and jerked him up and down like a salt shaker. Joaquin started coughing up all sorts of things, some of which may or may not have been the pills. It was hard to tell. Book and Toussaint let him down hard, and Joaquin squatted, palms on the ground, trying to catch his breath.

Toby looked at Book, sitting again and drumming on his knee, Toussaint standing over little Joaquin, his own reflection in the cracked mirror, the blank-faced girl blankly blinking. "He has a girlfriend, you know," Toby said to her. "I hope you haven't blown him yet."

What he thought might have been a facial expression came over her, as she turned and ran out the stage door.

"You fuck," Toussaint said, now facing him. "You're next."

"I didn't take any," he lied. "I don't know what the fuck any of you are talking about."

"You better not have..." Toussaint said.

Or else? Or else what? Toby wanted to say, but didn't. He had as much on Tous as Tous had on him. And he would have loved to see Tous, or Book, or both of them, try and pick him up. It didn't take much to toss Joaquin around. Even blank girl could have done that. But him, he was a big dude.

"Do not drag us down with you," Toussaint said to him. He was looking at Toby, but meant both him and Joaquin. He said this often to them. "Do not drag the band down to your level."

"I am so sick of this shit!" Joaquin was hopping and yelling, holding the front of his shirt out in front of him. "I got puke on my shirt." He looked at Toby. "They got puke on my shirt." He tugged the shirt again. "Look. Puke."

There was a weird colored spot on the front of Joaquin's tiny white shirt. He suddenly felt really sorry for and protective of the little pencil-mustached knob. It wasn't Joaquin's fault he was small. The bass would probably cover up the stain, but there was no telling Joaquin that, the way he was hopping around. And Toby was sick of Toussaint telling him not to drag them down, like he and Book were on some other fucking level. Fuck that.

Toby stood up and grabbed Joaquin's free hand like Joaquin was his son. "We'll get a new shirt from the merchandise table." He started walking towards the stage door, dragging Joaquin behind him.

"Yeah," Joaquin called over his shoulder. "I'm getting a new shirt from the merch table."

The club was packed. Toby squinted in the dark, but all he could make out were shapes. It was like the din overpowered his vision. A thousand conversations, a thousand cocktails. Too much.

Good acoustics, though, he thought and stepped forward onto a foot.

The owner of the foot moved his face into the light. *Glasses guy,* he immediately recognized, the characteristic black glasses and thick eyebrows there, then back in blackness.

Toby stepped over him and smiled to himself. Glasses guy was a good omen, like an albatross to sailors.

It meant a good show. He led Joaquin out to the bar without knocking into anyone else and let Joaquin order for the both of them.

The drinks came, and Joaquin had the new t-shirt in his hand, a black one, FIGUREHEAD in letters Toby hand-drew himself. Joaquin drank down his brown shot and then stripped off his white shirt, talking the whole time. Toby saw Joaquin's skinny chest, shiny and brown like he was coated in oil, then the shirt, unfurling like a tiny flag. He tried to follow what Joaquin was saying. Toby caught "I'm fucking sick of it" and "We don't even need him" and knew he was fantasizing again about kicking Toussaint out of the band. "He doesn't even have any talent." Joaquin spat as he spoke.

Toby nodded along, even though he knew it wasn't true. Book was a good drummer, and Toussaint wrote everything. The music, the lyrics, everything. At best, he and Joaquin were serviceable with their instruments. Neither of them practiced outside scheduled band time, and they never booked any gigs. The only consequences of one of them not showing up for a show would have been just dealing with Tous or Book, not because the performance would've suffered any. It was a favor, of sorts, that they hadn't been replaced. At least he felt like it was a favor, after quitting baseball like he did. So, he let Joaquin mouth off for a while, then drink Toby's untouched drink.

Until Joaquin finally noticed it'd been a solo show. "What's wrong with you?" Joaquin asked.

Toby thought about it. He was really tired and said so.

"You fuck," Joaquin said. "They're working on you, aren't they?"

He considered again. It took a lot of effort. He said they probably were, he didn't know.

"What does it feel like?"

He didn't know. He told Joaquin that. But Joaquin kept asking and Toby wanted to get away. It was hot. He tried to turn, guy behind him. Girl squeezing next to him. Arms reaching around him, credits dealt back and forth. It was too much. He asked when it got so crowded.

"Seriously. You are hi-ii-gh."

He was, he guessed. It was really hot and he was so tired. If it weren't for the bodies up and on him, he would have slid to the floor.

As soon as they let up a bit, he did. The first band was starting. He couldn't recall their name. They were the one with horns. Real horns, not samples. Crazy. Toby rested the back of his head against the wood paneling at the bottom of the bar. It was better down there. Cooler. Quieter. He tucked his legs in and Joaquin took off. Left him there. Little knob.

He closed his eyes. The floor shook with music and footsteps. Red and pink and purple lights went off behind his eyes. He watched up until it started to freak him out. What caused those lights? What kind of person collects old medications? What kind of knob lets his monkey knob talk him into taking them?

When he opened his eyes again, the blank girl was on all fours, peering into his face.

"Are you OK?" she asked.

He gave her gold brown eyes and freckles and then she was the most beautiful girl he ever saw. He nodded and she leaned in closer.

"So," she said. "Do *you* have a girlfriend?"

He shook his head, *no*. He didn't. He wanted her hair to be red and shiny and really soft, and when he reached out to touch, it was.

She slid down into the space next to him. "What are we doing down here?" she asked. Her neck was long and graceful, her shoulders delicately curved into a well-worn cotton shirt. He gave her a twisting Chinese dragon on her arm— no, a bouquet of roses, thorns dripping magenta blood— then he revised it again, just bare flesh, pink and firm, dotted with fine, gold hairs. She tucked her knees beneath her chin and crossed her feet.

Toby played with her fingers as he thought of an answer. Her fingers were long and thin, the nails healthy and well-cared for. She had a small gold ring on her index finger. He imagined slipping it off into his mouth and swallowing it, like a pill. When he spoke, his voice was clear and strong. "Plenty of room down here at the bottom," he said.

Something Between Us

They weren't going to get far on a tomato. Toussaint sat down on the sofa and placed his hands, palm down, on his thighs. The posture made him look trustworthy. "We will stop at my place," he said. "Then we'll get out of here."

"To someplace safe?" Chaaya asked. Sarcasm. She must've been feeling better.

"To someplace safe." He stood, and pulled her arm around him. She may have been feeling better, but she was still all weight and no sense. He had to hold her up and steer, up the stairs, which were steeper and longer than he remembered.

He propped her against the wall and tried his door. It was locked. He didn't have the key. He never had his key.

"I don't have my key," he said. He'd often forgotten his key, and Nani Gopal held a spare. "Where did Nani keep my key?"

"I have no idea." She was still pale and damp, her cheeks rusty with dried blood. "She had a key?"

Toussaint pushed the door. He kicked it, banged down on the doorknob, but it didn't budge.

"The locks here are still good," she said.

"Stay here," he said.

Chaaya slid down, back against the wall next to the door. She wasn't going anyplace.

The King didn't really want to go back downstairs to her apartment. He'd wanted to get both of them out of there. The body, the stillness. But, he had to get his apartment one way or another, and that 200 year old door wasn't moving.

He ran down the stairs and pushed back into the apartment. He halfheartedly rifled through drawers. He couldn't imagine where Nani Gopal stored keys. He opened a few cabinets, closed them, and then remembered: the gun. It lay where Chaaya dropped it; a few feet from the body, in a thick pool of blood that made the whole room smell sweet and metallic and a little like bad eggs. He tried not to look at the body, but couldn't help it. The girl laid face down, her head destroyed. He shuddered; a flash passed through him, Chaaya's arm out, gun flush against the girl's nose. If he didn't know Chaaya as well as he did, he would have assumed she shot the girl execution style.

He just never expected a gun would make such a mess. It would have been cleaner if she used a baseball bat.

He grabbed the gun—it was heavier than he expected—wiped the blood off onto the quilt strewn on the bed and dropped it into his pocket next to the small journal he'd taken from the girl earlier.

Back up the stairs. Chaaya hadn't moved. "Hey," he said, nudging her with his boot. "Wake up. Cover your ears."

"What are you going to do?" she asked.

He flashed the gun. "I'm going to shoot the lock off."

"Will that work?" she asked. She motioned for him to give her his other arm. He did, and then pulled her up.

"I don't know. It works in games. And movies," he said. It did, too, well; Toussaint had done it in at least 10 games and had seen it done in at least 50 movies he could think of. If Book were there, he could have thought of 500 more. He didn't know exactly how to do it, though. He turned the gun around in his hands, trying to decide how to hold it. "I've never held a real one."

Chaaya was so weak that she looked blurry, but she folded her hands over his, holding the gun. "I have," she said. Then she paused, waiting for something from him—a laugh? Then she continued, "I mean, before today. But I don't think it's going to work."

Toussaint slipped his hands away from hers'. She barely looked able to hold a mouse in her palm, but she took a deep breath. "This is only a 357," she said. "We may be able to shoot off the lock face, not much more. But we can try." She solidified then, less blurry, leveled the gun at the lock and said, "Take cover. There's going to be ricochet." Then she shot. The sound was short but deafening, and the reverb bounced around the corridor. Toussaint felt it through his ears into his teeth; it nearly collapsed his bad knee. She was right, the shot loosened and ripped some of the metal, but the lock held true.

"Shit," he said.

"One more time," she said. "Cover your face," and she shot again, this time destroying the knob. They both stared at it.

"It works in movies," Toussaint repeated.

"This is a pretty small gun," she said. "There's a concrete block by the front door. You'll just have to break the rest."

Toussaint found the block. He dragged it to the door and then used all his strength to chuck it at the lock.

It crashed, a close call from his foot, but it worked. The door swung open; the smell of gunpowder and cologne, dust, and the dishes he'd left flooded his mask. He took the gun from Chaaya and motioned for her to go inside. He followed, head and teeth and knee still pounding. If the Gopals had electricity, then he probably did too. He felt for the light switch. He knew this place with his eyes closed. He found the switch, hit it, and blinked into the light. Dust sparkled and reflected.

"I don't think you have food in here," Chaaya said.

"Did you look?"

"No, but you never did when you lived here."

He led Chaaya into the living room. "Sit down," he ordered, and it sounded like she obliged, a soft thud. "No. I just never cooked." In the kitchen, he opened cabinets, pulled out a can of pears and a can of meatballs, other cans, then brought out an armful and an opener. He arranged the cans down in a half circle before Chaaya, opened the meatballs and handed them to her. He watched as she immediately started digging out meatballs with her fingers.

She really was a good looking girl. A little thick maybe, no, strong, with really big breasts and dimpled elbows. She was dirty and pale, could use a shower and some rouge or something, and her eyebrows were drawn so tightly together in that funny, stubborn, sour, serious way. But he always liked her hair, a sheet of glossy black. And her smart eyes. And her smooth hands. He'd forgotten her smooth hands until he watched them shoot the doorknob. He couldn't imagine those hands shooting anyone, much less execution style.

He wanted to stand there and watch her fingers greedily pull meatballs out from the can and shove them beneath her mask, but he forced himself to stand up and dig into his MaGo pouch.

His supplies were limited, but she needed a second seeding. Food wouldn't be enough. He shook out a shell and unfolded his air syringe. "When's the last time you had a full seeding?"

"I have no idea," she said. "I've been crapping out bots for weeks, though."

He smiled at the "*crapping*," and then squatted beside her and held the syringe to her shoulder, opposite side from the one he had dosed downstairs. "This will help." He shot, dumped the empty shell on the carpet, and sat down next to her.

"Meatball?" Chaaya asked, holding one out.

"Sure," he said, taking it from her. He popped it under his mask. He was aware of her watching him chew. He swallowed. "Eat up," he said. "You need energy to get where we're going."

"Where are we going?" she asked.

"I told you. Out of here," he said. "Someplace safe." Then he reached for the can.

"And I told you, no such place," she said. She picked up the can of pears and poked them with an index finger. She was starting to look better and better, more color in her cheeks, less like a ghostly outline and more like a thick, solid girl.

"Let's finish this," he said. "Sunset is coming and we can leave under cover of darkness. There's two of us. We'll be OK."

Chaaya snorted at that. "Cover of darkness." But then she held the can of pears in a toast and said, "To someplace safe."

⏮ ⏸ ⏭

He kept sneaking looks over at Chaaya as they walked. Her gait was slower than his and he didn't want to call attention to it, although from time to time, he wanted to sweep her up and over his shoulder, carry her off, and not only because it would be faster. Fear was mingling with something else, something he knew very well, something he should know better to avoid in its implications and complications, but, like the smell of fresh donuts inviting gluttony and indigestion, he let himself be re-tempted by her. As they walked, he hummed a few bars of "Goodbye to Ashley."

He'd reached for her hand a few times, under the pretense of safety, and each time when he held it too long, she'd bat it away. Each batting seemed less and less insistent. So he liked to believe.

He'd loved this neighborhood, once upon a time. He spent most of his credits simply for the privilege of living among streets lit with nostalgic shaped street lamps, rehab after rehab bumping against modern complexes, all with good views of the lake. Once upon a time, these streets lived at this time of the evening. Young couples to and from dinner, students to and from coffee shops, exhausted day jobbers lugging home briefcases like trophies gone heavy and awkward. Everyone in their front rooms, gamesets strapped on, playing or surfing, comps on, waving through files. Street lamps burned; buses ambled lazily around cars with open windows blaring music or scraps of an argument or tails of cigarette smoke.

And through the lit front rooms of houses you could see dinners served and cleared, splayed bodies watching the news, or cats hunting the lights through the panes of glass.

Now, there was almost none of that. A few solar lights, here and there, enough to navigate the darkness. Little movement, scratching in brambles that turned out to be a family of Buddha-bellied raccoons, acrid smells from mysterious rotting piles.

They walked in silence, listening, breathing. He tried to breathe evenly, but fear made him huff like an old man, and his knee, still stiff from sleeping in the Rallye, sent sharp pains up his thigh to his spine, which didn't help. Chaaya made no sounds except the delicate scrape of her thighs against one another as she walked.

They were both surprised when they heard a voice say, "Nice evening."

He looked towards the voice and could barely make out a youngish man, his silhouette a darker shade of the darkness, lumpy with wraps and scarves. However, the closer the young man came, the clearer his smell—days of musky sweat, sweet smoke and something else Toussaint couldn't identify but that was familiar, like a baking potato mixed with camphor and pencil lead, although that wasn't quite it.

"It's really very late to be out," young man said, one side, his arm, fishing around inside his robes. *Was he going to pull out his dick?* Toussaint wondered, *or a gun?*

Toussaint felt Chaaya's gun and the leather journal heavy against his own leg, but instead, the man pulled out a flashlight, clicked it on and shone the cold blue light into their faces.

Time slowed and Toussaint huffed. Then he started to say, "Hello—" but Chaaya spoke loudly, right over him.

"Who are you?" she said. Her tone was sharp, the voice of a woman who, less than 6 hours before, blew someone's head off.

"This isn't your neighborhood," the man said. "I've been patrolling this area for weeks and I never seen either of you."

"Patrolling?" Chaaya said. "What the fuck are—" but she was interrupted by some cracking noises across the street, something moving towards the lake at great speed. A catch of light from the palace and they could all see it was a figure.

"Excuse me," the man said, and dropped the flash-light, tearing off running after the figure.

Toussaint and Chaaya stood there for a second, watching. "WTF," Chaaya started to say, but Toussaint clamped a hand over her mask and pulled her towards him, then backed up against the wall of a building into a splinter of complete darkness. He held her still, although she wriggled to get free; she wasn't that strong yet. She finally gave up and they watched, their hearts beating within a half second of one another's—thum-*thump*—and their eyes adjusted and they saw the young man that had stopped them, then another man and another and another creep from the bushes, out of the night, and the sounds of s scuffle and a scream, a woman's perhaps, and then a crowd of lumpy shapes dragged something from the lake into the middle of the street and beat it. Toussaint could barely see what was going on, yet knew exactly. The figures punched and kicked and struck and dragged, and as they did, a low hum came up from the mob, a low hum that started growing the more furiously they attacked, songs upon songs upon songs with no rhythm or sense or logic or sympathy. Toussaint wanted to plug his ears against the noise, which was worse, almost, than the sight, but he was too afraid to unclamp Chaaya's mask. He felt her mouth moving—counting probably, something she always did under stress or after sex—so instead, he tried to drown out the sound by feeling the moisture spread from her mouth wetting her mask and listening to their heart-beats, faster now—*thumthum-thumpthump, thuthuthum thumthumpthump.*

Eventually, the shapes stopped, scattered, left a pile on the street, and most crept back into the night. One, the one that stopped them, Toussaint assumed, came towards them and he held his breath and pulled Chaaya deeper to him, but the young man stopped at the flashlight, picked it up, clicked it off, and also disappeared into the night.

Toussaint finally loosened his grip on Chaaya and dropped his hand from her mask, but neither moved for a few minutes.

"No place," Chaaya said, "is safe." She looked at Toussaint. "Where will you take me? Where is this safe place?"

Toussaint didn't answer. He didn't know how long it took for them to sag back onto the sidewalk and start walking again. But they did, and they didn't look back at the pile on the sidewalk Instead, they moved forward. "Out of the city," he finally said. "To my friend, Book. He's in a town on the coast. We're going there. To Ocean Shores." He reached for Chaaya's hand. She definitely let him hold it for a few seconds this time before tugging it away. "Until then, I'll be someplace safe. I will keep you safe until we get to someplace safe."

She nodded, and he was happy. It was a victory, he knew, and he celebrated it. Chaaya never acquiesced easily. It'd been a recurring theme in their relationship. That she acquiesced now proved what he suspected since he watched her eat the meatballs: there was, indeed, still something between them. Something wonderful and magical, and for the first time since he'd run away from the Space Needle, since he shed his title as the King of Seattle, he felt hopeful and happy. He smiled at her—and tripped over a deep crack in the sidewalk. The pain was immediate, blinding and hot in his knee, then he felt the impact on the concrete as he slid, a different hot pain, wet, spread on the back of his thigh. He sat, suppressing a yell, and held his knee.

Chaaya squatted by him immediately. He would have appreciated the genuine concern in her eyes if his leg didn't hurt so fucking much. "Are you OK?" she asked.

He wasn't OK. He screwed up his face in the pain and tried to breathe through the pain, huffing until it subsided somewhat and his thigh began to itch. "I'm all right," he finally said.

She reached out to touch his knee, squeeze it, and he almost hit her as she did it, re-inflaming the pain in a spasm. "Hold on," she said. "Trying to make sure you didn't break anything."

Toussaint felt like he was going to throw up. His armpits were soaked and he was sure he was sitting in a growing pool of blood from the back of his leg. But he sat still as Chaaya poked around his knee, then finally shook at the kneecap. "You're OK," she said. "It's going to swell something awful, though."

He reached into his pouch. There were just a few shells left, between the two he'd given Chaaya and the one he was about to give himself. He hoped the rest of the journey would be smooth, because he'd need some shells to clone once they got to Ocean Shores. But the pain was unbearable. He had to be able to walk, so this one couldn't be helped.

He slipped a shell into the syringe and, holding one hand steady with the other, injected the bots into his thigh. That'd get them to the inflamed tissue faster.

"Give me a minute," he said, and they sat.

"You ready?"

He nodded again and she helped him stand and he tested it, putting weight on it gently, rolling his foot heel to ball. It was bad, but he could make it.

"I think I cut myself," he said, feeling the back of his pants leg. The fabric was rough, may have abraded off a layer of skin, but seemed fine. He took a step.

Chaaya held his arm around her shoulder to support him, and even though he had to stoop down for it, he let her. She bumped against his leg and the gun, stopped and took it from him, tucking it into her own waistband. "We should get to the Interstate," she said. "It's a long way to Ocean Shores."

"I have a plan," he said. "What do you know about hot wiring cars?"

"Really?" she asked. "That's your plan? We're going to hot wire a car?"

"Yes," he said.

"And you just assumed I knew how to hot wire a car?"

"Not an old one," he said. "But I bet, smart as you are, you could program a newer one."

She eyed him warily. He tried to look sincere.

Finally, she grunted something about she'd pick out the car then, and that it might take her a few tries, and some other things like that, but he only half-heard them. He concentrated on walking, on the feel of her shoulders and the pearls beneath his arm, on not putting too much weight on her.

"Where'd you come up with this plan? Wait. Let me guess," she said. "You've done it in games? Seen it in movies?"

"So many times," he said. "So many times."

|◄◄ || ►►|

The slick Jupiter truck had the color and sheen of a freshly pulled espresso shot. The exterior was misleading, though. The truck rattled them only as far as the rest stop at Elma before overheating some.

They pulled over to run a diagnostic on the truck and sat on a broken-down picnic bench. He played some songs on the Little Lady he'd brought, and they both watched the sun rise.

"I can't believe you still don't know how to drive," Chaaya said.

That held some definite subtext, unasked questions: *where he had been, why he hadn't come to get her faster?* He'd never forgive himself for staying away as long as he did; in a sense, he thought it was his fault Chaaya killed the girl. He imagined it for a second, Chaaya shooting the intruder, then he crushed it. It didn't matter any longer. Here they were, she was safe now, he was taking her to a brand new life, safe and sound. He decided to be straight with her. She'd understand. He set down the harmonica. "I was crowned the King of Seattle."

She cocked her head at him. "What?"

"It started at work. The hospital flooded with people. Hordes. There were sick everywhere. People with sick loved ones. People asking questions, people with nowhere else to go. The hospital began to run out of room and out of supplies. It was overwhelming. Doctors and nurses ran." He paused to let it all sink in. Then he continued, "It became dangerous for anyone to know you were a professional anything. They would mob you. But I stayed and gave shots. I bandaged wounds. I stayed as long as I could. A group. They decided I was their leader. We moved into the Space Needle."

"WTF are you talking about?"

"Where I was," he said. "Why I didn't come for you sooner."

"Oh God," she said. "You're sick."

"I'm not sick. It happened. I left because Joaquin and Toby— you remember them?" He waited for her to nod. "They were going to try and kill me. They wanted to take over. They always wanted to take over. They tried to kick me out of Figurehead a few times. You remember." He paused to let he nod again. "Well, it was just like that. So, I left and knew I had to find a safe place. And I wanted to take you there. And Nani."

"That's the craziest thing I have ever heard," she said. "And this has been an unusual week." She looked at him. "Really. I should have known."

Toussaint smiled at that. She knew and understood: she knew he had to take care of people. It'd been his responsibility. He hadn't tried to hold her hand since they saw the beating and he tried now. She shook him off immediately. She was still playing. He liked that and inched a bit closer to her. "Don't you think there's still something between us?"

Her eyes were mercury-slick and one color in the rising light. "I haven't thought about it." She sighed, and her slick eyes blinked. "It only takes one solid hallucination."

Toussaint grabbed her neck with one hand and flipped his mask with the other. The movement, the naked pink stunned her, and he flipped her mask and was on her before she could fight him. He kissed her with everything he had.

She finally got some leverage on his chest and pushed him away. He grabbed what he could to keep her close: the strand of pearls around her neck, but the cheap string broke with the gentle tug, and the beads flew, bouncing off the wood table and into the long grass. *No one can cook a gourmet meal or fall in love without breaking something*, he thought.

Chaaya was angry. He didn't know why. He reached for her again, but she slapped away his hand, stood up and straightened her mask.

"That wasn't fair," she said, and turned from him. "This isn't a movie."

"I'm sorry," he called after her, but she was stomping away across the unkempt grass, towards the old shacks that served as bathrooms. "But you can't tell me you didn't feel that."

"You're sick," she yelled.

Toussaint watched her go. He wanted to call after her that if he was sick, then so was she. They were sharing the same hallucination, the same psychosis, *folie a deux* (words he'd come across one day, and used in a song, as both the subject and the title). But he didn't. He leaned down. From up on the picnic table, the beads looked like jewels, catching light, half hidden and sprinkled into the grass. He bent, reached for one. Into blinding pain. Then nothing.

◄◄ ❙❙ ►►❙

His first thought when he opened his eyes was about how under most circumstances, he was incredibly ticklish under his arms. But he wasn't feeling ticklish. He felt gravel and sharp grass cutting his calves and thighs. The hands that held him up and dragged him were small and delicate, and didn't hold him up high enough not to catch the ground.

The hands dropped him onto broken, cold grass that smelled clean and dry, like hay. Then his attacker stood in front of him, leaning their small frame against a wooden baseball bat. He couldn't quite focus his eyes, but the shape was familiar.

"Eliza?" he asked.

"Hello, sire," the Eliza shape said.

He wasn't sure this was real. He tried to sit up into the pain, but couldn't move. He was hot and the grass so cold. His hand clasped around a pearl bead. He couldn't make his hand do anything except squeeze the pearl tighter. "What are you doing, Eliza?"

"I'm going by Ashley, now," she said. "It suits me better, don't you think?" She held the bat up and bobbed it in her hand.

If she wasn't real, she wasn't going away. He squeezed the bead. "How——?"

"I was in the bed of the truck," she said. "I climbed in and you and your fat girlfriend didn't even notice. I've been following you."

He thought she shook the bat after that, but everything was shaking.

"I even got to her house before you. You sure took your time getting there. I waited in that closet for hours, bored out of my skull."

Her voice seemed to be coming from farther and farther away. She'd been in Chaaya's house. That was why the door was open. He wanted to tell Chaaya. Where was she?

"I've been waiting for you to be alone, but that girl just would not go away," she said.

Chaaya, he thought. *Where was she?* Now his head was wet, and he coughed. The cough hurt more than anything he'd ever felt in his life, so he swallowed instead.

"And now, finally. Here we are."

Here. We. Are. Each word required translation, like a foreign language. "Why——?"

"Oh, your highness. You don't know?" She bent down closer to him. "I gave myself to you. Then you gave me away."

He couldn't understand what she meant. The pain was. It had just been sunrise. Now the sun set. Dark, purple dark. He opened his mouth to say something else, but Eliza already had the bat up.

"Say 'Goodbye to Ashley,'" she said and swung.

The hit came.

Purple everything. He was wet. Was he in a bathtub? He was a kid, in the bathtub, reenacting naval battles of World War I, then always, his play would end as the water cooled and he imagined he was one of the few survivors of the Battle of Jutland and this, his modest lifeboat, was sinking in the North Sea. His mother yelling in from the next room to wash well and hurry up.

Everything was purple. He was sinking. He heard a crack and a scream and something fell next to him. He tried to see. The Eliza-shaped Ashley was next to him. Chaaya was over her. It was real, solid. She had the gun. She was unloading into Eliza-shaped Ashley's head. He felt wetter. He always liked Chaaya's hands. Everything was getting less clear. And wetter, wetter. Was it raining?

He had a guitar in his hands. He tried to play a song. Purple Chaaya-shaped Chaaya was there. The rain was her hair.

He wanted to tell her that Eliza'd been in her closet. That she'd somehow jimmied open the locks and that was why the doors were open, which was why that girl had wandered in. But when he opened his mouth, he said, instead, "There is something between us." The words were literal. There was something between them. Time slipped away, he slipped away. He couldn't get to her anymore. "You've got to get to Book." He couldn't remember Book's real first name. He remembered Book's laugh, and his shaggy, dark hair, his chewed-up fingernails around the neck of a bottle of beer. He remembered Book nervously drumming on everything in sight. He remembered Book's last name. "Gomez," he said. He couldn't remember why it was so important to get there, but thought he held a hand out to Chaaya. "You'll go there."

Her mouth was close to his face, naked, pink and beautiful. They moved.

And although he wanted to rest, he translated her words: *You kept me safe.* And he dropped the guitar.

Excerpts from the Introduction to "Anything Is Possible: A Review of the Interpretations of Probability and Personal Bias": A Thesis Submitted in Partial Fulfillment of the Requirements for the Degree of Master of Arts in the Philosophy of Mathematics by C. Gupta-Lee / Portrait of the Artist

In practice, humans have demonstrated little talent at accurately estimating probability. Bias reigns over individual perceptions of chance and likelihood. The average person notices and remembers only particular events, forgetting others, and only puts to question events which challenge his or her preconceived notions, based on subjective world views, of what is probable and improbable.

Because of this, people create a narrative of probability based not on mathematical frequencies over an adequately-sized sample set, but on familiarity and recall. How closely the events correlate to what one already knows and perceives, as well as how thoroughly the recall of such events, determines both the importance an individual ascribes to the event, as well as his or her estimations on how frequently such events occur.

There are a number of conflicting theories regarding the origin and mechanism of these subjective false judgments, but the simple fact remains that mathematicians quantify these biases in order to bridge the gap between probability theory and cognitive heuristics.

Ashley looked over the scene before her and it moved her.

She had a pure and tender soul, the spirit of a poet, of an artist: faced with a landscape that pure and dazzling, a moment in time so perfectly illustrated, a tableau of such exquisite beauty that she, and she alone created, it was both a physical and material struggle for her to keep back her tears, to push down the emotion that threatened to choke her.

This was her best work yet. Her masterpiece. She wanted to sign it. She wanted a souvenir.

She wanted Toussaint's arm. The one with the tattoo.

Ashley held her foot against his shoulder for leverage and tugged, but his arm was too heavy, heavier than she was. She screwed up her face with concentration, stepped on his ribs with both feet, and twisted the arm hard. Bones cracked, caved in, his rotator cuff ripping as she fell back, hard onto the ground. His arm flopped down next to her like a prize fish tossed ashore.

She wanted it. She found a piece of jagged bottle and sawed through the skin, tendons and muscles. Ligaments stretched over the bottle's edge then snapped through. She pulled and pulled at the arm, but couldn't get it free. The bone arch joint was eggshell white and Ashley was momentarily sad to smash it with the butt-end of the bat. It shattered like a dinner plate, but the arm stayed attached.

She sat back on her heels, astounded at its resiliency —considering the fragility of the skull. A mental picture of the scene was all she'd get.

She searched his pockets. A seeding kit. She threw it as far as she could into the high grass. Then she pulled out a small leather book. More interesting. She flipped through it, but could immediately tell the handwriting probably wasn't his, unless he had the curly, ornate handwriting of a female who always got what she wanted. That made her angry, thinking about whose it could be (the fat girl's?) and why he had it in his pocket. She didn't want to be angry. She wanted to bask in her best work to date, so she threw it into the grass with the kit and the gun.

There, she thought, *mistakes erased like stray pencil marks.*

Toussaint's eyes were closed, and if she squinted, she couldn't even tell the back of his head was missing. He was sleeping, albeit on a tapestry spun of his blood and brains, thin waters the color of honey and drips of pudding-thick brick red. All of Greystone lingering wet on the tops of the grasses and dandelions before sliding down to feed the hungry ground.

This place would be her signature, her souvenir. She'd visit it year after year, even after she'd surpassed its excellence. It would be wild and abundant from the nourishment, a living tribute to her and her capacity for love.

She backed up to include the fat girl in her scene. Fat girl wasn't supposed to be a part of this. But the ability to improve, to be flexible in the moment to capture the moment was, Ashley supposed, what distinguished her as an artist. Her mother hadn't been supposed to be in her first piece. But she was. And Mallory had made it work. And if Mallory could've made that work, then Ashley could do better.

She should have killed fat girl in her apartment. But she hadn't. The guru once told Mallory that every challenge was an opportunity, if you only knew to seize it.

Mallory knew the words held meaning, just not how they were meant. They were meant to shut her down. Instead, she'd opened up, bursting like a fountain.

The fat girl was face down, one hand bent, reaching out like a claw. The fat girl's blood was a shade of purple Ashley couldn't name. And didn't like. She should have killed her in her apartment.

The fat girl's other hand clutched a gun. Ashley hated guns. They stripped killing of the art. She grabbed the gun from the fat girl and turned it over in her hands.

It was heavy. Ashley held it out like she saw the fat girl hold it. Ashley had been behind the drapes. She'd watched the fat girl kill with no art, no magic, and then be rewarded; Ashley had been barely able to stay hidden as Toussaint feed the fat girl meatballs.

Challenges, opportunities. A new piece. An impromptu, second piece to complement the first.

Ashley dragged the fat girl by her feet away from Toussaint. The scene was better with just him. She left the girl by the restrooms. That seemed better. The girl spread over the concrete. Her blood looked better there. Not perfect, but better. Ashley kicked the girl's legs wider, made her into a star. Not perfect, but better.

Ashley leaned on the bat like a cane and squinted at the girl. She wasn't excited. She decided the excellence of the work was dependent on the quality of the raw materials. She also remembered hearing that artists were not always the most objective critics of their own works. The important thing was to keep trying. Output and discipline. And passion. Ashley felt better as she stepped over the girl into the restroom.

The mirror reflected back a horror show. She was drenched in blood. Her hair was stringy with it. The water ran rusty and smelled, itself, a little like blood. Ashley rinsed her face and hair under the tap as she thought about the girls she'd been, the girls she would become. Ashley stripped down and rinsed her clothes in the sink. The tile floor was cold as she wrung out her shirt and skirt. The skirt was tie-dyed pink with blood and she admired it as she slipped it on. Her clothes clung to her and she turned and folded and arranged them so they clung in the best places. She half-stepped outside and stuck her finger in the fat girl's hair. She smoothed the purple on her liplike gloss, opened her eyes wide and blinked. She was ready.

She walked towards the off-ramp, practicing jumping up and down as she went.

⏮ ⏸ ⏭

That the average individual misunderstands or underrepresents scientific or mathematical proofs as anecdotal evidence to disprove the notion of bias as a purely cognitive phenomenon is not a new notion. In 1748, David Hume asserted that effects invariable follow causes, and contemporary mathematicians and engineers continue to canonize and implement this principle, treating causal relationships as objective features, deferring to the binary states of Boolean logic: true/false, yes/no, on/off. However, personal experiences illustrate that cause-effect relationships are inconsistent. Many causes are, indeed, not followed by expected results. And as the nature of quanta becomes part of the social largesse, Heisenberg's Uncertainty Principle is invoked: if one cannot know the precise and accurate state of a pair of physical properties such as the location and velocity of a particle, how can anyone quantitatively know anything?

|◀ ❚❚ ▶|

The truck driver looked at her wet clothes and didn't wonder why the hysterical girl was holding a bat.

"You've got to help me," she sobbed. "I was attacked." When she rubbed her eyes, her shirt stretched across her breasts. "I need help."

"How did you get here?" the driver asked, in a voice that let Ashley know he wanted to be asking other things.

"My car," she said. "It broke down." She rushed to his side and leaned in the window. "There's a maniac. He attacked me." She glanced back at the rest stop, and, just knowing her work was right there over the horizon made her tears start again. "Please. We don't have much time."

The driver popped the lock and waved her in. "They're still here?"

"I don't know," she said. "We've got to go."

"Who is that?" the driver asked, pointing. "That doesn't look like a maniac."

Ashley followed his finger towards a moving shadow, lumbering and clumsy like a zombie. It was the fat girl, and it was true surprise erupted as a scream. "Go," she said. "Please go. Go now."

The driver looked panicked. He revved the engine, but then stopped as the fat girl moved closer and it was apparent she was a fat girl and not some sort of maniac. "Is she with you?"

Ashley wanted to scream and curse and slam her foot down on the accelerator and run over the fat girl who she hadn't killed twice so far. She wanted to yell that she was the maniac, but knew the driver would never believe it.

Fat girl looked like a victim. Ashley wanted to beat her for her weakness. So, instead she said, "Yes. My sister." She grabbed the driver's arm. "Thank god. My sister is OK."

Then the fat girl fell. Anyone else, Ashley would be sure they were dead for sure, but no more chances, no more missteps. Opportunities. Flexibility in the moment. "We have to get help," she said. "She's going to die."

Then the driver said the first sensible thing since he'd pulled over. "Are you two sick?"

It almost made her respect him. "No, we aren't." She opened her eyes wide and blinked like she had in the mirror. "She should go in the bed. She needs to lie down."

"I can do it," he said. He pulled the truck close to where fat girl lay, and then walked over. He was thin and ropy, and Ashley could see his Adam's apple in sharp silhouette. He grabbed fat girl under her arms and lifted her up. With a few squats, he had her over his shoulder. Ashley was impressed the driver was that strong. She slipped from the passenger seat and told him so while he placed fat girl gently into the bed.

"I wish I had something soft," he said. "She'll get banged around in there." He shook his head and continued. "We should put her in the cab with us."

"Whatever you say," Ashley said. It wasn't going to change anything.

The driver got fat girl back onto his shoulder and then pushed her into the cab, right where Ashley had been sitting. Ashley tucked the bat under her arm casually like a long baguette of bread and slid her skirt up her leg. The driver opened his mouth to say something, but changed his mind and just looked at her bare thigh.

"What are your names?" he managed.

"I'm Ashley. *She's* Eliza." She empathized that she, herself, could never be named something as frumpy and plain as Eliza. Then she smiled at him but he was still staring at her leg. She tucked the end of her skirt into the leg of her underwear and he licked his lips.

He never saw the bat. It wasn't a great swing, being inside the cab and all, and having to work over the dumb fat girl, but she hit the mark best she could. His head burst like a pimple. The spray was a ghastly fireworks.

|◀ ❙❙ ▶▶|

Two hundred years after Hume, John Venn delineated the problematic nature of categorizing cause and effect relationships, stating that every event has an indefinite number of attributes and, therefore, belongs to an indefinite number of categories.

We must notice, however, that Venn used the word "indefinite," not infinite. Indefinite commonly describes situations with unclear, vague, or imprecise limits, while the concept of the infinite refers, in both theoretical and conversational language, to that without limits.

There is a wide gulf between an indefinite number of categories and an infinite number of categories. The connotations of this expose that familiarity and recall are only two of the underlying suppositions that skew human perceptions of probability. There is an additional innate inclination that must be considered: people simply do not, innately, understand the idea of what constitutes a sample set. People routinely neglect to consider adequate set sizes and to consider their individual selves (each person's 'I') as a unit subject to probabilities.

Even the most unexpected coincidence must occur over a long-enough time span across a large-enough sample size, of which all individuals are members. Events will occur with no less and no more than their appropriate frequency, no matter how little any single member expects, because events calculated as rare or infrequent per person occur with frequencies astounding to average people when the number of interactions is increased to global levels, or a simply larger set.

The classic birthday problem never fails to impress. The fact that within a group of 30 randomly chosen people, the probability of two of them sharing a birthday is ~70.6% feels nothing short of miraculous. Birthdays, in western culture, are events that celebrate the uniqueness of the individual, and we internalize a sense of ownership over "our" day. However, the fact that—excluding Leap years—there are only 365 individual members of the set equaling all possible birthdays should make the figure less surprising.

In other words, we can take the equation out of ourselves, but we cannot take ourselves out of the equation.

⏮ ⏸ ⏭

First bump they hit, fat Eliza woke up. "Where am I?" she asked. Or Ashley thought she asked. It was hard to tell. Fat Eliza was slurring drunkenly. It made Ashley a little sick and she didn't answer.

"Who're you?" fat Eliza asked her.

Ashley held the wheel tightly. She started at the road, but could see the fat girl trying to move out of the corner of her eye. "I'm Ashley," she finally said.

"What happened to me?"

Ashley sighed. She watched the road go by. "I don't know." What she meant was that she didn't know what she was going to do with her. "What do you remember?"

"I was with Toussaint," fat Eliza said. "And we were going somewhere."

Ashley waited for fat Eliza to continue. She was so slow. "Where?"

"To the coast," fat Eliza answered, in a voice that sounded like the answer surprised her. "Ocean Shores."

Ocean Shores. Ashley scanned the GPS, but the signal was a flat line. She'd have to wing it. The road felt west, and Ashley had the instincts of a bird, of a prize fighter, an intrepid explorer. "Why there?" Ashley demanded. "What's in Ocean Shores?" She looked at fat Eliza. The only part of her that was clean was a roll of brown stomach showing above her waistband. It looked soft and unbaked. Ashley looked away.

"Book," fat Eliza said, or so Ashley thought.

"For a book?" It annoyed her. "What book?"

"He's a person. Toussaint was taking me to Book. We would be safe there with Book."

"Safe from what?" It made her uncomfortable to think that Toussaint spoke of her to fat Eliza when she wasn't there. "Safe from what?" she repeated.

Fat Eliza made a noise. Ashley couldn't understand it. She wished the girl would just speak clearly and keep her fat stomach covered. She glanced over at her, avoiding looking at her middle. "What did you say?" She asked.

But fat Eliza didn't answer. Her eyes were closed. Ashley forced herself to push her fingers onto Eliza's neck. Alive. The fat girl was still alive. That should have enraged her, but she had to admit she was curious, too. She had the curiosity of a kitten, the whimsical imagination of an excited child.

The digital signs were dim, but Ashley could just catch what it said. "Ocean Shores, 51 miles," she read and stepped down on the accelerator.

Knight-Errant

Sundays were a relief.

Book always hated Friday and Saturday nights. And even though he'd technically gone out Friday night, seen a friend, even, had dinner, and then drank himself out, he woke up with the same sense of Sunday lightness across his chest.

Sasha never understood his hatred of the weekend. Or of birthdays or New Year's Eve or Halloween— or even the innocuous Labor Day and Memorial Day weekends. Sasha could enjoy things without second thought or restraint or, more pointedly, without unrealistic expectation, although she feared things irrationally and completely.

Book had a handle on his fears, but was doomed, no matter where he was and what he was doing, always to feel like he should be having a much better time, in a much better place, with much better people. Even when he was in Figurehead, playing a tight venue, seats filled with pretty girls, he thought of it as work and looked at all the people not working, but, instead, dancing to the music he was making for them. He made their good time possible.

Sundays, the pressure was off, at least for another week. No one expected anyone to do anything during the week. Reasonable, successful, admirable people could watch a movie, read a little, and then go the hell to bed. If you went out on a weeknight, it was cake or naughty, or both. But not expected, and not something Book tallied in his mind the way he did the weekend.

And this was heightened, double, triple time since he'd been home. Friday and Saturday nights seemed to throw in his face that he'd never quite bloomed to anyone's expectation. It also made him feel old and dried out and mortal, a sad, middle aged guy staying home with his parents. It didn't matter he had good reason to be home with his parents, either, and it wasn't as if there was any place to go or anything to do, unless he wanted to start beach fires or go to Aberdeen.

And his night at Davey's should count in his mind. That was what most people would consider a good time. And at his age, he knew, that was rare.

He'd never told anyone about any of this, aside from Sasha. He tended to not strike people as particularly restless, but she knew him for what he really was. He wished she'd come home already. But, at least, it was Sunday.

The one night at Davey's threw off his sleep schedule. It was really early; his mother wasn't even up yet. The light streaming through the windows was pale pink. His father was stacked on the couch like a pile of sticks covered by a blanket, squinting at an old paper book, holding it out so he could get the full effect of the sunrise.

"That's no good for your eyes," he whispered to his dad.

"I couldn't sleep anymore," his dad said. "Your mother's snoring. What are the chances we have coffee?"

"Slim to none," Book answered. "But I'll look." He went into the kitchen and rifled around in the cupboards. He found a dusty, open can of chicory his mother must have bought for some recipe or another back in the day, and he remembered his father, in fact, telling him how dried chicory roots were used as substitutes for coffee during the 30s Great Depression. "How about some chicory?"

"Why do we even have chicory?" his father asked.

Book went in and handed his father the can. His father propped the book on his lap and squinted at the can, and Book took the opportunity to look at his father and worry. It could be Addison's Disease, wouldn't be surprising if his adrenal glands were going next, or a cardiac tamponade, fluids flooding the tissue of his ventricles. So many possible complications. Or the blood he stole was hemochromatic and his dad was storing iron like a war factory.

"Let's try it," his father finally said. "Why not?" He handed the can back to Book. "Better than dandelion coffee. Poor Civil War soldiers had it bad enough, and then had to drink brewed dandelion leaves. Horrible, I hear."

Book set the water to boiling and loaded two mugs with water and chicory. It looked black as motor oil and smelled malty. He was dubious but he brought it into his father, who patted the edge of the couch and motioned for Book to sit.

Book sat, and some of the blanket fell away. His father was so thin and delicate, wearing his skin rather than occupying it. His father took the mug, his hand loose and muddy grey, and Book wished he'd taken the time to study nanotech. He could have been a doctor, as his mother often liked to remind him, or a scientist. He wished he could at least transform his blood type, and inwardly he squeezed and pushed like he used to when he was a child wishing to be taller. But he was A positive, like his mother and his sister, incompatible with the O his father needed and no amount of trying or wishing or wanting it bad enough was going to change his blood or whatever was going on inside his father. He hated that he knew that. Sasha was the one that always believed in wanting and wishing and fairies and spirits and karma and faith, not him, and maybe that was what his father would need now.

"Yikes," his father said, into the mug.

"Is it terrible?"

"It's earthy," his father said. The he looked at Book. "Did you strain it?"

"Was I supposed to?"

His father glanced over his shoulder at the bedroom door. He lowered his voice. "We need to, you know—"

"No." Book could feel his father looking at him.

"How much longer, really, can we do this?" his

father asked.

"Forever." Book thought of Shin, out of blood, out of options, but he shook his head.

"Avoiding it isn't going to keep it from happening," his father continued.

"It might," Book said.

"You sound like your sister." His father set down his mug. "Listen to me. There's some money, but I don't think that's going to matter any. You'll have to make a plan. Read up on farming and native plants." He looked at Book. "Your mother is going to lose it for a while. But she'll pull together."

"What will I pull together?" his mother said. She padded into the living room. In her pajamas, wiping sleep from her eyes, her littleness made her look like a child.

"Nothing," his father said, then shot Book a look he hadn't seen since high school, when his father caught Book smoking pot pilfered from his father's stash, an I-won't-tell-if-you-won't-otherwise-we-both-get-screwed wince.

Book stood up, holding his mug awkwardly.

"What are you drinking?" His mother stood on her toes to peek in the mug.

"Alastair found your chicory stash," his father said.

"Chicory?" She stopped and thought, then made a face. "That has to be at least ten years old. We bought that for that Mardi Gras party." She took Book's mug from him and slipped it beneath her mask. "Yuck. Tastes as good as it did then."

She tried to hand the mug back to him, but he shook his head. He needed to get away from there. "I'm going out. Taking the car."

His father held up a hand.

"OK," his mother said. "Be careful." Then, as if she knew something, she kissed his forehead.

◄◄ ❚❚ ▶▶

Book drove fast. He never drove fast. Then again,

he'd never lost his father. Or anything, really: never lost a bet or a fight. But he never picked battles he didn't think he could win.

His knuckles were white and numb from squeezing the wheel, so he slowed down. He thought he was headed for the beach, where he usually went when he had to think things over. He'd walk the beach and play catch with the surf, tossing in beach rocks then picking up others that rolled in with the tide, until the wind and salt left him sticky and tired. The sun was coming up—it would make sense to head to the beach.

Instead, he found himself at the turn for the Shore Harbor Clinic. He pulled into the parking lot, turned the key, and sat up on the hood of the car.

He'd been excited to get his first dose. It made him feel grown up. The syringe had looked enormous, nearly old-fashioned in its shiny brass casing, but it hadn't hurt and he'd gotten to choose the flavor of lollipop afterwards, rather than getting stuck with some flavor he didn't like. He was an expert at it by the time Sasha turned ten. She hadn't looked forward to it like he had. She wanted to stay a kid forever. Their parents let her cry herself out before they left for her first dose, and she rode the whole way, holding her knobby knees, snuffling and terrified. He'd managed to distract her by challenging her to a cloud race. It was a perfect day for cloud racing, a blue sky filled with bulging cumulus clouds and a steady west wind. He even let her pick the best cloud. By the time they'd parked, pretty much in this exact spot, Sasha wasn't exactly looking forward to her first dose, but she'd made some sort of peace with it. Just to make sure, he gave her his lollipop too. It was a mango one.

Lies. They were all lies. The big dupe. He was seized with overwhelming anger over it, the unfairness, not of death, but of being assured, promised, and sold the idea that death was always to be distant. Not eliminated, but too far down the horizon to worry about. He was completely unprepared. They were led down the proverbial garden path and told it was a road.

His parents led him. And he led Sasha.

He remembered his grandparents' funerals. He was sad, but he hadn't really known them. He held Sasha's little, sweaty hand while she cried at the very idea of death. Relatives told him what a good brother he was. Such a good brother.

Something was keeping Sasha away. His parents weren't done pretending this was typical Sasha behavior, but he was. She would have been home by now, even dragging her feet. If she was coming home at all.

Book slid off the car into the soft sawdust-covered landscaping. The entire parking lot was hemmed with carefully manicured mud and driftwood, and he bent over and picked up a long, thick branch, blanched with salt and sun and time into near weightlessness. It took nearly all the matches he saved for his cigarettes to get the tip to burn, but then it caught, and he held the torch aloft. He wasn't sure what he was planning to do with it, burn the place down or just stomp around like a cartoon caveman, but then he caught a flicker through the clinic's windows. Just a flicker, nothing more, but it was enough to move him towards the front door, holding the torch in both hands in front of him like a broad sword, a knight errant.

He pushed the door open with his foot. The sound was gentle, unsystematic. Maybe raccoons, he thought, black curls of smoke and smell as the torch singed the ceiling. An examination room with the door open, a bobbling flashlight. He squeezed the lit branch and moved towards it.

Book heard the voice, "What the fuck? WTF? Who the fuck are you?" then saw the eyes, yellow and runny. He knew the eyes. The guy was drug sick, the son of the woman who ran the Oyehut wildlife refuge. She'd been corralling and caring for him since Book was in junior high school. He looked at Book like he was trying to place him and couldn't.

"Get the fuck out of here," Book said.

"What you want, man? There's nothing here worth anything. I've been looking." The guy talked too fast, scratching his cheeks and forehead. "What you doing, man? You gonna set fire to me, to the place?"

"I said, get the fuck out of here." Book held the torch in front of him and tried not to blink, even though the smoke in the room was starting to make his eyes tear. "Go. Get the fuck out of here."

"Who are you, man?" The guy slid past him, both smiling and muttering. "Who are you to tell me to go? Not doing nothing. Who you? You the sheriff?"

"Maybe I am the sheriff," Book said, then shook the torch at the junkie. "Not going to tell you again to get the fuck out of here."

The guy muttered again. Book caught "...tin star..." but then the guy was running. He'd scared him. He listened to the junkie run over the sawdust, fall in the mud, and then keep going. He waited until there was nothing but silence, and walked to the examination room sink.

The water spluttered, but then ran brown. He dowsed the torch under the stream, then laid the rest of the branch in the sink. Book splashed water on his face and sat down back out in the waiting room, on the couch with the nubby tweed fabric, holding his head in his hands. He wanted to cry or something cathartic, but instead he was consumed with the thought that this place needed to be protected, that to put together the future, the raw materials lay in these walls. He stood up, found the custodial closet, and swept up the bigger chunks of broken glass and human waste, then bagged and tied it. He set the robot vacuum to cruise, and dragged the bag of trash out back to set it on top of the bulging dumpster of uncollected trash. He went back in and secured what he could, and as he left, slipped three or four lollipops from the reception desk into his pocket.

He drove slowly, but with purpose. He obeyed every stop sign, paused at the dark traffic lights, then pulled into a legal parking spot. He looked both ways down the empty street before crossing over to the guard booth.

Fareed McCarthy shaped his fingers into a gun and

aimed at Book. That meant he was pleased to see him. He greeted everyone that way, especially Book's mother, who he always admired from afar at the Eagles happy hour, and had once, she'd say as she repeated the story in certain companies, pinched her butt after he'd thrown back a few too many. Mr. McCarthy was considered an elder in town, though, so no one found it creepy, only funny. Book was never sure he thought it was that funny.

"Heard you scared Todd the Toad pretty good," Mr. McCarthy said. "He came running down the street like he was being chased. When I got hold of him, he was yammering something about a sheriff in town. Then he described you."

"Todd the Toad," Book repeated.

"Poor kid's always been a little off," Mr. McCarthy said. "His poor mother always looked out for him. Now he's wild and all on his own. He described you. Or it could have been the Pickell kid. David. You two are the last two young men. Last good young men. That I know of anyway."

"Yeah," Book said. He could tell Mr. McCarthy was waiting for him deny or confirm, and if confirmed, to tell him the story. He didn't know what to say or really want to say anything.

"So," Mr. McCarthy said, breaking the silence. "It was you. You want to be sheriff?"

"I wanted to sign up for a few shifts here," he said.

"I think you should, son." Mr. McCarthy made the finger gun at him again. "I'll call a meeting at the Eagles. I think, considering, it's as easy as that to make a sheriff."

"Maybe start with a few shifts—" but Book could tell this was already out of his control.

"We need to check the charter. But this town needs a sheriff. Good old fashioned western justice," Mr. McCarthy said. "Your father would sure be proud of you."

That made him want to talk. That made him want to break off McCarthy's gun—and presumably, pinching —fingers. "My father isn't dead," Book snapped.

Mr. McCarthy held up his gun pointing hand, but

loosely, palm up. "No, no. Of course not. Not what I meant. You'd even be perfect, with your hair-trigger temper. Look at you. You look about ready to rip my head off my neck."

Book wanted to say more, but a car, farting smoke and exhaust, rambled around the corner into view. McCarthy gave Book a curt nod. "I'll call a meeting. And get word to you. Sheriff." He picked up the clipboard and turned towards the incoming car. "Send best to your parents." He glanced at Book. "Both your parents."

"Fuck you, McCarthy," he said.

"That's the spirit," Mr. McCarthy said.

Book crossed back to the car. He slid in and poked his leg on a lollipop stick. He peeled the warm, sticky candy out. A red one. He always hated red. He unwrapped it and stuck the lollipop beneath his mask.

He drove just over the posted speed limit. He rolled through crosswalks and glanced at stop lights. He wasn't in any particular hurry to get home, but he didn't have any place he wanted to go. He thought again about heading to the beach. The sun was afternoon high, getting stronger, and the idea of standing in sunlight and sweating sounded better than heading back. He decided to take the long way back to his favorite beach, a stretch behind the abandoned hotel. Thickets of forest thinned around abandoned houses, then back into verdant walls.

Then he hit something. He didn't see it, but it felt deer sized.

"Mother fucker." He was annoyed, then realized he could drape it over the front of the car, Davey could dress it. Make it a thing. His mother would be pleased, and his father wouldn't be able to get him alone again. He pulled over.

It wasn't a deer.

He'd hit a girl. "Mother fucker," he repeated, this time full of panic.

He bent over her. Mud was packed into her hair, smeared down her face and neck, soaked into her clothes, a golem of a girl. He smelled her, counterpoint to the sweet, rotting leaves, some deathly scent of iron. The ground was black, the asphalt wet between them, and he knew somehow that it was blood, and that was what he smelled, blood in the air as strong as if he were passing close to an abattoir.

"Mother fucker." A whisper.

Then she coughed, face down in the mud.

"Miss?" he asked. "Are you all right?" It was idiotic; it was obvious that she wasn't all right, and that his having slammed into her with his car was only the most recent of her problems. He stepped back and a bell tinkled beneath his foot. He rolled a tiny, tatty stuffed elephant with his foot. He picked it up and looked back at her. "Miss?"

She jerked a bit, and he felt horrible noticing that her ass was wide and flat, but not bad at all. Wide ass, wide hips, small feet and a curve to her back. Then he felt worse because he panicked. He felt himself panic and become two people: one who moved to help, who rolled her face up and who gave her first aid, and the other, the other one, the one who slid back into the car. Both versions of him said: "I'll send help." But then one foot was on the gas and his hand curled around the elephant, the hook and bell cutting into his palm, and he was speeding away, towards the beach.

Then he pulled over again. *Some sheriff,* he thought. "Mother fucker." This was his life now. He looked in the rear view mirror then yanked the car into reverse. A u turn and he was back to her. He placed the elephant into his pocket next to the lollipops, parked sideways across the street, put on flashers, and hoped no one would come tearing down the stretch.

She looked soft but was packed dense. He struggled her up and dumped her in the backseat. Her mask was gone and he couldn't help staring at her lips for a second. Then he scanned her face. She was pretty, best he could tell, under the mud. High cheekbones and chubby cheeks. Asian probably. And something about her was familiar. He'd seen her before. Somewhere. Then again, pretty faces always felt a bit familiar in their prettiness; it was probably just that. He'd seen pretty girls before who had the same bold features. Instead he looked for obvious contusions and didn't see any. The blood on her forehead didn't look serious. He wondered what he'd smelled.

Her eyes fluttered open and she licked mud off her lips. "I heard someone say they'd send help. Are you help?"

"I am." Relief flooded him. She was OK. Filthy, maybe bruised, a few cuts. Maybe something broken, but nothing on her pointed the wrong direction. "Are you OK?"

She tried to sit up and winced. Then she pulled herself up, slowly. "I think so. Considering." She then realized her mouth was bare, she clamped her hand over her lips. She muttered something behind her hand, then said, "Do you have an extra mask?"

"I can give you mine," he offered. Then he'd be bare, but that didn't bother him as much as it did her.

She shook her head.

Her face, covered with her hand, looked more familiar. There was something about the black, shiny eyes looking out of the mud. "You need to get cleaned up and checked out. Can you hold for a few minutes?" He plopped into the driver's seat, suddenly exhausted. He looked at her in the rear view mirror. "You don't feel anything broken?"

She shook her head again.

"I also don't care," he said. "I've seen a woman's mouth before."

"Not mine," she said. Then she said, "Some place safe," and laughed, a spiny laugh that became a cough. She covered her face with both hands, and then sniffed in hard. She looked up, into his eyes in the mirror. "OK." She looked down again.

And he knew who she was.

"Chaaya?" he asked.

"Book?"

"You didn't recognize me."

"You didn't recognize me," she said, distantly, as if she was repeating what he'd said. Then she continued, "I was hit by a car. You hit me. I don't remember..." She slid to the edge of the seat to get closer and dropped her hand off her mouth entirely. "That's crazy. I didn't recognize you. It's been—. That's crazy. What are the odds...?" She repeated that again, dropping the question mark, as if the odds were something she, indeed, could calculate.

They really were, and he said so. "Pretty good actually. This town wasn't very big even in good times. So, how did you get here?" He glanced back at her, but she wasn't in the mirror.

She hunched over, gagged, and then coughed. She sat up slowly, wiped her naked mouth on the back of her hand, and said, "I just threw up a little. I'm sorry."

"Don't worry," he said. "I don't blame you. Are you OK?"

She held onto the seat with a wet hand. "I don't know." She coughed and said. "Toussaint brought me. But I don't know." She squinted, like the answer was in the mirror, writ small.

Book slammed onto the brakes. "Toussaint brought you? Where is he?"

Chaaya shrugged, ducked back down to vomit again. Book pulled a second u turn, sped back to where he'd found her, and pulled over. He jumped out of the driver's seat, door open, car motor on, and started calling for Toussaint.

Nothing.

He waded through dead leaves, moss and grass, rifling like he'd lost his keys instead of a full grown man. He searched until his shoes and pants cuffs soaked through, starting at two sounds with hope and fear: the first an adult buck disturbed from a mushroom feast— Book could see him deciding whether or not to charge before darting deeper into the woods. The second sound was Chaaya lurching towards him, unsteady and leaky.

Tears and snot cleaned paths down her face, her black eyes wet and bright. And he knew.

He held her, even as she threw up on his shoulder. He patted her and she caught her breath. "I don't know where he is," she said. "We started in a car. We stole a car. We stopped in Alma."

"Elma," Book corrected.

"He still doesn't know how to drive, did you know that?"

"Is he out here somewhere?" Book asked.

Chaaya let go of his arms and slid down into the leaves, holding her head in her hands. "I'm really tired. I think I have a concussion."

The trees absorbed the sound of the truck, careening towards them. The silence and speed made it look like a cartoon. Book stared at it for what felt like a long time, then jumped like a cat over Chaaya— a release of breath, deep splintering, and a hard thud onto ground, scraped with dead leaves and sticks and sharp grass. A spray of gravel and rocks peppered the back of his neck and where his shirt pulled up, and he waited for a blow that never came as the truck swerved back onto the road.

He waited to roll off, and when he did, she was white beneath the mud, lower lip fat with slack, with shock. She sat up and looked at her arm, wrist back at an alarming angle.

He stood up and then picked her up, carrying her to the car. He opened the back door with his knee—but she had her head on his dry shoulder and he didn't want to put her down. "I broke your arm," he said. "I'm sorry." He looked at her face. Her swollen lips were shaking, talking.

He leaned in to hear. She was counting. "341, 561, 1105, 1729, 1905, 2047."

"Numbers?" he asked.

She barely nodded.

He recognized them from a school project on special numbers. He hadn't understood the theory, but liked the mysterious elegance, how strange unrelated numbers had such exceptional relationships. "Euler Base 2 pseudoprimes," he added, and slid her carefully into the back seat.

And as he did, she looked at him like no one had ever looked at him before.

"Keep at it," he said. "You need to stay awake."

He drove carefully, slowing over pothole and cracks he knew by heart, so as not to jostle her. A mile down the road, smoke climbed in black taffy streaks, and he slowed to see the truck, flipped over, flames sizzling on wet brush. The same truck that swerved towards them. *No one could have survived a crash like that*, he thought with cruel satisfaction, stopping fully for a second. He should stop, see if the driver was OK. It was his duty now. But, he also knew time was a real factor in saving Chaaya. So, he chose her, the driver that swerved towards him, he would swear on his life, on purpose, be damned. He's come back later, after he got Chaaya home. *Control, alt, delete.*

Across the road, the buck leapt deeper into the trees, a brown shadow nearly as big as the truck.

He started the car again. Chaaya had her broken hand laid on her lap. She was still pale, but mouthing her numbers, and they cruised in silence. A few blocks from his parents' house, it all hit him. Chaaya, Toussaint, the truck, the deer, his dad, everything. He suddenly needed a cigarette. He pulled into a driveway, the brown and purple rambler that used to belong to the Fishers. Book fished out the pack, rolled down the window and yanked off his own mask. He lit his cigarette and turned around in his seat.

Chaaya looked at him. It felt physical, almost as if she were touching him as well. "Do you want a cigarette?" he asked. "Or a lollipop?"

"A lollipop?" She looked like she didn't understand the word for a second, then said, "OK."

He pulled one out of his pocket and handed it back to her. A mango one. The best flavor. "Sugar may help you in the short term."

She turned the lollipop over in her hand and held the lollipop up to the light. It was transparent as stained glass. "Can you really take me someplace safe?" she asked.

Book took a long drag off his cigarette. Each one he smoked burned less and less, which meant he should probably stop. He tossed the butt out the window just as

Chaaya put the lollipop in her mouth. "Yes," he said. "I'm taking you home."

Anoneira
Part II

Didi could spend the whole of a day taking care of the cats: fill water dishes, portion out food, and sift through the litter and dirt she used to extend the litter, comb the long haired Iras, and wipe up hairballs and vomit. By that time, the water dishes needed refilling, the next mealtime was approaching, and the litter boxes stank again.

Daylight carried obligations, expectations—she felt guilty for not showing up to work for, *how long now?* She wondered. *A week?*—A vacuum she filled tending the Iras and Mrs. Lopez. But nighttime carried no such suggestion of responsibility; she'd get a fire going and some candles burning, and start a kettle for hot tea. Then she'd sit on the couch and make a scratching gesture in the air until Ira moved beneath her hand for petting.

Didi could now keep the cats straight: the calico Ira was the neediest, and would follow her around mewling and butting his head against her leg until she picked him up. The ginger Ira with the freckles and silver Ira with the chubby cheeks were the best hunters, and would leave dead slugs, headless birds, or even a few praying mantises all over the house. Tuxedo polydactyl Ira used his two extra toes to open the doors and windows. White Persian Ira trilled like a Spaniard when she was happy, Ira the Russian Blue joyfully licked anything crinkly or plastic, and Ira, the emerald eyed tortie Ira purred loudly as a diesel truck. And always there was lame, game Mrs. Lopez, who kept after Didi like Didi was her own lost kitten: grooming Didi's hands and hair, holding Didi's cheeks in her arthritic paws and looking deep into Didi's eyes like she could read something there.

This night, Didi set the water to boiling and dozed off, waking to the kettle screaming and the cats scattering in confused panic. Didi pulled herself up, took the kettle off, decided against tea, and sat back down.

The candles flickered at the knock on the door. First, she stupidly thought it was Sasha, but Sasha never knocked. Didi couldn't think of who could be knocking, so she approached it carefully. "Yes," she called, trying to sound confident and calm.

"It's Bob, Didi," the voice said through the door. She opened it, and there he stood, Bob Hughes, RN, holding a pot of something. He also had a bag slung over his shoulder.

She should have known he'd come eventually. She probably did know.

"Where have you been?" he asked.

"Oh, Bob." Didi sagged. "I'm sorry. Things have been strange."

"Can I come in?" he asked, but he was already coming in, stepping into the dark foyer into a sea of cats who scattered and brushed up and hissed and meowed.

Didi closed the door behind him and followed him into the living room.

"I heard about the DeVotos and saw your bike there and then you didn't come in. I thought you needed some time, but it's been nearly a week, so I got worried." He blinked, eyes adjusting to the candlelight. "Who's all this now?"

"These are all Ira," Didi said. "We couldn't keep them straight when we got them, so we call them all Ira."

"Ah," Bob said. "Is there a place to put this?" He held up the pot. "It's a stew. A mélange."

"Sure." Didi took the pot from him and set it on top of the stove.

He set the bag down and immediately a few Iras

started sniffing at it. "So. No offense. I knew lesbians had a thing for cats, but—this is unexpected."

"Sasha started taking them in," Didi said. "Then they started appearing. Sasha couldn't turn them away."

"Where is Sasha?" Bob asked. "I brought some molasses cookies over for her. She went crazy for them the last time."

Didi didn't know if Bob could see her expression in the low light, or if it was just that he was so sensitive, so kind, and trained to take care of people, but in that next moment, he said, "What happened, Didi? Where is she?"

Didi sat on the floor and motioned for Bob to take the chair. He sat and waited for her to talk. She opened her mouth a few times, but each was a false start.

"You know, I brought some whiskey," he said. "It's in the bag. Give me a second." He stood up and went into the kitchen cabinets and found two cups, pulled a bottle out of the bag and poured both glasses near full. "It's lousy whiskey, but whiskey."

Didi took a sip. It felt hot in her throat but she forced it down, then took another sip. It immediately began to work. "She's gone, Bob. She left me."

"Why didn't you tell me?" he asked.

"I'm sorry, Bob," she said.

He waved his hand. "Let's eat something."

Didi stood up, spooned out bowls of the stew into deep dishes and set them at the table. Bob lit as many candles as he could find, tended to the embers in the stove.

They sat and ate. Didi was hungry, and the whiskey made her head feel like it was attached to her neck only by a string.

Bob kept the conversation going. "This is a nice place. Shaker style, yes?" He fed scraps to the Iras beneath the table. "Hand done pegging?"

Didi ate and drank and nodded along. The Iras climbed up on the table, smelling the stew and whiskey and Bob. They both slipped the Iras bits of meat from the stew.

After a while, Bob changed tone. "When did she

leave?"

Didi pushed the last of the stew around on her plate. "I don't know. A few weeks ago." She dropped her fork. "I can't seem to get it together."

Bob shooed white Persian Ira out of Didi's cup, then refilled it to the top.

"I'm going to get drunk," she protested.

"Might do you some good."

She shook her head but took a big sip.

"Good girl," he said.

"I don't know what to do," Didi said.

Bob tipped his cup at her. "Maybe you should go after her."

"No." Didi's eyelids felt fat and heavy from the whiskey. "I couldn't."

"Why not? You two were together for how long—?"

"Three years." Didi sighed.

"I'm living at the office," Bob said. "I don't know if you know."

Didi nodded.

"If I could've gone after Vicky, I would." He reached down and pulled tortie Ira onto his lap. He concentrated on the tiny cat's head and her purrs echoed through the kitchen. "Good Ira."

Didi took another sip of whiskey. Everything was getting dark around the edges. "You really think I should go after her?"

"I really do." He picked Ira up onto his shoulder. She settled in like a sleeping infant. "Where do you think she'd go?"

"Her brother lives in Seattle. Her family's on the coast. Ocean Shores. Probably either."

"Then it's settled."

"She took the car. I have my bike. And there's work. And the cats. I can't just leave the cats."

"I have a truck. You can have the truck. I have a lot of fuel at my house." He looked sad. "It's probably all there, secure. I haven't checked. But you can take it. The car, fuel, supplies and everything."

"But work. And the cats."

"Work?" Bob looked at her with a crooked smile. "You haven't shown up in a week. You're fired. And I can take care of the cats."

It was all more than she could process. "Bob."

"We'll go to the house," he said. "Tomorrow, though. I'm plowed. Are you plowed?"

She nodded. "I'm plowed."

"Excellent news." He let tortie Ira leap off his shoulder onto the table. He stood up, unsteady. "Wow. I need to lie down."

Didi forced Bob to sleep in the bed. When he protested, she told him that she didn't really sleep there since Sasha left, which he understood. She changed the sheets and he fell asleep, an Ira across the top of his head and Mrs. Lopez wheeze-snoring by his hand before Didi was even done folding extra blankets at the foot of the bed.

Didi lay on the sofa, and soon she was covered in Iras herself, their warm naked bellies on her skin, purring, she fell asleep and slept all night, her head a dark, dreamless place.

When she woke, Bob had already boiled water for coffee. "I couldn't figure out your system," he said, "for feeding all the Iras."

She fed and watered the cats, took some lickings on the back of her hand, and then sat down and drank the strong hot coffee. Bob jiggled his leg, but this time it wasn't because he had something to tell her. She knew he was nervous about going to his house.

"Are you sure about this?" she asked.

He bobbed his leg, took a big sip of coffee, and stood up. "You'll go get her and bring her home," he said. "It'll be fine." He looked at her, but kept fidgeting. "You're all the family I have left. Let's do it. Let's go."

Didi wanted a shower, to change the clothes she'd been in since yesterday morning, but she put down her cup. "OK," she said. "Let's go."

She'd only been to Bob's house once before, when

the office was bright and busy. He held a holiday party for all the employees and some of the more mobile clients. She remembered it was big, with a wraparound deck and a private dock on Useless Bay, down from Deer Lagoon with sweeping views of nesting eagles and mild-mannered mule deer that ate Vicky Hughes' rosebushes. A fancy place, but one he was always careful to explain had been in his family since the 1990s. He drove in silence and Didi looked out the window at the abandoned farms and quiet dark woods.

They pulled into his driveway and the garage door automatically opened. Didi looked at it, then at Bob, who furrowed his brow as he pulled in. Then he flipped the truck into park as the garage door closed. He took a deep breath, but before Didi could ask him if he was OK, he was out of the truck and punching something into a keypad at a door. He opened the door that led inside and waited for her to go through first.

The sensors turned on lights, climate control. She could hear the fair whir of the generator. Bob stood, shaking slightly, in the doorframe.

She went over to him and led him inside by the hand. Then she started talking to fill the quiet house. "This is such a beautiful place," she said. "I remember it from that holiday party." She walked into the kitchen, opened the refrigerator which was humming cheerfully, when as she opened the door, a sour and rotten stench emerged like smoke, so she quickly shut it again tightly. "The views here are so beautiful and I remember there used to be an alpaca or llama farm up that way, but it hasn't been there for a few years now, right?" She looked through cabinets and found glasses, hand blown glass with artful swirls and bubbles and she turned on the tap. It coughed and choked, but then the well pumps kicked in and it dripped red water, then spit grey, then ran clear.

Didi filled the two glasses and handed one to Bob. "You loved them and now they are gone. Tell me about them. I only met Mrs. Hughes the once and your son just a few times."

Bob began talking. He told her about how he met Vicky, how she liked eating the crumbly part of coffee cakes and leaving the rest, that she couldn't sleep at night without a glass of white wine and was afraid of strange dogs, that she loved the color yellow and that she always wished that she had freckles. He pointed out her collection of souvenirs from places she'd never been. He talked and they walked into Vicky's garden, and he pointed out each plant and flower and herb. The deer had gotten to almost all of it, but there was still some chard and some spinach greens and she and Bob picked them and fried them in some oil. They ate and he talked about how they were so afraid they weren't going to be able to have a child, and just when they gave up, Vicky became pregnant with Noel. How even though he was late and came in January, they called him Noel because they couldn't agree on another name but could agree to pronounce it "Nole" instead. Bon described when Noel came out, he was long and pink as a hot dog and ugly as a politician, but he fell utterly in love with him. He told Didi that Noel's first word wasn't *mama* or *papa*, but *crumble*, and they could never figure out how that happened. Bob talked until the late afternoon, and then he cried. Then he went and washed his face in the master bedroom's bathroom and handed her the truck keys.

"Go get her," he said, and hugged her close. Didi nodded into his neck, then he said, "Good girl."

⏮ ⏸ ⏭

People were living on the roads, out of the backs of cars, like an apocalyptic tailgate that stretched across the Deception Pass Bridge and well onto state road 20. A few places where she couldn't pass on the shoulder, she had to politely wait while folks moved their settlement slightly to the left or right. She went slowly, even where the roads were deserted and quiet, so she had no idea why she flipped the truck a few miles outside La Conner. One second, she was driving, the next, there was a shower of glass, a hard knock on her head, and she was upside down with her legs thrown over her shoulders. At first, her gasps for air came fast and strong, but then she was getting very relaxed, the relaxation, she decided, that happens before death, allows people to die with a soft smile. Death, death —she was trying to breathe again, too deep and too fast— and she kicked and pulled herself out of the broken window onto the wet grass of the median.

She looked at the sky and at a tree overhead and then at her hands, which were far away and the wrong color, the light link of her palms streaked with lavender. The lavender and pink of flowers—*were her hands always this beautiful?*—Like the Kellogg lilies that grew wild in island forests. Didi bent and straightened her fingers, a time-lapse film of Kellogg lilies bud to bloom, and she was relaxed and happy. Bend and straighten. Bend and straighten.

She was sure she'd soon float away, blown into the wind like the pollen off the pistil of a Kellogg lily, if she waited long enough. She was sure, and she was happy about it. Bud, open, bloom.

She barely heard the voice telling her to come along or the wool blanket around her shoulders. She came to her senses in a tub of seemingly hot water beneath the steady green gaze of a strange woman. The woman sat cross legged on top of the toilet, twirling a section of her black and white hair around a finger as she watched Didi. "So, you're back then?" She asked, and uncrossed her legs, scooted forward on the toilet.

Did tried to sit up, but everything hurt. She was naked, but she was too weak to do anything about it except be meekly embarrassed, although the woman didn't seem uncomfortable. "Where am I?"

"You're in my bathtub. You were in an accident." The woman leaned closer and held a cool, dry hand against Didi's cheek. "You wrecked your truck."

"Why am I in the bathtub?" She kept trying to sit up, to push herself up and out of the tub or, at least, above the water. She couldn't tell if anything was broken or if she was bleeding.

"You felt cold. I was afraid you had hypothermia." She stood up and opened the mirrored cabinet over the small sink next to the toilet. The woman closed her eyes as if she were meditating.

"It's June," Didi said, but the woman kept going in and out of focus. She didn't know if she passed out or fell asleep, but she came to again as the woman was digging under her arms to help her out of the tub. "Come on, darlin'," the woman was saying. "Time to get up."

Didi let her help, and then stood in the tub as the woman dried her with a fitted flannel sheet. She was apologizing about not having clean towels, but Didi was barely listening. She was sore all over, and she was acutely aware of all the hairs that stood up, her lumpiness, her body, and she was worried somehow that this woman would find her disgusting and how ridiculous it was that she should be self-conscious right now. But the woman was drying her gently and didn't seem to even notice anything on Didi's body, like a nurse or a mother. The woman tossed the wet sheet onto the bathroom floor, and then wrapped Didi in the matching flat sheet. She held Didi's elbows and Didi was aware of how short the woman was, maybe Sasha's height, and wondered how the woman had gotten her in, gotten her clothes off and into a tub because Didi didn't remember helping her. She didn't remember anything except pushing off, and the bright blue sail, lavender and lilies, and didn't have any idea why.

But she held Didi's elbows firmly. "Let's get you into the living room."

Didi stepped out of the tub. She was ashamed again, but not of her body—instead, of how much weight she placed on the tiny woman's hands as she limped into the living room. The apartment was dark but warm, and the woman led her down a narrow hallway and onto a futon. The futon was covered with a chenille throw, which felt cold and smooth and liquid against her exposed skin, and as soon as she sat down, the woman started grabbing from piles of blankets and draped them around her. When she

was satisfied that Didi was either well covered or too
weighed down to run away, she sat down on the floor in
front of the futon and nodded her head. "You'll be ok," she
said. She smiled a bit, relieved, and then looked surprised.
"Oh," she said. "My name is Eden. I didn't tell you that.
You must have been wondering." Eden pointed out the
window. "I saw you crash. Looked like your truck was
doing cartwheels."

"Did I hit something?" Didi tried to see out the window, but the afternoon light was bright. There was no
sense of how long she'd been there, if it was the same day,
the next, a week later.

"I thought you'd gotten a concussion," Eden said.
"What's your name?"

"I'm Didi."

"Hello, Didi. Are you hungry?"

Didi didn't feel hungry, but she nodded. Eden stood
up and put her hands on her hips. Didi got a good look at
her. She was one of those kinds of women it was difficult
to age, with long, thick dark hair well striped with grey—
which was why it'd looked black and white. The grey hairs
stood out a bit as if they were electrified, and they caught
the light nicely. She was a bit heavy, but just the heavy of a
thin woman whose metabolism had finally slowed with
age, small, small breasted, and in a long, layered, dress of
different fabrics and laces and prints. She looked like she
was definitely someone's mother. She also might have
taught art at some point.

"Good. Soup?" Eden asked, but didn't wait for an
answer. She went into the next room, the kitchen presumably, and returned a few minutes later with two steaming
mugs. "Soup." She handed one to Didi.

The steam filled Didi's nose and the back of her
throat. It was still hot, but good and salty, filled with
mushy chunks, and she finished it before she even realized
she had. She drained the cup.

Eden smiled and took the mug from her. "Good.
That's an excellent sign." She set Didi's empty mug and her
own half-filled one down on the carpet and folded her

arms in her lap. "Now, darlin' Didi. Where were you going?'"

"I don't really know where to start."

"At the beginning, the middle. We have time."

The blankets and sheets slipped off her shoulder and Didi took her time straightening them and secured them under her arms, which still burned a bit. "I'm looking for someone."

Eden waited, and when Didi didn't continue, said, "We're all looking for someone," but not impatiently. She picked up her soup mug with both hands and started to sip. "You're safe now."

Didi looked at Eden, calmly drinking her soup; the living room, decorated with the kind of bohemian insouciance that was either the sign of a single, well-traveled woman or one that could afford a decorator with a retro sensibility and a good import contact. It was probably the former, not the latter, because the batik sofa looked sat upon and the carved camel end tables were dusty. The light streaming through the window illuminated a few stains on the multi-colored carpet, nothing sinister, just the stains of muddy feet and spilled food and maybe a few pet accidents. Framed art lined one wall, but all in shadow, so Didi couldn't tell what they were: paintings or textiles or family jpegs, printed out, framed, and fading. If Eden was crazy, Didi couldn't tell. She didn't seem to be. She seemed to be concentrating fully on her soup. "It's so nice to have company," she finally said. "I've been alone for a while. I used to get things delivered. Then, my neighbors brought me things. I didn't know why the deliveries stopped," she explained. "Then my neighbors stopped coming over. I knocked on their doors. They were all gone. I kicked in their doors. I'm stronger than I look. They were all gone and so I took whatever I could. It's lasted me awhile. Will last awhile yet." She picked up the edge of one of the chenille blankets. "These were Soraya Johnstone's. She lived in 207. She had lovely taste. I miss them. I've been alone here. I haven't even been outside in years."

Didi looked around the room again. It looked different now, mismatched, looted, random—and it made her suddenly a little sick to her stomach. "But you came and got me outside—"

"Yes. I did. But you were on the road. I can go to the road, but no further. Haven't been further in years." She squinted her eyes as if she were trying to remember the last time she had. "Years."

Didi didn't know what to say. She nodded and hoped she didn't look as scared as she felt.

"You look exhausted, poor darlin'. You should get some rest. I should let you rest. I'll be in the other room, if you need me. I'll give you some quiet."

Didi nodded until Eden left the room, and then she listened: shuffling and the squeak of an old wooden bed frame, then snoring, surprisingly loud snores for such a small lady.

Didi sat up. Her entire body felt tender and bruised, even the bottoms of her feet. She didn't know where her clothes were. She pulled a small throw blanket off the pile and knotted it around herself like a sarong.

She started looking around for clothes or something she could use to get out of there.

She found papers, disks, books, figurines shaped like animals, scarves, and a collection of shoes by the door.

Didi rifled through the shoe pile. All different sizes and styles, but not many seemed to have mates. She quietly tossed each aside as she looked, until she finally found a pair—some men's black watch plaid slippers, far too big even on her giant feet.

On a small stand by the shoes was a mason jar. It was filled with change and keys, fat wads of mismatched keys, including a few obviously ignition keys for old cars. There had to be a garage of some sort, maybe a key would fit a car there. It wasn't a great plan, but she didn't know what else to do.

"What are you doing?" Eden asked. She didn't seem angry or surprised.

Didi dug her feet deeper in the slippers. "I was— I'm sorry. I can't stay," Didi said. "I'm grateful to you—"

192 THE BIRTHDAY PROBLEM

Didi tried to hide the keys in her hand.

"But you have to find your someone."

Didi nodded.

"I understand," Eden said. "But you're not in any shape you drive anywhere. You should lie down."

"I'm really OK. I may have bruised some ribs, but I think I'm OK."

"I'm afraid you have internal bleeding."

"I really should go."

"Then—" Eden said. "Sit down. You should eat something more before you go. You only had soup. Eden went into the kitchen. "I saw you found the car keys. Mr. Torsello, he lived in 312, he collected older cars. Far as I know, they're still all parked downstairs. Do you like tuna fish? I have some tuna fish. I can make us tuna fish sandwiches."

Tuna reminded Didi of the Iras and Mrs. Lopez. She forgot tuna was something humans could eat. She sat down on the sofa and played with the keys. "I like tuna just fine."

"This is great," Eden called, over some banging and busy noises in the kitchen. "I like taking care of you. It makes me feel good."

"Thank you," Didi said. "You've been really kind."

"I love to cook," Eden called again. "My ex-husband always said I had no talent for it." She came into the room, holding two plates triumphantly. "This will give you some protein." Eden balanced a plate on Didi's knees, then she sat on the floor below her. She took a big bite of her sandwich and smiled.

Didi held the sandwich to her lips and bit down. "It's good."

"Thank you, darlin'. Enjoy. Eat up." Eden swallowed. "So tell me all about this someone."

Eden told her. It came out in a stream. She told her about Sasha and their life, a quiet one—librarian and serial hobbyist, retired basketball player, living comfortably off Didi's savings credits which should have lasted them several more years.

Eden listened, nodding in places, looking expectant. So Didi continued, told Eden about her job, caring for the seniors, which became, unexpectedly, hospice care for the infirm and the sick as time caught up exponentially. Then she told her about the cats, all the cats, and a little about Bob and how he was with the cats. But when she tried to go on, and tell her about how much she wanted to find Sasha and bring her home and make everything like it was before, she felt dizzy and a little nauseated. She looked at Eden, but it was hard to focus on her.

"You look pale," Eden said. "How are you feeling?"

"Woozy," Didi answered.

"Any pain?"

Didi felt her arms, her legs. She wasn't sore any longer—just unable to move. "No," she said. "No pain, but —"

"No pain?" Eden asked. "Good. That's the morphine. You know, drugs really don't ever go bad."

"You drugged me?" It took a lot of effort for Didi to form the words.

"Spencer in 223. He was a historian. Pharmaceuticals. Had an impressive personal collection." Eden reached over and took the keys from Didi's lap. "I ground them up. Xanax, some Klonopin and morphine." Her voice echoed, like across a canyon. "In the tuna fish. You couldn't even taste them."

Didi felt herself start to slide down off the sofa, onto the floor. Her mind was clear and empty, just like when she was asleep. She saw Eden standing above her, a big smile on her face. "If you like," she said. "You can call me Sasha."

In the Changed Rain
(an unread journal)

September

The rain has changed from when I was a little girl. I used to sit in on my bed with my feet up on the wall, watching rivulets of water gather and run down the windowpanes. I'd watch for hours, until my mother would give me a chore or my father would make me do my homework or read a book or something good for my mind or my brother would come in and make fun of me.

I was never good at chores. I would again get caught in a dream, only doing it halfway or with halfway effort. And for all that which was good for my mind, I am losing it now. And my brother, well, I will come back to him. Figuratively, here. Literally, soon.

The rain has changed. It used to be more forceful, bossy, something to believe in and love and tolerate. When the sun peeks out, when there is a cool, bright spring morning or a blazing hot summer day, no true northwesterner can really enjoy it, any more than someone can enjoy the last moments before they die. You know what is coming next and you almost want to just get on with it, because the sun is fickle and deceitful, and can hide again in an instant. And the rain always returns.

It took a certain type of person to love this kind of rain. The northwest was founded by opportunistic merchants, optimistic fortune seekers, loggers and captains and men made lonely by war, whores and wives and the women in between. Their heartiness and industry and

checkered pasts were not what distinguished our settlers
from other regions; instead they're set apart by how they
came to love this rain, marry it, take it as a loyal life mate
bringing moss and mold and fat white mushrooms.

Now, I don't quite understand how we can all call
this wet the rain. Rain implies droplets, drips and dribbles,
storms filled with light and noise. The rain now is an
abstraction, an idea and a feeling and a wet, all the implications of water falling from the sky without the falling. It's
still dependable and present, and there's intermittent
downpours of actual drops, sometimes determinate
drizzles, and even the occasional storm filled with light
and noise. But the rain has changed since when I was a
child.

When I think of the rain, and I think of the rain a
lot, I don't think of this cold humidity, the bright white
sky sucking the color from everything else. I think of the
water streaming on the glass, making patterns like a language, and shapes like pictures. I don't think of the sus-
pended mist, which, if you let your eyes relax and go just
so, moves like smoke.

That is how it is raining right now.

That is the rain I am leaving in. Out the front door
and into the night, wearing dampness like a second
sweater.

But first, I will write this down. I've always been a
dreamer, a rain watcher. It's not that I can't remember
anything; it's just that I never have. And now, it seems
important to write this down, so I will know where I have
been. So I can know where I am going and how to return.

I got ready to go by watching my Didi sleep. I
looked at her every inch. From her feet, the broken toe
healed up like a nutmeat; up her legs, lengthened by thin-
ness; over her stomach, animal-round. I touched her big
hands; her hair, all froth and suds; and her eyelids, thin
and violet and perfectly still.

I want to remember her, so I am writing it down.
I'm getting sicker, and what was once my dreaming and
rain watching is getting to be a gulf between me and

everything else. It used to be harmless, something my brother would make fun of. I could lay and watch the rain, while he was so restless and always needing to be fed. He remembers everything. He can recite conversations to you word for word, romantic sonnets and sports scores and the conversion rate of meters to inches to fathoms. I would leave dishes to pile up wherever I've eaten, towels on the floor whenever I showered.

Yet, my brother, hungry and restless, was always steady as a house, jangled only by extreme circumstances. I made my decisions without reservation or caution, but immediate intention.

I think I am still 36 years old.

Didi is so still when she sleeps. She doesn't dream. She slips away at night into nothing. Eyelids and stock-still limbs, long and thin. She goes someplace I have never been. Then she wakes up, still a bit tired, but back to this world, the only world there is.

She is as still as the cats are fidgety. There are so many now that I've lost count, there are so many that they answer to the same name. Didi thought I gathered them from a place of maternal love. Someone had to take care of the cats as the town emptied out. It was s puzzle not worth solving.

But it isn't true. I've raised an army, all in her honor. Because I love her.

My army will guard her. My army will keep her safe. They will give her a reason to get out of bed, to set her long feet on the floor and go on. I gathered them all and gave them instructions. Stay with Didi, I told them. Guard her with your lives. I couldn't leave her if I had to leave her alone, no matter how far I am from everything.

I haven't told Didi my plans. I haven't told her I'm sick. I may have told her once about the rain.

Didi loves me in this, her only world. I studied her to remember. I leave dishes: I've eaten; I leave towels: I've showered. I will remember her, like I remember watching the rivulets of water.

I haven't told her that I'm going, where I'm going. I

stayed silent. I didn't tell her I was already away. That I was already gone.

The cats see me out. They will watch over her. They will make trouble like I used to, they will make decisions without reservation or caution, memories cloudy, and she will have to get up. She will have to live. She will have to love them like she could love me forever.

I'm sick. I'll go to my brother in the changed rain. To my brother. He will remember what to do, tell me in a voice deep with bass and butter. My army stands ready.

Out the front door. I leave, I walk, I steal away out into the mist and steam, northwest rain, take me home, if you love me, take me home.

September, still

Today is the next-next day.

I left, like I said. And as that night ended, and the day began, my shoes felt thinner and I was less and less sure of anything else. I reread what I wrote before I left and it makes me feel better.

I waited for the ferry until the ferry didn't come. The higher the sun, the lower I sank. I didn't trust that sun. I covered my head with my arms, and my arms with my legs, to wait out the ferry or the night. I hoped they'd come.

The rain, I knew, would arrive soon.

Fingers traced my spine. I uncovered my legs from my arms and my arms from my head. From a nimbus of light, he asked me, "Are you hurt?"

I was hurt. "No," I said.

"The ferry hasn't run in..." he said, then sidestepped the light so I could see him better. "A while." His hair so gold it was nearly green. His knees dimpled like a child's. "You need to get across?"

He looked at me. I sat up and smoothed my hair. "I do."

"Are you sick?"

I am. "I don't know," I said. "Are you?"

His face is fat. It takes up more of his face than his face. He shook his head and I blinked at the light thrown by the gold and green. "Not so far. But I'm not afraid of the sick. I can take you. I can fly you across."

I looked at his arms and his dimpled knees. *He is too heavy to fly.* But he meant a seaplane. Parked down the beach. *I missed it when I'd covered my head in my arms and arms in legs.* "I don't have any money."

"No one does." He looked at me again. "I live on a farm. Maybe you can help us with chores for a day in exchange? Before you get going to wherever you are going."

I am bad at chores, but I didn't tell him that. I write it down here instead. Even so, I couldn't help already liking the idea. Then he asked me, "Do you like goats?"

I do. "I do."

His name is Roomy and mine is Sasha. Roomy squeezed my hand instead of shaking it, and I like him. Roomy suits him. Then we were inside the plane, taking off. *Once we were closer to the sky, I liked the sun a little bit better.*

We landed on grapes. I walked through grapes until Roomy pointed out where the goats ate a path. The grapes are dying out but sweet.

"There used to be vineyards here," Roomy said. "Now they grow wild. The farm was a restaurant and a hotel. A fancy one."

We followed the path past a broken down sign. "The Herbfarm," I read.

"We're here," Roomy said.

There's a courtyard between a farmhouse and the remains of a big fancy building, overrun with blackberries. Three or four people and short, shaggy goats greeted us. A woman took one of my hands as a goat licks the other. "Yes," I say. "We are."

This is a place for the sick. Roomy told me this over dinner. The woman didn't let go of my hand until I asked her to, so I could eat the bread and goat cheese and grapes, drink vinegary tea.

The sick can get better, Roomy thinks, and he wants to prove it so. It will take time and a safe place to be. Food and water and a purge of nanobots to kill the ones that make us sick or to allow them to find a balance. He believes they are good. By good, he means, I understand, clever enough to figure out how to keep us safe.

No host, no life.

So Roomy finds the goats and the sick and he brings them home. I think of the cats. I think of my Didi.

"You are welcome to stay here," Roomy said. *He could see me getting better, and thinks it could be soon. I am not so far gone. I can also leave. He invited me to look where I'd like and to sit with the goats to consider my options.*

There are books across every wall. Paper books, Books like my brother. I run my fingers along a row of thin volumes, then pull one, Poems by Rumi. I slide it back and go outside to the grass and write this all down.

The woman sits behind me and when I lay down, I lay my head in her lap. The air smells of turning grapes and cole slaw. The sun begins to set and the clouds roll in before Rumi joins us.

"I left Didi for a reason," I say. "It wasn't to come here."

"Where will you go?"

"To the city," I say. "Where my brother lives." *I am not so far gone; I could get better, so I admit:* "I don't know exactly where."

"That's a problem," Rumi says.

"What is his name?" *the woman asks. I'd forgotten she wasn't a part of the grapes and the fields, and that she could speak.*

"Alastair," I say. "I named him 'Book' when we were children. Book Gomez-Larsen."

"I don't know him," *the woman says, with great sadness.*

But Rumi laughs, open-mouthed, bigger than the face that dominated his face. "Does your brother play the drums?"

I jump up, then back down and throw my arms around Rumi. He is warm from the last of the sunlight and smells like the tea.

"I don't know Book," he says. "But I know Grey-stone Toussaint."

"You can tell me how to get to him?"

"I can," he says. "We can fly."

The rain starts again. I hold my hand to catch it, even though I know very well it won't be that sort of rain. "I thought your name was Roomy," I say.

Rumi smiles. "That works too."

I'll go to my brother in the rain. To my brother. I'll fly over the wet and the water. I smile back at Rumi underneath the misting rain.

Also September

This is the second time in two days that I've been to the sky. The only thing more exciting is playing at not being excited. I betray myself bouncing in the seat and Rumi has to hold my knee until I stop my bouncing. But inside, I still bounce.

From the sky, everything looks organized, deliber-ately placed. Rumi knows the way by sight, he says. He lived in Seattle until the sickness grew, engineering bots at a research hospital. This is how he knows Toussaint, and by default, my brother.

He doesn't know my brother well and asks me about him. It is hard to tell the story of my brother without telling mine.

Baby girls in happy families have a birthright to be adored. But my restless, hungry brother took that title and its associated remuneration and responsibilities.

I named my brother Book, a name full of bile and offered as a gift. I hated him and I loved him. It wasn't until later that I understood all siblings were born this way, portions of hate and love and memories and angst, gifts and bile.

My brother's worn the name like he's worn his

memory: with rigidity and delicacy, with respect towards, if not knowledge of, arcane subjects. There was nothing he couldn't remember. It wasn't until much later that I understood he couldn't forget.

When he and I played together, we played at disaster. The floor was made of lava. Our parents' bed shook in earthquakes, bobbed as a raft riding a tsunami, a treeless desert island darkened by hurricane. I played nurse when he was wounded in war, fire fighter to canned explosions, and policeman to murderers. These games should have some meaning, but they don't. We were no better prepared for disasters than anyone else.

When I dreamed alone, I thought I was alone. But much later I understood how close he was. Always close to me, always watching, and not always making fun. He painted a tiny door on the floor of the kitchen and there I sat, waiting for fairies. I watched water bead and run down the window panes. Always, my brother, a few feet away—both of us trying to find patterns, but in the most different of ways.

In another family, I would have been adored. I realized, much later, how I was.

The city should be drunk with lights and color and busy. Instead, it is a dark afternoon. As we swoop down, I can't make anything out from anything else, and it is only because I feel Lake Union pulling down on the pontoons that I am sure that we've landed.

Rumi writes Toussaint's address on my hand in bright blue ink, copying carefully from a small notebook. His notebook is a lot like mine. I copy the address from my hand here:

2800 EASTLAKE AVENUE EAST

We're actually very close, he tells me, and is sad because he cannot stay with me, cannot go visit, can't spare even more than a few hours before having to go home and watch the sick until they get better. I don't understand his desperation or devotion or his worry. I think he should get some cats, maybe better instruct the goats.

"Will you be OK?" he asks me again and again, and I look at the letters and numbers on my hand and on this page until I am sure that I understand them.

"I will," I say. On the shore, the soles of my shoes feel thicker again, and there is a slight chill disappearing from the air as the sun fights its way from behind a cloud.

A fat, beautiful cloud, a perfect racing cloud, and I name it Rumi and watch it hopelessly chase Rumi's plane. Rumi cuts right through Rumi, and then, is gone.

And then I do it. I sit down on a rock and write this all down again. And writing forces me to think.

My head wants to gibber instead, meeting the sound of water dripping and flowing somewhere nearby. It wants to sing songs and recite movie lines and remember the smell and taste of a hot turkey sandwich and look at the tortured machinery rusting across the water in Gas Works Park. It wants to make my knees itch. But, no, I have to think, so I close my eyes and squeeze my brain. Hunching down helps.

When I open them up again, I'm crying over Didi's long hands and long feet and plum colored nipples and her one weak knee and dreamless sleep and her kiss that pulls desire right to the surface like Lake Union gripping the pontoons of a seaplane. Then I can't stop my thinking.

Unless I am on my feet. On my feet, I run.

The numbers get larger and the cracks in the sidewalk get bigger, the home get older and the lots tighter. I can't believe how far I can run, so I run past the apartment and past a knot of chanting voices just to see how far I can go, which isn't much further than that.

Wet with tears and sweat, I'm stepping in time to the protester's rounds. The front door of the building isn't where I thought it would be, so I walk around the entire perimeter, panting, until I find it, and when I find it, it is exactly where I should have known it to be.

The doors are heavy and wood and they vibrate with humming. The landing is old and sparkles with bits of broken glass and silicon. I look at the bottom of the door and think there, there should be a fairy door. This is

the kind of place fairies really would live if fairies still existed. I lay my hand on the door and feel the tremble. It is
the purr of electricity which feels just like a happy cat. I
push a bit to feel it deep in my hand and the door, the
solid door gives under my palm. It swings inward and I
step in and follow.

I don't know which way to go, so I follow the humming down the hall to a front door with a woven welcome
mat. I lay my hand on this door in the very same way and
push.

"Toussaint?" I ask.

No one answers. I think I see a shadow of a little girl
against a wall, but I shake my head and she's gone. I see
her again from a corner of an eye, but turning chases her
away. It's my head again. My head smells old paint and
dirty clothes, sings "Happy Birthday to Me," hears electricity like a sweet angel cicada. I hear snoring from a bedroom. It is a delicate snore, the snore of someone not as
asleep as they could be, only drowsing in the artificial yellow light coming from a corner room. And so that's the
way I go.

I write this down, and next I am going in there. I
will call out, "Hello? I'm looking for my brother, Book."

Epilogue: Balancing the Books

These would be the last blackberries of the year. Most were already overripe, wouldn't come off clean, even picked gently; they burst instead, spraying the sugary purple juice irresistible to gnats and indelible as wood stain.

Chaaya Lee-Gomez filled half a bucket and she already looked like she'd spent the afternoon on the wrong side of a paintball gun. Felt like it too. Swollen ankles, swollen knees, swollen elbows and wrists, never mind the timpani of a belly, stretched impossibly tight. Chaaya had been having nightmares about bursting open from the pressure in her belly. She didn't say anything to anyone though—it would have unnecessarily worried her husband and he had so much on his mind already, and would have given her mother-in-law, Bonita, license to increase her micromanagement over Chaaya's eating, sleeping, peeing and blood pressure.

Chaaya moved like a clay golem. The second bucket served well as a seat, and that's the position she was in, mauve fat legs splayed to hold up her mauve fat belly, swatting away the cloud of gnats with her fat mauve gloved hands, when the van drove into view.

Chaaya hadn't been long enough in her new life to trust that strange vans didn't only mean bad news. Chaaya wasn't used to good news yet. Strange vans, unfamiliar faces, groups of strangers on bicycles, lightning storms, rustling in the bushes. She feared them all. She yelled for Bonita, and recited the Padovan primes to herself and her baby: *2, 2, 3, 5, 7, 37, 151.*

Bonita made it to her quickly. She hadn't been far, and Chaaya suspected Bonita been watching her pick blackberries the whole time, keeping track of how many times she sat down and how many times she ducked behind the biggest of the bushes to pee. It was her first grandchild, after all. Bonita had a gun tucked in her waistband. "It's OK, *hija*." They watched the van stop and start its way up to the house. The driver held up a palm in greeting.

"Who is it? Chaaya asked.

"Don't know." Bonita pushed Chaaya slightly behind her, as effective as a duck protecting a moose. She called out, "Can we help you, friend?"

The driver turned off the ignition and opened his door. Bonita continued to hold Chaaya back with one hand. Her other one was on the gun.

He was an older man, thin at top and soft from the belly and hips down. It was hard to tell how old he was; over fifty more than likely. He wiped his forehead with the back of his hand. "Good morning," he said. "I'm looking for Boudicca VanNess."

Bonita started to pull the gun out. "No one here by that name, '*migo*."

"How about Sasha Gomez?" he said. "Does Sasha Gomez live here?"

Bonita dropped her hands. "Sasha?" she asked. Her voice cracked a little. "I'm her mother. You know Sasha?"

The man came forward. He held out his hand. "Robert Hughes. I knew Boudicca and Sasha on Whidbey Island. Boudicca worked for me."

"Didi," Bonita sighed. "I didn't even think, Boudicca. Didi. Of course." She looked at his hand if trying to figure out what to do with it. Then she took it. "I'm Bonita Larsen-Gomez, Mr. Hughes." She stepped slightly aside as if she were blocking more of his view of Chaaya than she actually was. "This is my daughter in law, Chaaya."

"Bob," he said. "Please call me Bob." He held his other hand to her. "Pleasure to meet you, Chaaya." Then he looked at her belly and smiled. "My. You're just about there."

"A few weeks," Chaaya answered. His hand was warm and moist. "Although if he decided to show up early, at this point I wouldn't argue."

"Shush that," Bonita said to her. Then she made the sign of the cross for Chaaya's benefit. "Mr.—Bob. Won't you come out of the heat?"

"Thank you," he said. "I wasn't sure if I had the right place—"

"Our old house burned down after—" Bonita started, swallowed, and then continued, "My husband died. This is actually our neighbor's property, although they haven't—" she paused again, "lived here in some time. We've taken it over. All the way to the canal."

Bonita led Bob to the house, pointing out the gardens and the orchard, the chicken coops and the stable. She was as proud of the ranch as if it were Versailles.

Chaaya followed behind with the bucket barely filled with the soft berries. Chaaya rinsed the berries in the kitchen and listened to Bonita make small explain that they didn't see too many visitors and then talk about how she refused to rest, blackberry picking and gardening so far into her pregnancy, and describe how her son, her husband, Book, was out hunting along with Cassie and Davey, who also lived here. Bonita was trying to build up to talk of Sasha and Didi and Bob was letting her. Chaaya decided he was probably kind.

Chaaya looked out the window at the van. It appeared to rock slightly. She hadn't gotten too much sun, Chaaya didn't think, so she wasn't imagining it. Chaaya splashed some water on her face and looked at the van again. This time, she was sure she could see it sway and heard some soft cries coming from the back. She held her ear out the window. It sounded like babies. It made her breasts hurt. She wondered exactly what type of kind he was. "Mr. Hughes? Bob?" Chaaya called, wiping her hands on her stained pants, and waddling to the living room. "Your van is rocking and crying."

Bonita froze in horror, but Bob smiled. "That's Ira and Petey." He stood up. "Let me show you."

Bonita and Chaaya followed him to his van. Bonita had her hand back on her waistline just in case.

"The last time I saw Didi, she left in my truck to go find Sasha," he said. "And she left me in charge of these guys." He opened the back of the van and stepped aside.

Inside, there were cats. Striped, grey, brown, black and white, tan and tortoiseshell. Chaaya couldn't count them all. The van was upholstered in layers of carpet and cats. He'd built some shelves onto the van's walls, and cats perched on each level, stretched out across the floor. A wooden box divided the back, up against the partition to the front seat, and inside there was scratching, which flung bits of litter out the door. "Sasha took them in at first," he said. "She and Didi named them Ira because there were so many, they couldn't keep track."

Chaaya held out her hand. A few hisses, but more than one seemed fascinated by the smell of blackberries. She started petting random heads. "How many are here?"

"Fourteen. We lost some of the original Iras," Bob said. "And Didi's favorite, Mrs. Lopez. But two Iras had babies. I call the next generation Petey."

Bonita gingerly held out her hand as well to pet one of the Iras or Peteys. "So, Didi left you."

"Yes. She went after Sasha, who'd already left. I'm afraid I don't know how much of a head start Sasha had."

"And you never saw Sasha or Didi again?" Bonita asked in a small voice.

"No, not after that." Bob touched Bonita's shoulder. "I waited for them to come back, but no one ever did. I was hoping to find them here."

"They never came here," Bonita said. "I prayed for her to come home. I still do."

"I started looking for them in Seattle," Bob said. "Didi seemed to think Sasha went there."

"*Ay.* Why would she do that? Go to Seattle?"

"I assume to see your son."

"Yes," Bonita agreed. "They never come to their parents first."

"How's Seattle?" Chaaya asked, but they heard and smelled the truck coming. It was a good, solid truck, but the engine had to be cleaned every day or it would be loud as a jet's, burning off impurities from the vegetable oil fuel. And no one ever cleaned the engine regularly. "They're home."

Then they could see the truck. They pulled in behind the van, and Davey, Book, and Cassie all jumped out, holding tiny, slack bodies in their fists. Bunnies. Chaaya could see and smell them when Book rushed over to give her a kiss. He managed to get her cheek as she broke a fast, cold sweat, turned away and vomited up frothy blackberry juice. He shoved his bunnies to Cassie and held her shoulders as she finished. "Sorry," he whispered. "I didn't think."

"Nope," Chaaya said and threw up again.

"Can I help?" Bob asked. "I am a registered nurse. I haven't had much occasion to practice recently, though, except on cats."

"Everything makes her puke. Poor *hija*," Bonita said. Then she introduced Bob to Cassie, Davey and her son, Alastair. Book waved briefly then returned to holding her up.

"She's OK," Book said, and then whispered to her. "My fault. Right? Dead rabbits and pregnant wife, not a good combination." and Chaaya nodded.

Someone brought her a glass of water and Chaaya rinsed her mouth and spit a few times. "I'm fine." She tried not to look at the dead rabbits. "I feel a little queasy. Maybe I'll just sit out here with the cats."

"Cats?" Cassie asked.

"You feel queasy because you push too hard. Always with the picking or the gardening or something." Bonita waggled her finger at Chaaya, and then turned to Bob. "I think we can bring them in. Shouldn't we? I mean, no one here's allergic, I don't think, and it seems cruel to keep them cooped up in that van."

"Once we bring them in, it'll be hard to herd them

all up to leave," Bob said.

"Well, of course," Bonita said. "But you're staying for a while, yes? We have some old pig troughs I think we can use for litter. Or they can go outside?"

Bob looked surprised and pleased. "Outside is fine."

"Cats?" Cassie repeated.

"You'll see," Chaaya said.

Chaaya perched on the bumper while Bob and Book carried in Iras and the Peteys two at a time. Cassie was skinning and cleaning the rabbits by the door, and her eyes got wider with each cat delivery. "We should roast one of these plain for these, uh, other guests," she said to no one in particular, giggling at her own joke.

One of the younger or smaller cats, a silvery-haired girl with pale green eyes tried to find a comfortable place on her short lap. She wedged herself underneath her belly and started purring. The heat on her stomach felt good.

"That's Petey," Bob told her.

"Hi, Petey," Chaaya said as the little cat began to knead her thigh.

Book stopped to look at her with the cat on her lap and smiled. "I'm glad we weren't considering Ira or Peter as names." He pulled the small cat out from beneath her stomach and first she hissed, then smelled his face and purred again. "But we are having a girl."

"You can name a girl Ira or Pete," Chaaya said. "Besides, we're having a boy."

"A girl," Book said. He started ticking off on his fingers. "You're carrying her high, which means she's a girl. You keep craving sweets, which means it's a girl. Your left boob is much bigger than your right—"

"*Hijo*," Bonita broke in. "Where did you hear all this garbage?"

"I don't know," he said. "I read somewhere. We're having a girl. I just know it." He looked at Chaaya. "And we'll name her Ira Peter."

"Lovely," Chaaya said. "I love it."

They followed the last Ira/Petey inside and watched them spread out to explore the house. Soon, each nook, corner, and hiding place was filled by a small furry body.

"Well," Bonita said. "At least we have these of Sasha. You know, we don't even have any jpegs of Sasha. They all got lost in the fire. After my husband passed away."

Bob scooped up one of the cats, an older, slow white long hair, and started to pet her. "I know I have memory cards in the van. At least of Didi, and probably of Sasha too. My wife used to throw these big holiday parties."

"Your wife?" Bonita asked.

Bob kissed the top of the cat's head then let her jump to the floor. "She also passed on. Some time ago."

"We also do not have any photos of my father," Book reminded Bonita. "Or of me as a child. Or of…"

Bonita squeezed his arm and he was quiet.

"It smells good in here," Bob said.

"Davey's a good cook," Chaaya answered. "He does most of it around here."

"I learned from my dad," Davey called, dishing up bowls. "I'll dish for people if someone serves the cats."

Bonita started filling small plates with a heap of shredded rabbit meat down in a row for the cats.

Chaaya was first to the table, not because she was hungry, but instead the opposite. Chaaya was nauseated and wanted to get dinner over with so she could lie down for a while. She must have gotten too much sun after all, done too much.

Davey had made good use of her sad blackberry harvest, cooking it down into compote that went over the rabbit quite nicely. It was good as long as she didn't look at it—then she could see the lifeless bunnies swinging from Book and Cassie and Davey's fists. Chaaya wondered how long she'd be able to keep it down as cats weaved in and around her legs.

"As you were pulling up, Bob was going to tell us news of Seattle," Bonita said. "He'd been there first to look for Sasha and Didi. He said Didi thought Sasha went there to find her brother."

"Or hit some bars," Book murmured.

"What?" Bonita asked him, and then turned towards

Bob.

"It's going to take Seattle a long time to recover. Parts of the city are still in ruins." Bob took another bite of the stew. "God, this is delicious. Anyway. Some small enclaves have sprung up though, little cooperatives. Best I can tell. In fact they helped me resupply for the trip out here. They seem to be doing ok. They're all being run by one guy. Beluga Grace, I think his name was."

"No way," Book said.

"You know of him?" Davey asked.

"I know him. He used to be a fan of the band, ages ago. Little nerdy guy." Book looked at Bob. "I used to be in a band," he explained. "If it's the same guy. Must be the same guy." He looked at her. "What do you think the odds are that there are two guys named Beluga Grace in same area, Chaaya?"

He knew as well as Chaaya did about the probabilities involved in that. He remembered everything he read. But he was always aware of spilling out too many factoids and information. He tried to pretend sometimes that he didn't know all that he did. Usually Chaaya could sympathize with her husband not wanting to be an asshole, but instead, she felt a little annoyed at him for not just letting her sit quietly and feel sick to her stomach. "There's too high of an obscurity factor. It's probably the same guy."

"Well, good for him." He grinned at Bob. "Chaaya's a mathematician."

"I was. I mean, I was studying to be one. Not much call for mathematicians these days."

"She keeps our books," Bonita says. "Makes sure everything balances. It's important, you know, with farming." Then she added, as if she needed to convince everyone of its importance, "I mean, we don't count on money yet, but we will. And she does great."

Chaaya stood up. She knew she was being rude, but she felt like she was going to vomit again. Chaaya burped through her mask. "Will you all excuse me? I need to lie down."

"If it's heartburn, don't lie flat," Bonita said, then she looked at Book. "Go with her, *hijo*. Take care of your wife."

Book followed her up the stairs. Chaaya flopped onto the bed with a crash.

"Are you OK?"

"I'm tired," Chaaya said. "I'm achy. I'm huge."

"You're perfect," he said, stroking her hair. You're beautiful."

"I feel like I'm going to throw up again. My tummy itches. The soles of my feet itch. I have a headache. I pee 300 times a day. I'm huge."

He snuggled up to her. "You're the perfect balance of beautiful and huge. The golden ratio. Walking *phi*."

Chaaya smiled. "Stop using my math against me."

"You are in divine proportion. I bet if we measure we'll get...oh, 1 point 6180339..."

"Show off."

"88749...join in. You know it too."

"I have to use the quadratic equation," she said, sitting up. "I have to pee again."

"One second," he said and pulled her back down next to him. "I have a surprise for you."

"What's that?"

"We rolled by the library. That's going to be a big salvage job. I worry about the books. They're paper. And some of the files I can tell are trashed. But anyway." He rolled to the side and pulled a small book out of his pocket. He laid it in front of her. "I looked for a Korean one too, but they only had Hangul dictionaries. I'll have to try in Aberdeen."

Chaaya looked at the title. *Speak Hindi from Day One.*

"*Kurta hoon*," he said.

"I love you too," Chaaya said. "And I don't speak Hindi that well. And I don't know any Korean."

"I know you miss your Nani. And your parents." He looked at her so earnestly that she melted.

Chaaya laid her hand on his chest. "*Dhanyavad.*"

Book grinned. "You're welcome, my dearest."

"*Meri jaan*," she said.

"Huh?"

"*Meri jaan*," Chaaya repeated. "That means my dear. My *nani* used to call me that all the time, especially when I pissed her off."

"*Kurta hoon, meri jaan*."

Chaaya peed twice and tried to snuggle with her husband, but on cue, as if she knew that she had just that second found a comfortable position where her belly didn't crush her lungs or force the baby to sit atop her bladder, Bonita called up to the room: "Come down, *niños*. Bob has jpegs of your sister."

Downstairs, they all sat in the living room as Bob fiddled around with one of Book's old gamesets. Chaaya could feel Book trying to hold back from volunteering assistance, but finally data began to condense. "These photos," He said. "Don't be shocked. Our house had full HEPA in every room, so you may see some naked faces." He waved through the files. "Here's one of Didi," he said, and signaled it to open. The photo expanded, showing a tall, thin, beautiful black girl with high cheek bones and bright eyes that dominated her face above her mask.

"She's so beautiful," Davey said. They all murmured agreement.

"You never met Didi?" Book asked Davey.

"Nope. I would remember. They got together after Sasha moved, right?" Davey asked.

"Yes," Bonita said.

"She used to play basketball," Book said.

Bob flicked to the next photo, one of him and the same girl. "Look," he said. "I had more hair." He flicked again. "Yes, here's one of Sasha." The photo expanded, and Bonita cried, "Sasha!"

The woman in the photo had a bare face. It still jolted Chaaya see full faces. But the woman was really pretty, with the same creamy skin as Book, the same caramel colored hair, only hers more cut boyish than his, short and slicked back. Her almond eyes were dwarfed by huge old-fashioned black rimmed glasses, perched precariously on an upturned little nose. Her lips were large for her face, pink and full.

Bonita stood up and reached out to the jpeg, blocking her view. "Oh, baby," she said. Then she sat down on the ground.

Chaaya looked again at Sasha's face, but kept being drawn back to her lips. Glossy, heart-shaped.

Her stomach seized with pain. .

Bob waved through the next few photos, other guests at that particular party. But those lips were burned onto her retinas. Chaaya knew those lips. Chaaya knew them as well as she knew her own. She felt frozen in space and time—no one else was. They all moved normally.

Chaaya dreamed of those lips. She had nightmares of bursting open and she had nightmares about those lips. Chaaya felt lightheaded and heavy at the same time. Chaaya couldn't lift her hands, move her feet, but she managed to vomit a little acid in her mouth and swallow it again.

"Chaaya?" Book held her shoulder. "You OK? You're pale."

"No," Chaaya whispered. "I don't feel well."

Above her, everyone went into a flurry of activity, Chaaya heard Bonita call, "*Hija? Hija?*" and someone slipped their hands under her arms, helping her down to the couch.

Chaaya knew those lips. Chaaya dreamed of those lips.

"Should I boil water?" Cassie asked, to no one in particular.

She killed those lips.

She started counting. The Hilbert numbers: 1, *5, 9, 13, 17, 21, 25, 29, 33, 37...*

Then it was just Bob holding her wrist. His mask rippled. Chaaya realized he was counting too.

"Your heart rate is a little high," he said. "Her heart rate is a little high."

"We've been watching for hypertension," Book said.

"I was pretty sure she was out of danger for preeclampsia."

"She is," Bob said. "But her heart rate is definitely high." Then back to her: "Chaaya, I want you to take a few good, deep breaths for me. In through your nose, out your mouth."

She tried, but her chest hurt. *25, 29, 33.*

Bob gently tugged on her shirt. "May I?"

She didn't remember nodding, but Bob had her shirt up and he pressed down on her belly, feeling for the baby. Then he did a few other things, but Chaaya didn't keep track. She kept seeing the lips.

Sasha. Chaaya killed Sasha. Sasha all those years ago, looking for her brother. She couldn't remember what number came next in the Hilbert sequence. *37. 37. It was 4n + 1.* Chaaya couldn't remember. She tried simpler math, powers of 3: *3, 9, 27, 81, 243, 729, 2187...*

"Everything seems to be all right," Bob said. "The baby's low. I think you're starting to go into labor." He looked up. "She's going into labor. It's all right."

Chaaya forced some words out: "It's not all right." She banged her head against the couch pillow, trying to shake the lips out of her eyes. She didn't know how she was going to tell her husband that she killed his sister. She didn't know how she was going to tell Bonita that she killed her daughter.

Another wave of pain. Before it was over, Book had her hand in his. "I'm here," he said.

"Should I boil water?" Cassie repeated.

More number. Cubes. 1, 8, 27, 64, 125, 216, 343, 512, 729.

"Not yet," Bob answered Cassie. "But we should time these. Chaaya, Tell us when it hurts again."

"I didn't know what I was doing," she said.

"It's OK," Book murmured to her. "You can do this."

"I didn't know." Chaaya said to him. She clutched at his shirt. She needed him to understand. "I didn't know what I was doing."

"It's OK," she heard Bonita say. "No one ever does."

Chaaya knew Bonita was talking about the pregnancy, but she could almost pretend she wasn't. "Do you remember when I came here?" she asked Book.

He tried to loosen her grip, comfort her, but she held on him harder. "Do you remember?"

"Of course," He said. "Toussaint brought you here. He gave his life to get you here."

Another wave of pain swept over her.

"I'm timing," Cassie yelled, and Bob tried to pry Book away from Chaaya, telling her to relax and breathe. But she wouldn't let go. "You know why?" she asked. "You know why I left Seattle? You know why he took me here?"

"It wasn't safe," Book said.

"Yes, but also—" Chaaya tried to think of the words to tell him. She didn't think they existed. Not in any language. "The books are not balanced," she said.

Then Bonita was close to her face. "*Hija*, shush. It doesn't matter now."

"It does," Chaaya said. She started to cry.

"It doesn't. It really doesn't. The books are fine." Bonita reached over Book and wiped away Chaaya's tears. "Whatever it is, whatever you did, it doesn't matter now. The books are fine. We have you now. We have you."

And then Bob whooped. "All right, Chaaya—" he said. "Here we go. Your waters just broke."

"Push, *meri jaan*," Book said. "Push."

ACKNOWLEDGMENTS

Chris Sumption: this one, like the others I hope will follow, is for you.

And to: Frank Fuller, the real King of Seattle; the Speculative Literature Foundation for awarding me a Gulliver Travel grant to finish needed research; Hedgebrook, for the time, space, and nourishment, both literal and figurative; Elizabeth George, for financial support via her foundation; Centrum, for a cabin on the beach; the SYBHEL consortium, sponsored by the European Commission's Science & Society Program, for publishing portions of "Glasses Guy"; The Center for Wooden Boats' Heron Scott, for patiently explaining the currents around Whidbey Island; Pamela Rentz for backing my horse and tuckerizing Bob, The Herbfarm Restaurant for the meal of a lifetime; Inner Chapters Books (RIP) for a comfy booth and Mexican mochas; Cat Rambo, Eden Robins, and the members of Horrific Miscue, Seattle, for reading, rereading, and then reading again; my dear editor Bill Racicot, who made medicine taste like sugar; and Rose Mambert for taking a gamble and playing through; I thank you. Because of you, I feel like Pierre de Fermat when he wrote, "I have discovered a truly remarkable proof but this margin is too small to contain it."

ABOUT THE AUTHOR

Caren Gussoff's fiction has been featured in anthologies and magazines such as Serpent's Tail, Seal Press, Hadley Rille, *Fantasy Magazine, Abyss & Apex*, has earned her an Octavia E. Butler scholarship, a Village Voice "Writer on the Verge" nomination, an Elizabeth George award, a Seattle Post-Intelligencer "Geek of the Week," and a Speculative Literature Foundation grant, among other things. She lives in Seattle, WA with her husband, SF artist Chris Sumption, her cats Molly Bloom and Paul Atreides, and some unnamed dust bunnies. She is everywhere online as "spitkitten."

Gussoff is also the author of *Homecoming* (High Risk Books) *and The Wave and Other Stories* (Serpent's Tail). *The Birthday Problem* is her second novel.

Other science fiction titles available from
PINK NARCISSUS PRESS

DARKWALKER
A post-apocalyptic crime novel by Duncan Eagleson
A supernatural killer is stalking Bay City. City Boss Micah Roth summons the Railwalkers – an Order of warrior shamans – to hunt for the killer the newsfeeds have dubbed "The Beast."
ISBN: 978-1-939056-04-7

DAUGHTERS OF ICARUS
New Feminist Science Fiction and Fantasy
"Throughout, the authors explore themes of gender, identity, and autonomy, with characters as diverse as miniature clones, stripper vampires, aggressive mermaids, and mystical crones. Many of the stories focus on gender roles and the pull of relationships, whether parental, familial, or romantic, among all

kinds of people." —*Library Journal*
ISBN: 978-1-939056-00-9

IMPOSSIBLE FUTURES
Return to the Future that Never Was!
"This wholly satisfying collection delivers an entertaining, engrossing, even exhilarating reading experience." —*ForeWord Reviews*
ISBN: 978-1-939056-02-3

NARCISSUS IS DREAMING
A science fiction novel by Rose Mambert-
Banned from Earth, Shapers live hidden among us. When Earthman Thomas Echo breaks Dahlia's heart, the Shaper's revenge leads to its discovery. Forced to comply with the agency's demands or be "cleansed", our hero/heroine must use all its resources in order to escape.
ISBN: 978-1-939056-05-4